*Charlotte Carter*

# BEAUTY IN
# THE BLOOD

Charlotte Carter is the author of an acclaimed
mystery series featuring Nanette Hayes, a young
black American jazz musician with a lust for life
and a talent for crime solving. Her short fiction
has appeared in a number of American and Brit-
ish anthologies. Charlotte Carter has lived in the
American Midwest, North Africa, and France. She
currently resides in New York City.

# BEAUTY IN
## THE BLOOD

# BEAUTY IN THE BLOOD

*Charlotte Carter*

VINTAGE BOOKS

A DIVISION OF PENGUIN RANDOM HOUSE LLC

NEW YORK

A VINTAGE BOOKS ORIGINAL 2025

Library of Congress Cataloging-in-Publication Data
Names: Carter, Charlotte, (Charlotte C.) author.
Title: Beauty in the blood / Charlotte Carter.
Description: New York : Vintage Books, a division of
Penguin Random House LLC, 2025.
Identifiers: LCCN 2024043483 |
ISBN 9780593467282 (trade paperback) | ISBN 9780593467299 (ebook)
Subjects: LCGFT: Gothic fiction. | Paranormal fiction. | Novels.
Classification: LCC PS3553.A7736 B43 2025 |
DDC 813/.54—dc23/eng/20240917
LC record available at https://lccn.loc.gov/2024043483

**Vintage Trade Paperback ISBN: 978-0-593-46728-2**
**eBook ISBN: 978-0-593-46729-9**

*Book design by Nicholas Alguire*

vintagebooks.com

Printed in the United States of America
10 9 8 7 6 5 4 3 2 1

*For Darby and Gene*

# BEAUTY IN
## THE BLOOD

## CHAPTER I

# Southeastern Georgia, 1865

In the daytime, they kept low to the ground, watching, not speaking much. It seemed safer to travel that way. So, by night, they were walking black ghosts.

Five of them left the ravaged Clarkson place together. The pitiful livestock had long ago been slaughtered for food. The big house was ransacked, nothing of use left behind. Some of the newly freed slaves stayed among the ruins. Others, destined never to see the day of their freedom, had dropped dead of exhaustion and hunger. As for Master Clarkson and his remaining kin, they'd vanished long ago, riding off in the middle of the night.

This band of five had been on the road for three days now. In their flight, the five of them—Preacher Jack, Monroe, Henry and his son Abner, and Ruben—had raided abandoned homes, looking for any food or tools they could lay hands on. They were now living, for the most part, on the berries they picked.

They'd heard all kinds of rumors: Seek out the Union soldiers, they'll help you, give you something to eat. Keep away from the Union troops, they're mean, tired of fighting, resentful. Some of them never even seen nobody look like us before— might shoot you thinking you some kind of animal. And woe be unto you if you come across any deserting Rebs, wounded and half crazy. They'd just as soon kill you as look at you.

Monroe was hungry. He was so hungry, nothing else mattered. So when Brother Jack told him to wait a little while longer before he lit the fire, for the first time ever Monroe disobeyed the older man. Earlier in the day, he had found and skinned a possum, and Monroe meant to have some of it now.

They tore at the charred flesh, sucked at its bones. Hungry as they were, Jack had made them say grace before eating. As a respected elder, the preacher who knew how to read some, the only one of them who had ever been more than ten miles away from his birthplace, he was looked to for guidance, and the other men were trusting in him to lead them on to freedom.

The important thing was to keep moving toward that freedom. Even though they didn't yet know where that was or how long it would take to get there, they figured they'd recognize it when they saw it. Like Jack had said a hundred times, God wanted them to go into the wilderness. And God would help them find a way out. They were the children of the Israelites.

The preacher was a big man, over six feet, and in his youth, long before Monroe was born, he had brought top dollar at auction. Clarkson, like his father-in-law before him, had worked Jack like the horse of a man that he was. Jack had been broken like a horse too. Branded, lashed, and near-hobbled for trying to run away. But for a long time now, more mule than stallion. He had seen eight of his children sold off. Monroe was his sister's grandchild.

Jack was old now, and a long way from virile. He still had a voice like thunder, though. And when he talked to the others about God and sin, good and evil, it was not hard to understand why so many believed the word of the Lord was booming out of his throat.

Henry took a careful swig from the water jar and passed it to young Abner. But the boy was asleep. Thirteen-year-old Abner had come out of Henry's wife, by way of Master Clarkson's son. That made no difference to Henry. Abner was all he had left; his natural son had been sold long ago, and his and Ruth's little daughter had died of fever before she was six years old.

The fire was out now. Henry shook Abner awake, and the band of men took to the trees.

## CHAPTER 2

## *Midtown Manhattan, 2000*

The March air was wonderful, bracing. Yet it had a milder hint of the coming change of season. Sarah felt good in her coat. She turned into Bergdorf's and headed for the escalator.

Halfway up, she felt a blow of terror strong enough to buckle her knees. Between the teeth of the moving stairs, something animal was showing its filthy mouth. Whatever it was, it was releasing a dank and suffocating odor.

Against her will, she reached toward the thing, just for an instant, but a horrible sound from somewhere deep inside it made her pull back.

She flew off the escalator and onto solid ground, struggling to keep herself from screaming.

"Are you ill, miss?"

The voice that came out of nowhere belonged to the young

white man who caught her as she stumbled backward. That word, *ill*, hardly conveyed the panicky thumping in her chest. *Ill*. When a reeking, wet monster had just come after her . . . in Bergdorf's?

Sarah pointed toward the escalator. The young man followed the movement of her hand with his eyes. "What? There's nothing there."

He was right. No monsters anywhere in sight.

"Should I get a doctor?" the stranger asked.

She looked at him, dizzy, confused. But the pounding in her heart and ears had ceased. She inhaled deeply. The foul odor was gone now. Nothing but the flowery scent that wafted up from the main floor.

"I'm all right, thank you."

The whole thing had to be a carryover from some nightmare. Surely that explained it. She'd had a nightmare about some sort of reptilian monster, repressed it until now, and suddenly the creature from the dream scenario had come slithering into her waking mind. She took another deep breath, and another. There, that was better. Everything was all right now. In fact, she almost felt giddy.

The first thing to catch her eye was a deep purple jacket with a cinched-in waist. Pretty, in its way, attention-grabbing. But certainly not at all her style. Yet she couldn't stop looking at it. And the more she looked, the easier it was to imagine herself wearing it. Sarah saw the red-haired saleswoman head in her direction.

The new suit would have to be altered. But her two new sheer blouses were wrapped in tissue inside the lilac shopping bag swinging from her wrist.

Her next stop was the cosmetics counter at Bendel's. The affectless saleswoman applied mascara to Sarah's eyes while enumerating the merits of the different shades of blush. When she suddenly paused and looked quizzically into her face, Sarah knew exactly why. The woman had just realized Sarah was black. It was the ivory cast to her skin that so often threw white people. Other black people seldom made the mistake. The saleswoman resumed the makeover. Sarah thanked her and then proceeded to buy a full complement of Chanel cosmetics and bath items.

Her final stop was Saks, where she spent eight hundred dollars on a marked-down pair of Jimmy Choos and then picked up a rust-colored silk bra, matching bikini panties, and an assortment of Swiss lace camisoles.

Out on the street again, she doubled back toward the apartment, stopping to do more window-shopping, striding confidently along the avenue.

Sarah had never been much of a drinker. But, standing outside the spacious bar attached to the new hotel on Fifty-Sixth, she was suddenly aware of a strong desire for alcohol. She pushed in through the heavy glass door, took a quick survey of the room, and headed for a booth. The waiter, a gray-haired black man with stick-straight posture, soon appeared at her elbow. He stood there cocking his head in anticipation. Sarah just then realized she had no idea what to order. The waiter never moved.

"I suppose I'll have something in a martini glass," she said tentatively.

"But not the martini itself. Is that it?"

"Yes. I think so." Oh for heaven's sake, she chastised herself, you're talking nonsense.

"A Negroni? Cosmopolitan?"

"I don't— Yes."

It was after four o'clock by now. The bar was virtually deserted. Sarah luxuriated in the booth, taking off her coat to reveal her favorite sweater, powder blue cashmere with a silk ribbon at the neckline. She took out her compact to tidy her hair and freshen her lipstick, and as she was replacing it in her bag, she noticed the well-dressed black man two tables away. He was thumbing through a sheaf of papers in his open attaché case. At her glance, he looked up and smiled at her. She returned the smile, and instead of looking away, her standard response to the attentions of a stranger, she held his eyes with her own. Not sixty seconds later, he was standing over her, asking permission to join her at her table. Going against her every instinct, she consented.

The well-built stranger in gray Hugo Boss introduced himself as Crawford, a native New Yorker who was now living in Atlanta.

Unbidden, the waiter brought them a plate with an assortment of hors d'oeuvres to accompany their third round. He nodded slyly at them as he walked off.

"Thanks, brother," Crawford called to the man, then he turned back to Sarah. "I guess there's some perks to being black, after all," he said.

Sarah laughed out loud, and then realized how strange her own voice sounded, oddly robust. She let herself laugh again, enjoying the unfamiliar ring of it. "Now, tell me, what is it you do in Atlanta?"

"I'm V.P. at a restaurant supply company. We sell all kinds of special kitchen equipment. You like to cook? I can get you a deal on a fantastic Viking, or even one of the French ones."

"I've never been much good in the kitchen. But I have been *very* bad there." She laughed at her own lame joke, but clearly he didn't get it. "Let's get back to you. You said you were raised in New York."

"Yeah. Born in the projects in Bed-Stuy."

"Why did you go to the South?"

"That's where the jobs were fifteen years ago. I guess I always figured I'd come back up here to live after a while. But the years kept going by. I've done pretty well for myself down there."

"You actually like it there? You don't find it dull? After living in New York, I mean."

"What you think, I live on a farm or something? Let me tell you something, lady. Atlanta is a banging place. You come on down sometime and I'll show you I don't lie."

Ordinarily, Sarah would have been mortified to think she had insulted the man. But now she merely laughed. "I just may do that," she said.

Crawford was curious about her work too.

"What do you think I do for a living? It'll be more fun for you to guess."

"College teacher," he said.

"Why that?"

"I don't know. 'Cause you speak so nice. Educated."

"What do I teach?"

"Let's see—English?"

"Right. Good for you." She felt a strong tickle then, in her left ear. Like a reminder that it wasn't nice to tell a lie. She ignored it.

He grinned and started to ask another question. But he stopped short when Sarah placed her hand on his thigh and began to slide it upward. She saw the shock in his face: English teachers in little blue sweaters didn't act the way she was acting.

"Are you by any chance staying here at the hotel, Crawford?"

"I sure am. Got a beautiful room."

He signed the bar bill in short order and gathered up his things along with her shopping bags.

As the elevator traveled up, that featherlight feeling returned, but now it was mingled with the effects of the alcohol. Sarah was woozy and took extra care to walk upright on her heels. I feel good, she thought. This doesn't seem at all tawdry. It doesn't feel at all like me, but it does seem right. Now, how could that be?

They got off the elevator on the eighteenth floor. He fumbled, juggling the packages at the same time as he worked the electronic card that opened the door to his suite.

"No wedding ring," Sarah noted. "You're not married, Crawford?"

"Divorced," he said.

He settled all the packages on a table nearby.

"This is a nice room indeed," Sarah said, tossing her coat on an armchair.

"Want a drink? The bar is full. Got some good bourbon in there. Or I could call down for you another one of those red things."

"Don't worry about it."

Crawford had just removed his suit jacket when she came at him. Her mouth on his was like a succubus. She gave him no chance to breathe. In another moment she was reaching for the buttons on his trousers.

"You in a hell of a hurry, baby," he said. "I was just about to— Hey! Hey! Girl! Lord have mercy— Ah . . . Oh. Oh shit, girl!"

Crawford had a good, manly chest. Sarah lay across the bed, watching him as he toweled off after his shower.

He was popping cashews from the room's gift basket into his mouth while he dried himself. "You kind of a strange sister, Sarah. You know that?"

"Am I?"

"Yes, ma'am, you are. I sure never met any sister like you down in Atlanta."

"Is that a good thing or a bad thing?"

"Huh. I don't know yet. But I got a second wind now. Let's find out," he said.

"That sounds delicious," she said. "You come over here and find out."

Crawford let the towel fall onto the carpet and stepped toward her. And Sarah rose up to meet him.

---

I must have dozed off, she thought. She sat up in the tousled bed. The late-afternoon sun was flooding the room. "I could swear I heard someone screaming," she said. "I must have had a bad dream. I didn't make you scream, did I, Crawford?" she asked playfully.

There was no answer.

She looked around the room, called his name twice. Silence. She didn't recall the room being so cold. Then she noticed the smashed window and the blood-tipped shards of glass on the carpet. She started toward the window, tiptoeing to avoid the glass.

*Stop.*

Who said that?

It was the voice in her head. Shouting.

*Don't look. Don't look down there.*

She tore away from the window. Dressed and pushed into her shoes in seconds. Snatched up her shopping bags and ran. The door closed soundlessly behind her.

———

Joseph, the second-shift doorman, tipped his cap toward her, and Sarah smiled back at him. It wasn't until she was riding up in the elevator that she noticed all the shopping bags she was clutching. Where on earth had they come from?

She came into the apartment, flipped the double lock, and then hurriedly emptied all the bags onto the sofa. A blizzard of tissue and ribbon. Shoes, camisoles, silk, crepe, lace. She could only stare at the booty.

Yes, she'd been experiencing some memory lapses lately. But this? Hundreds and hundreds of dollars' worth of new things she had no memory of buying. Earlier in the day she'd been contemplating a shopping trip, *contemplating* it, but she had no memory of accomplishing it.

I didn't actually go shopping, did I?

And where else have I been all day? God, what's the matter with me?

Don't be stupid, Sarah told herself. You know what it's about. These blackouts started right after Mom died. That's when all this blurry kind of forgetfulness started—though *forgetting* is hardly the right word anymore. You were knocked for a loop by her passing, and for some reason you can't admit it. But you'd better shape up. Just get yourself in hand. You haven't even given a thought to work.

But she was wrong about that. That morning, Sarah had

indeed been thinking about work, and about her mother, and even about shopping. All those things had been on her mind as she stood at the window looking down at the busy street below. Then, a bit before noon, she'd dressed, put on her coat, and taken down her briefcase, meaning to head to the law library downtown. But then she'd abruptly returned the case to its spot on the closet shelf. She'd suddenly made the decision: No library today. No work, period. *I'm going to buy a new suit, new shoes, and possibly some indulgent, costly lingerie.*

She smiled. *Maybe there's a sale at Bergdorf's.*

CHAPTER 3

# Kew Gardens, Queens, 2000

Yvonne Howard did not have many heroes in life. But one of the few she did have was Julia Child. Why? Because that legendary cook had, like Yvonne, come to appreciate the joy of food fairly late in life.

But that was about where the similarities ended. Child had lived in Paris, had risen to worldwide recognition, respect, and wealth. Yvonne was a forty-three-year-old black woman living in a rent-stabilized apartment in Queens. She had never traveled farther from home than Buffalo. And she was surely nobody's idea of a celebrity; she often thought in fact that if she were to die at home, no one would miss her until the apartment started to stink. Yvonne—a smart woman who liked to read but was not college educated—lived a quiet life and looked like a thousand other women on the F train.

Until the age of thirty-nine, she had worked as a corrections officer at the women's prison on Rikers Island. Year on year, the ugliness of prison life had scoured at her. True, she had begun the job in her twenties thinking that she might make a difference in the lives of the miserable women who ended up in the system. But as time went on, it looked more like the joke was on her. She came to loathe the work and most of her fellow officers, loathe the system and the role she was forced to play in it, and, saddest of all, loathe the luckless inmates themselves.

By the time she gave up and quit the job, she had enough savings to do nothing but sit in the comfort of her apartment and try to recover. She had her lending-library books and she had her big-screen TV with all the cable channels she could order. It was an ad on the Food Network that got her interested in the Institute of Epicurean Arts.

She took to the work at once. And two years later, certificate in hand, she landed a job with a restaurant in the Village. Sea Grass, a popular place on Washington Street, was actually a soul food restaurant—collard greens, smothered chicken, slow-cooked pork, and so on—but all done in highfalutin style; fusion, as some of the food people called it. High and low. And pretty damn costly.

Yvonne was assistant to the pastry chef. She had so impressed him that she was now allowed to make the banana tarts, the olive oil cake, the biscuits, the miniature sourdough loaves for the complimentary bread baskets. When Hugo, her boss, took a week's vacation in the Bahamas, he left her on her own: "I know you can handle it, Miss Girl. Just do the mixed berry cobbler every night. If they don't like it, fuck 'em."

The restaurant was hopping. The late-dinner crowd had discovered Sea Grass and business was booming. Yvonne had been on her feet for hours and she was exhausted. Around one in the morning, the volume of orders dropped off. She was leaning against the cold room door, deep breathing, eyes closed, when one of the hostesses came back and called out:

"Client wants to see you, Yvonne. Table nine."

"Me? What for?"

The girl shrugged.

"Don't tell me somebody wants to complain 'cause the biscuits were cold. I am not hearing that tonight."

"I don't know. She just asked for you. She knows your name."

Yvonne straightened up. She didn't have but a handful of friends, and the chances were pretty remote that one of them was stopping by the restaurant to see her, especially at the tail end of the night.

Still wearing her apron, she followed the girl out through the kitchen door and into the dining room.

The young hostess didn't have to point out the mystery guest. Yvonne recognized her immediately. She felt a cold wind sweep through the big room and settle in her chest. A blast from the past, Yvonne thought acridly. Like they say, the past is never past. Sooner or later it comes back to bite you in the ass.

The coffee-colored woman at table nine was surrounded by a party of people who were drinking and eating lustily—black folks who were dressed up just enough to seem out of place in the Village. The woman who had summoned Yvonne looked appraisingly at her and pursed her lips.

Bitty Willetts had not been particularly violent, but she was one of the more annoying inmates, a frequent guest at Rikers. Always bitching about something: her sore back, suspended privileges, indigestion from the bad food. She had been convicted of a variety of confidence scams, petty larceny, prostitution.

The sight of Bitty almost made Yvonne sick. She turned on her heel and started to walk back toward the kitchen.

"Hold up!" Bitty had left her table and was trailing Yvonne's steps. "Hold up, woman. I just wanna talk to you."

"I won't even ask how you know I work here," Yvonne said. "But . . . how the hell did you know I work here?"

"Biggs," the other woman answered.

"What?"

"Biggs. Fat dyke guard from the joint. We stay in touch. She heard about what you was doing these days."

Yvonne clucked her tongue. "Look, we got nothing to say to each other. I treated you like you deserved to be treated and you got no business looking for payback. What the hell do you want with me?"

"I'm gone tell you, bitch, if you just shut up for a minute. I don't have nothing against you. I swear. Can we go somewhere and talk—just for a minute?"

In the warmth of the kitchen, Yvonne pulled out a tall stool and used her foot to push it over to Bitty.

"I got a problem," Bitty said.

Yvonne stopped her there. "Can't help you. I don't have anything to do with the department anymore. Can't you see I'm living a different kind of life now?"

"No, no, no," Bitty said. "Not a problem with the law. Well, in a way it is. But I'm not in no trouble. That's not what I mean." She began to rummage in her purse then, until she found her pack of Salems. "Okay to smoke back here?"

"No."

"It's my little brother," Bitty said. "He was killed."

"I'm sorry."

"Yeah. Everybody sorry."

"Who killed him?"

"Nobody seem to know that—or care. My baby brother Crawford was about the only good thing ever came from our raggedy-ass family. He put himself through school, got a degree in business. Got himself a good job down in Atlanta and moved away from New York long time ago. He comes back through here from time to time, though. Used to make the trip up here more often when our mama was still alive. Now, he don't make it to New York that much, only when he got business here. But when he does, he always visits, comes by to see how I am and everything. Turned out to be a beautiful man—at least he was."

"So what happened to him?"

"A couple of weeks ago he was in town, staying up at a hotel midtown. He went out a window."

"Jesus. That was your brother?"

She nodded. "They saying it was suicide. That's a lie."

"How do you know?"

"I know Crawford, that's how. I saw him just the night before. We had a good time talking and laughing. He even took me to a show. Wasn't a thing about him to make you think he was about to jump out a goddamn window. He did not kill himself, Yvonne. Somebody murdered him."

"But the cops don't agree with you?"

"Damn right they don't. Claim he mighta been with a prostitute, but there's no evidence she did anything to him, except maybe rob him. Come talking about he tried to make it with her and couldn't get it up, or something, and killed himself 'cause he was 'despondent.'"

"How do you know that didn't happen?"

"I know 'cause it's bullshit. Crawford was straight as a arrow, and fine. He didn't have to pay for no pussy. And he wouldn't let no woman rob him. More than that, he couldn't stand ho's. Why you think it hurt him so bad when I was hooking? No, something else happened to him. And the cops ain't hearing it at all. They just don't give a shit about him."

Yvonne sighed. "Well, I'm sorry. I'm real sorry, but—"

"Just a minute. Don't say there's nothing you can do, Yvonne. There is something you can do."

"No, there isn't."

"Yeah, there is. Police say the case not officially closed yet. You can ask around for me, see if they even playing like they interested. You in a better position than me. You could even go over to where he was staying, and ask around—"

"That's ridiculous. I can't. I can't find out who killed your brother. *If* that's what happened. The police say it's suicide, the medical examiner must've said the same thing. But you know different."

Bitty held up a placating hand. "Okay. Say you find out it didn't happen like I think. If you can prove that, it'll be good enough for me. I'll stop bugging everybody and accept what you tell me. Just ask around. Ain't you got any favors you could call in from somebody on the cops? Somebody who might give you some help? I'm trying to get some justice here."

"Jesus Christ, Bitty. You expect me to go sticking my nose in police business for you?"

"I'm not asking you to do it as a favor. I can pay you for your time."

"Pay me?"

Bitty withdrew a plain white envelope from her bag. "Look. I told you I don't expect no favors." She crammed a slip of paper into the ties of Yvonne's apron. "Take this, it's my phone number. And here. Look in that envelope."

"Girl, there's a thousand dollars in here. Are you insane?"

"Take it."

"No!" Yvonne shoved the envelope back into her hands. "Where did this come from, anyway? You trying for a life sentence now?"

"It's clean, Black! I manage a club uptown for a niggah I'm tight with. I make crazy good money."

"Good for you," Yvonne said, stepping away from Bitty. "You and your niggah keep on keeping on. But I'm not in it."

Bitty was crying now. But her angry tears just hardened Yvonne's will. "That boohoo routine didn't work in Rikers," she said, "and it don't work now, Bitty."

Bitty exploded then. "Okay, Miss Yvonne. I get what you saying. You saying you think you better than me."

"Girl, get outta my face with that shit."

"No, that's exactly what you saying, Yvonne. It is. When you was a screw, you didn't have no choice. You had to be in jail with us garbage. But now you done moved up in the world. You can't even stand to smell us. Well, fuck you."

Yvonne tried to answer. But now it was Bitty who turned a deaf ear. She stormed out of the kitchen, banging the door behind her.

Goddamn. Three years since Yvonne had had to walk into that hellhole every working day; swimming in all that ignorant brutality and hopelessness. It had taken two years to feel like the grime of it was off her skin. Now somebody was trying to pull her back into it, talking about murder, no less.

And how did Bitty know it was murder? How could she know what happened in that hotel room? She wasn't there. She claimed to know what her late brother would or wouldn't do. But one thing Yvonne had learned: you never really know other people. You think you can trust them and then they turn around and betray you, laugh at you while they do it. Most cons live in a delusional world; think they're so goddamn slick. But they get everything backward. And then they're surprised when they end up wearing a number. Bitty was no different.

And as for all that cash—Yvonne didn't believe for a minute

that Bitty had a legitimate job that paid her enough to throw around coin like that. She was doubtless into some kind of mess.

Yvonne didn't have the education to become a social worker or a doctor, the things she had wanted to do as a young girl. But she thought she might do some good in the world by working in the prison system. Well, those were her delusions. It was like Bitty said—Yvonne had been "in jail" just like the inmates.

She picked up the pale blue mug she always drank her coffee from and threw it against the wall.

## CHAPTER 4

# Southeastern Georgia, 1865

Milk. Ruben said he could hardly remember what it tasted like. Not like this, for sure not like this. The five men had come upon a wooden pail half filled with yellowed milk, flies skating on the surface of it. Ruben bent down, lifted it to his lips. The liquid was vile. Henry watched young Abner drink greedily from the dirty vessel.

After they'd drunk their fill of the sickening muck, the preacher made them all kneel and thank God for the sustenance. And while they were praying, he took the opportunity to quote Scripture.

Monroe was tired of praying. What should he thank God for? The nightly searing ache in his knees? Being ripped away from his mother at age twelve? It seemed to him that his life of uninterrupted weariness and heartbreak and paralyzing fear was nothing to be thankful for. But he wasn't about to go against Preacher Jack. The preacher knew the territory better than any of them, and if they were to stand a chance of walking away still living, it would surely be Preacher Jack who'd talk them out of the trouble.

———————

Monroe woke with a start. Propped up against a giant stone at the edge of the campfire, he had dozed off during the preaching. He looked over and saw that Ruben, Henry, and Abner were sleeping as well. Only Jack was awake. But the big man's big voice had fallen into a whisper. He was still quoting Scripture, but now there were no amens from his flock. Monroe tried to concentrate on Jack's words. He could only make out singsong snatches, but he guessed Jack was telling about the white man's God: *Live according to my laws . . . peace in the land . . . I shall turn toward you . . . as I am your God, you are my people . . . to lead you out of Egypt so that you should be slaves no more.*

Preacher Jack was staring deep into the campfire as he talked, leaning into it, almost as if he were listening to the crackling sticks talk back to him.

Monroe turned away, no longer listening.

## CHAPTER 5

# *Midtown Manhattan, 2000*

Sarah arrived at the restaurant a few minutes early. She was wearing her purple suit and stiletto pumps. She told the host that she would wait at the bar for Mr. Bender. Heads turned as she took a seat and crossed her legs.

Her mind kept going back to that blurry, lost day when she experienced the terrifying hallucination on the escalator. She was attempting to piece things together. How had that day begun? Oh yes. She was standing at what she called her thinking window, morning coffee in hand:

Far below, twelve floors down, the traffic rolled along Fifty-Seventh Street, steady and noiseless. Out there was the fray—taxis honking, hurried movement and anticipation, people meeting and parting, life and death. Observing it all was the thing Sarah liked most about living in a high-rise building at the center of town. With the double-glazed windows closed, you could watch the drama of the city with the volume turned off.

She pressed one hand hard against the glass, and for a moment she felt as if she were falling right through. The sensation was so startling that she jerked away from the windowpane.

She looked down at the spreading coffee stain on her gray cotton bathrobe. Her mother bought the robe for Sarah's first year away at college. She had never spilled so much as a drop of water on it until now. Sarah Toomey had walked and talked and eaten with unnatural care all her life.

She poured herself another cup of coffee and again took up her post at the window. There was a lot to think about these days. Like the intricacies of the child custody case she was handling. Both spouses were affluent, old-line WASPs with good manners, seemingly reasonable people who had weathered the early stages of their divorce with equanimity, and who were presently shredding each other bloody over the future of their young daughter.

Then there was her mother, Lila, only four weeks dead. Sarah's grief seemed to be behind her now, the passing time lessening it day by day. In fact, the most troubling thing about this haze she seemed to live in currently was that she was fast losing all memories of her tall, mournful-faced mother.

And yet, despite the dimming of the details, Sarah had the strong feeling that everything she did now was somehow connected to Lila, that Lila was almost a presence in the apartment. In all of Sarah's time in New York, Lila had never once come to visit. She hated to travel, so Sarah made regular trips to see her in Wilmington.

She had gone right back to work after Lila's death, trying to lose herself in the job. Jeffrey Bender, her colleague and superior at the firm, had been noticing her exhaustion for weeks. Finally, he took a hand, ordering her to cut back, take time off from work.

"Play hooky," was how he put it. "Go lay in the sun some-where, Sarah. Hell, I'll come and join you. I'm tired of looking like a saltine cracker. Be nice if I could get just a tiny bit of a white-guy tan. Get you out of that pinstripe suit. I see you in one of those string bikinis."

He laughed as he said it. But Sarah knew he was more than half serious. He was constantly giving himself away. Light touches of the hand across the conference-room table. His steady gaze at her when she spoke at meetings, the brief bumping of knees on those uncomfortable stools at the cramped coffee place across from the office. Consulting on the more complex cases meant they spent a lot of time together. Then, one evening shortly before her mother's death, Jeffrey dropped by Sarah's place to pick up some documents, and as he left he hugged her and said how sorry he was that her mom was sick. And then he kissed her lightly on the lips. Before that happened, she had not allowed herself to take his attentions too seriously. But they'd exchanged a very long look after the kiss, and the jagged burst of heat she'd experienced made her think for a second that she was actually holding fire. They made a plan to have dinner together the fol-lowing evening, but that never happened; Sarah received the news that her mother's condition was grave. She canceled the dinner and took the train for Wilmington.

Jeffrey seemed to delight in teasing Sarah, who knew he con-sidered her overly prim and proper. And he wasn't the only one in the office who thought that. Most of her colleagues did too.

Her female co-workers often wanted to fix her up with one eligible man or another. Her answer was always the same: no, thanks. They just didn't get it. It had nothing to do with being prim, a goody-goody little overcompensating black girl. Well, not that alone, anyway. Other women her age seemed to be con-stantly on the lookout for lovers, husbands. They were on some kind of quest to fix an incompleteness in themselves. Sarah felt anything but complete, but she knew a man wasn't the answer to her sense of displacement, her imbalance.

Now, if only she knew what she did want, what she did need—if only she understood what it was that kept her at odds with herself and the rest of the world.

Since she had never cared much for children, maybe it was just as well she paid little attention to men. But even Sarah herself recognized how odd it was to assume all your life that you will never marry. Her mother had not exactly frightened her off men, but Sarah had been raised in a world nearly male-free.

Lila Toomey had appeared uninterested in men, except for her revered late husband, Sarah's father. He died before Sarah was born, and she had long ago stopped wondering about him—what kind of people did he come from, was he as loving and kind and strong as her mother said, or had all that been a rewrite of history, a fantasy?

A woman of so few words, Lila had maintained two jobs—bookkeeper and cook for a posh caterer—in order to send Sarah to a well-regarded girls' prep school where young Sarah excelled at her studies. She went on to a scholarship at Mills College, and then to New York for law school at Columbia.

There had been two or three young men in Sarah's life during college. A few dates and then mutual acknowledgment things were going nowhere. In every case, a roommate had pushed her into the relationship; *I told him how pretty you are, he wants to meet you. Plus, he's really good-looking.*

Jeffrey Bender was good-looking. And kind. And strong. He had a solid, well-muscled frame, though he wasn't especially tall. He'd helped her out of a cab once, lifted her from the back seat so effortlessly, as if she weighed nothing.

"Should I lay my cloak across that puddle for you, fair lady?" he said.

"That's very gallant of you, Jeff. But it isn't raining."

Have an affair. Clearly that was what he wanted. But what about her?

*Affair.* The word sounded so lighthearted. But in truth, didn't love affairs go sour sometimes, wreck lives, cost more than anyone could ever have predicted?

No, best not to take things with Jeffrey any further. Because, after all, she had neglected to add the most important item to that list of his attributes: He was married. Married with children.

Sarah caught her reflection in the window. Here it is, she thought, eleven in the morning, and I'm still in my robe. She rubbed at her forehead. That feeling, that damn feeling. Not exactly a headache. It was the sensation that had become so familiar, like coming out of a daydream and not quite knowing where you are.

---

Sarah heard someone talking, as if from a long way away. She was pulled back into the present. The young white bartender was smiling at her. "Apple martini," he said. "Am I right?"

"I'll try anything once," she said. And that was exactly how she felt today. As if she could blithely meet any challenge thrown at her.

As she sat with her drink, she looked out across the avenue, eyes traveling upward toward the roof of a building.

She realized then that she was gripping the edge of the bar, and that once again the bartender was speaking to her.

"Sorry. What did you say?"

"I asked if you'd like some olives. Or how about some peanuts?"

"Thank you, no."

He was almost good-looking enough to be a menswear model. "Are you a visitor in town?" he said.

"What makes you ask that?"

"Just saw you looking over at the hotel. Wondered if you knew about the big scene that happened there."

"Scene?"

"Yeah. Guy jumped out of a window. Man, what a mess. All hell was breaking loose. People screaming, cops, blood everywhere. We thought at first it was a terrorist thing."

"How terrible."

"Yeah. But, hey . . . New York. The next day? Like nothing happened. I already heard about twenty jokes."

"What sort of jokes?"

"About the jumper. I guess it sounds kind of cruel—I mean, the guy did die and everything. But some of the jokes are pretty funny. The jumper was buck naked, see, so you can imagine . . ."

Sarah nodded. "Yes, I can imagine."

Her eyes were registering the tight fit of his jacket. By the time their gazes met, she could see the flame inside his innocuous expression. Ah. He wanted her. As she was learning, there was a wicked thrill in lighting a match to a man's desire, watching it grow.

A minute later, Jeff Bender came in.

"Sarah?"

She swiveled on the seat to face him.

"Jesus, Sarah. I wasn't sure it was you. I mean, you look terrific. You've done something to your hair."

She laughed. "Haven't you ever seen a black blonde?"

"Yeah I have. And I approve." He leaned in close to her ear. "Liking the S&M shoes too. Nice, Miss Sarah Toomey."

As soon as they were seated at a table, Jeff ordered wine.

"I asked you to come out and meet me because I was afraid you were spending your time off work just sitting around your apartment feeling—Hey, you're drinking. Wine."

"I like wine."

"You do?"

"I do now. I'm finding I like quite a few things I never liked before. Why are you looking at me that way?"

Rather than answer, he merely clinked his glass against hers. "Here's to finding out what you like," he said.

He watched while she finished her second glass. "How about some pasta now?"

"No. I'm not hungry."

"Really? Are you sure? Because, you look amazing. But you also look . . . Are you sure you're okay?"

The lightheaded feeling was back. It was coming and going all the time now. "Jeff, I'm not sure if I ever thanked you properly."

"What for?"

"Being nice to me. Caring. I know how hidden away I've kept myself. I'm just shy that way. But still, I've always had the feeling we might . . ."

"What?"

"Be friends," she said. "At the very least."

Sarah drank more wine while he ate his lamb chops. Over coffee, she fell into a melancholy silence.

"What are you thinking about?"

"My mother. Sort of."

"Yeah. It's the worst when your mom dies. I was really close with mine. I didn't just love her, I admired her. You feel like you'll never get past it. But you do."

She shrugged. "I can't say I was 'close' with her. But she was the only family I had."

"Did you mean what you said a while back? About us being friends?"

"Yes."

"If we were friends, I would know what to say to make you feel a little better. But I don't know a damn thing about you. Why don't you tell me something real about yourself."

"All right. What do you want to know?"

"You seeing anyone?"

"No. And don't you think about anything other than sex?"

"Okay. Just curious. I'm not a total dog, Sarah. I'm just bothered you don't get any love. So let's move on to something else. Like, I don't know—What kind of things do you do to unwind?"

"I don't knit or play bridge, if that's the kind of thing you mean. I've always liked reading about wildlife, architecture. Once in a while, I go to the theater. I enjoy that. In fact, I'll tell you something, if you promise not to laugh."

"Okay."

"I did a little acting myself when I was in school. You know, stagestruck college girl."

"No kidding?"

"No kidding. I even played Blanche Dubois in a school production."

"Whoa. I'd pay a lot to see that."

"You're laughing at me, but it's all right. I came to my senses."

"Maybe you're too sensible for your own good. Maybe you let go of Blanche a little too soon."

"It didn't end well for her, remember."

"That mysterious smile thing you do. Makes me nuts, you know? I'm gonna figure you out though. You watch."

"I'm tired, Jeff," she said. "I think I'd better get home now."

"Okay. But we're going to see each other again, right?"

"Yes. And you can go ahead."

"With what?"

"Go ahead and figure me out."

"Already on it. But for now, I'll just sit here for a while and fantasize."

---

"You were very good, Sarah," the gawky middle-aged man said.

As was her wont when she received a compliment, Sarah looked down at her shoes.

She and a young actor from the local theater troupe were doing a run-through of a play by Leonard Melfi. The perpetually boyish-looking drama teacher, Mr. Haysbert, had given her the lead. He'd called her "especially sensitive," and said she was a natural actress.

It was not only natural; it was a relief for Sarah to disappear into a role—just about any role. Her classmates seemed to be falling in love every other week, or dieting recklessly, or trying to write novels, or running off to Sri Lanka with their archaeologist boyfriend. Every girl she knew seemed to be caught up with an all-consuming something or someone. But Sarah, even with the long hours spent at her studies, still found herself with time on her hands, and no direction, no passions. Most of the time she felt like a ghost, a cipher. No wonder the attraction, the ease, of inhabiting a fictional character's skin.

When she saw the notice on the English Department bulletin board announcing auditions for an arcane Strindberg play, something took hold of her. She had worked up the courage somehow, and when the day arrived, she propelled herself into the little theater and onto the stage, where she read for Mr. Haysbert and his student assistant. She wasn't cast in that play, but she was invited to join the group as a kind of apprentice. Instead of going home to Wilmington at school break, she'd spent the summer reading plays and biographies of theater luminaries, going to foreign films to study the great European actresses. In no time she was doing walk-ons and understudying second female leads.

The theater group was as close as Sarah had ever come to belonging to a clique. Occasionally she joined the others for beer at the hangout bar, and of course she took part in group excursions to San Francisco to see new work on one of the top-ranked professional stages.

Mostly, though, she threw herself into the parts she was given to play. After a while, her fellow students gave up on trying to push her into dates, parties, anything. Sarah became known to some on campus as the willowy, brilliant black girl who had pledged her life to the theater. Others, noticing her distracted manner as she wandered through the halls, almost as though she were sleepwalking, thought she was a bona fide head case. Every time she had a new role, she walked and dressed and spoke differently offstage as well as on. Even her handwriting would change.

Marty Haysbert approved heartily of her singleness of focus. Always generous with his time, he became her mentor. In Sarah's junior year he seduced her. They'd traveled together to La Jolla to see an experimental play written by a friend of his. He introduced her to the author and the director, presenting her as his "discovery," and then the two of them had gone on to a long and sumptuous meal at a nice place on the water.

Sarah was still acting as she lay beneath him on the motel

bed, breathing excitedly, making little cries of pleasure, kissing him hungrily as he made love to her. She'd seen enough movies to know the drill.

The teacher lit a second joint after they were done. "You're still in that pony stage, aren't you?" he said. "Long legs and fragile ankles, and those amazing big bashful eyes. I wonder if you know what an irresistible quality you have. Sometimes it does seem like you're from another place, though. Like you haven't quite gotten used to the air on planet Earth. You're a little scary sometimes."

"I am?"

"Yeah. Like the night we were doing improvs and you fainted."

"I fainted?"

"Yeah, you and Todd were doing a thing where he was an intruder and he was threatening to hurt your kids. You let out this bloodcurdling scream, and then you fainted dead away. We thought it was part of the bit, but then we realized you were really out. Scared the hell out of us. No memory of that?"

"No."

"See? That's what I mean. Alien." He pulled her to him. More long kisses. He slipped a finger inside her. "By the way, what's the deal on Planet Sarah? Don't you guys ever come?"

As he stroked, she took a demure toke from the cigarette and smiled. Enigmatically.

"Only one thing keeps us from being a living cliché," he said.

Sarah waited for him to explain.

"You know how it works in the movies—beautiful, ambitious young actress with older man. He does a Svengali. Molds her, guides her career until she hits the big time. Pretty soon she's the toast of Broadway. Then she flies off to Hollywood and leaves him in the gutter."

She laughed appreciatively.

"Not bloody likely you're going to be the toast of Broadway, Sarah. You know that, right?"

She didn't answer.

"I think you could be a wonderful actress. I don't say it just because I want to be between your legs. But no matter how good you get, you have to be realistic. This is a fucking racist society and the parts you'll get to play range from A to B—or B minus. And, because a lot of people'll think you look white, kind of—well, it'll just confuse the shit out of them. It stinks, but there you have it. Believe me, I know what it's like to be an actor with that kind of fire and no place to show it. Just kills you."

Actually, he'd said nothing that had not already occurred to her. The goal for Sarah was to find someone to be, and to play the part well—to be very good. To be, as Mr. Haysbert was always reminding her, *available.* If by some chance she did find herself with a career in the theater, that would be fine. Maybe it would be the route to feeling she belonged somewhere. On the other hand, she could just as easily see herself with a job in corporate America. Or as a professor on a tenure track at a respectable university. She knew, though, that no one was likely to understand that it made little difference to her.

Mr. Haysbert slid down to the foot of the bed, gently parted her thighs. "My beautiful Sarah," he said, "let me discover more about your planet."

Sarah went on to more dramatic triumphs during her senior year, including Gwendolen Fairfax in *The Importance of Being Earnest.*

## CHAPTER 6

# Kew Gardens, Queens, 2000

Yvonne set her pencil down and looked up at the high vaulted ceiling. She was having trouble following the lecture, unable to concentrate.

Once a week, she attended the class on the African diaspora that took place in a side room of the local public library. All the lecture series she had signed up for had been worthwhile—the one on Peruvian art, the one on textiles. But this class was particularly interesting. She was learning a lot about her people's past.

The lecturer was a learned black man in his early forties. When Yvonne first saw the multicolored cap he often wore, she assumed he was either African or a Muslim. No, not at all, he had told her when she asked, he was about as American as you could get: he had lived in New York all his life. Mr. Collins, who told the class he preferred to be called Kofi rather than Kenneth, his given name, was also a writer. He reviewed books and recordings for a number of magazines and weekly newspapers.

Kofi's talks were so interesting that Yvonne and a few other attendees had jumped at the chance when he'd offered to help anyone interested in tracing their ancestry.

Kofi always had something fascinating to say, whether he was talking about traditional West African masks or architecture or hip-hop. So it wasn't boredom that was making Yvonne fidget in her seat. She was simply distracted and agitated, and had been ever since the confrontation with Bitty.

*"Miss Howard?"*

Yvonne was startled to hear her name called. She looked up to find she was alone in the room with Kofi.

"It is Miss Howard, right?" he said. "Or is it Mrs.?"

"Plain old Yvonne," she said. "I'm not married."

"I'm not sure if I mentioned it," Kofi said, "but neither am I."

Guess I wasn't imagining those little looks he was giving me the last couple of weeks, she thought.

"I hope you're not thinking of dropping out of the class," he said. "You don't seem too interested in things anymore."

"That's not it," Yvonne said. "I just have something on my mind. Just thinking about it . . . I guess I haven't been good for much else lately."

He gathered his notes and zippered them inside his leather case. "I've always been a good listener," he said. "How about catching a cup of coffee with me?"

"You got time to listen to somebody else's troubles?"

"Not everybody's."

They wound up in a little Greek place where the coffee was thick and powerful. Kofi ate two pieces of baklava while Yvonne outlined her years as a prison guard, her second life as a baker, and finally Bitty's appearance out of the blue and her crazy demand that Yvonne look into her brother's violent death.

"I remember seeing that in the papers," Kofi said at the end of the story. "That's a lot to ask, what she wants you to do. A lot to ask of somebody who doesn't owe her a damn thing."

"No lie," said Yvonne. "Bitty always did have a pair on her. But the thing is, I don't know, much as she got on my nerves, I keep asking myself if I do owe something. Not just to her. To all of them."

"The women in jail, you mean."

"Yeah. It's no kind of life for a human being. Once I got away from there and put a little distance between me and that hellhole, I realized it was even worse than it seemed at the time. I mean, I saw there was about a minute's worth of difference between them and me. One little turn here or there in life and I could have been inside the cage looking out instead of the other way around."

"I seriously doubt that," he said.

*Oh, do you really? I guess you think you know who I am.* "Where was it you were raised, Kofi?"

"The Upper West Side."

"Um hum."

"I think maybe I said the wrong thing."

"Don't worry about it."

"Seems you've already made up your mind to help this woman. That's really honorable of you."

Yvonne looked up at him as she stirred more sugar into her coffee. "Does seem like that, doesn't it? I must be crazy. It's not like I don't have enough to do."

"I hear restaurant work is one of the hardest jobs you can have. You must go home exhausted," Kofi said.

"Yeah, man, but I love it. Maybe one of these days I'll have my own place. I'm thinking of a bakery."

"I believe you'll make it, Yvonne. And maybe one day you'll cook something for me."

"Well, just come by Sea Grass. Food's good."

"Oh. Right."

She knew full well what he really meant—her making a meal just for him. The guy has all that book learning; stands up in front of dozens of people and teaches all over the city; shit, he's a *writer*; and he still can't say what he means. Can't tell you what he wants. One thing you could say for prison: folks usually got right to the point.

"About this woman—Bitty—I think you're going to do whatever's right. Maybe I can help you. If you need it."

---

*"Bitch, you let me catch you taking my cigarettes again, Ima kill you."*

Yvonne, nightstick on one hip and state-issued weapon strapped to the other, had looked down at Bitty, who was grabbing another inmate by the collar. The TV room was crowded with women in their gray prison smocks, all riveted by the doings on *One Life to Live*. Yvonne had always despised the soaps, never understood as a child why her mother was addicted to them. And her mother had followed every one of them. Yvonne could recall Mama and her housing project cronies discussing the fate of the characters in "their stories" as though, with their plastic good looks and ghost-white teeth, they were living people. As though their absurd problems were just as for-real as the ones eating at every welfare family on the block.

"Quiet down, Bitty. Take it easy," Yvonne barked.

"That's right, Bitty," echoed the woman who had apparently filched a cigarette from Bitty's pack. "Take it easy. We trying to watch the story." She grinned evilly at Bitty and held a finger to her lips. "Shhhhh."

Talk about soap operas, Yvonne thought as she patrolled the room. There were enough plots, enough drama, sadness, and insanity right here in this room to keep a daytime story going for fifty years. No-tooth dope addicts, half-wit girls knocked up and alone, career hookers with AIDS—not to speak of the ones who had driven knives through some man's back.

Inmate Bitty could be a real pain in the ass, but she was no fool, and she could be funny sometimes. She was a straight-up crook, but she still managed to hang on to some humanity. More than once she had jumped to the defense of another inmate who was getting beat on, and she never joined in the hundred little tortures some of the women visited on the weak ones. Bitty did her share of greasing the guards and trusties for her regular deliveries of weed and extra grub. Still, she knew better than to approach Yvonne with any of that nonsense.

But, hell, any of the other, older ones were more human than the girl bangers. Those hard young bitches were in another league. Yvonne hated them and their violent bullying, their stupid tattoos, and their filthy mouths. She never gave them any kind of a break and she never turned her back on them. The hefty Juanita Biggs, Yvonne's co-worker, had beaten one of them senseless when the foolish young girl threw a plate at her one time. Yvonne was no freak; she got no charge out of inflicting or witnessing pain, but she had stood there watching in a kind of trance as Biggs landed the blows across the girl's face.

The gang girls were a horror show. And it didn't take much imagination to figure they had come out of horror shows of abuse and neglect. A girl who hadn't been criminally misused, who had been shown some decency and affection, could not turn out like them. Yvonne kept telling herself that, and it didn't help one bit.

At the end of her shift each night, she would pour herself into her secondhand heap and drive back to Queens. Too tired to cook at home, she'd stop for takeout, usually something that was no good for her blood pressure, and then she'd indulge in a long hot bath, trying vainly to soak away the anger and loathing in her bones—along with the guilt she knew would wreck her sleep.

## CHAPTER 7

# Midtown Manhattan, 2000

Jeffrey arrived with half a dozen dainty white cardboard containers in a shopping bag that looked like a lacquered jewelry box. He took the gamble that Sarah would go for Japanese food. Something spare and exquisitely presented. Between the time he buzzed her over the intercom and the time it took him to ride up to the twelfth floor, Sarah had changed out of her jeans and into a short emerald green dress. As the doorbell rang, she ran a brush through her hair.

Jeff's gamble paid off. She finished the sashimi and the eels in a flash and then went after the seaweed at the bottom of the container. They clinked glasses and drank some of the cold sake that he had picked up at the wine store on Sixtieth Street.

He set his glass down on the coffee table. "Sarah, I know what I said before, but I can't help it."

She did not ask what he meant. She knew. She had known it the minute she heard his voice over the intercom.

He reached for her and she went immediately into his arms.

They made love on the sofa. He undressed her quickly and barely took the time to get his own clothing off. It was a furious thing. They rolled onto the floor, Jeffrey still inside her. She had one hand across her mouth to stifle her moaning. He brushed the hand away. "Good solid walls," he said. "Neighbors won't hear you." Soon they were both baying and crying out like cats.

"Just occurred to me," he said later, as they drank more sake.

"What?"

"We didn't even take the time to kiss. You know what I'm saying, Sarah? We never even had a real first kiss before the big game."

"Yes, I see. I want mine now, then," she said.

A while later, he picked her up and carried her into the bedroom.

He devoted himself to her pleasure. She wept at the end, trembling so hard that he held on to her and wiped her forehead with tissues, as if she were in the grip of a fever.

"Wow. Tell me if I'm wrong, but it's like before tonight you never—"

She blushed crimson and turned away from him.

"I'm sorry," Jeff said. "No, I mean I'm glad. Don't be embarrassed. Yeah, Jeez, I'm glad, big macho me, right? I made you come. A lot. Look at me, will you? Something I want to say to you."

She took a deep breath and then complied.

"But you better stop before you get me crying too."

"All right. What do you want to tell me?"

"I think maybe I'm in trouble here, Sarah."

"What trouble?"

"I think I need to be with you. Or rather, I think I belong with you. And not just the sex, which, incidentally . . . Jesus. I mean the not being able to stop thinking about you. I don't know where this is going."

"Maybe you're thinking we shouldn't have done this, that it isn't worth the trouble."

"Lady, I'd say this is the best kind of trouble anybody could be in. No?"

"I guess so."

"And what if things could go further with us? Is that something you might want?"

She could not quite answer. Two or three short words came out, but put together they made no sense.

"I'm going too fast for you. Sorry. Maybe I'm going too fast for me too. I get like this. When my real heart's on the line, it's like I'm twelve years old."

"That's lovely what you just said—your *real* heart."

"Tell me what's in your heart now."

"Mine? I'm not sure. Sometimes it feels like there isn't anything there. I think I'm hollow."

"You're not. That's loneliness."

The tears welled in her eyes again. "Something's wrong with me. That's for sure. It's like they say, I'm broken."

"I'll fix you up. You'll see. Stop thinking like that. Meanwhile, you have any music?"

"Excuse me?"

"Music. You know. Tra la la."

"Oh. Yes."

"What do you like to listen to?"

"I don't know. Sometimes I play Miles Davis. The album inspired by Spain."

"Oh. God. Have you been to Spain?"

"No."

"Oh, Sarah." Face breaking into a grin. "Wait'll I take you. It's like . . . like you never knew what the sun— I'm— It's— Just you wait. Anyway, go find Miles now. While I get us something to drink. We'll fuck to Spanish music. How cool are we, Sarah?"

———

Jeffrey eased himself off the bed and found an oversized towel in the bathroom. He wrapped it around his midsection and crept past Sarah, who was sleeping like a corpse.

In the living room he found his suit jacket and took from the breast pocket one of the honey-colored cigars a client had passed to him earlier in the week. He lit it and began to survey the room. He took down from the bookcase a fat volume on New York skyscrapers, flipped through it. He went into the kitchen and helped himself to a wedge of cheese, then put the kettle on.

What the fuck, man? The fuck are you doing?

Sarah Toomey was a challenge he had made to himself. She was this shy woman with luminous skin and eyes like precious stones, long legs and pretty tits, and he had decided to bed her. She was fair game.

That was how it had started, anyway. Then his reaching out to her had switched from pure seduction to genuine affection, and finally to a kind of pity, a fierce protectiveness. Now that he had slept with her, she was truly under his skin. The sex had been marvelous, like the realization of some fantasy ideal he didn't even know he had: she was all passion and willingness, and yet she had next to no experience. As though she'd been waiting all this time to be wakened by Jeffrey Bender. Dr. Jeffrey Frankenstein had created not a murderous bruiser with a bolt through his neck but his own personal sex kitten.

A few of the other men at the firm had made barroom comments about her tight little butt, but as far as he knew, none of them had ever asked her out. Well, there was her goody-goody demeanor. No reason to think she would be up for a casual affair. With one exception, none of the other lawyers were what you'd call racist, but it simply wasn't in their makeup to date a black woman. Too much of a hassle, and maybe just plain fear of the Other. He'd gone to school with idiots like that.

Jeffrey, always aware of his good looks, had made the Cook's Tour of interesting women on the Penn campus and off. He could barely think of a type or a color or an ethnicity he hadn't sampled, with the exception of Inuit. His interest in all kinds of people, he came by naturally. His late mother had been a much-published anthropologist, a bohemian-spirited looker from a nice white-bread family in Minneapolis, and his father, Jewish, a leftist attorney who had retired, remarried, and was now living in Italy.

In the car that day, when his mother was driving him to college to help him settle in, she'd said, "Heed my words, O handsome devil of a son. As you set foot on the sexual playground, screw as much as you like, but don't be a rat. Remember, it's not just the woman who wants to be taken. Let her take you as well. Give as well as get. Otherwise you're just a good-looking asshole who screws around."

In addition, she made him swear that he would never date a girl who was a racist, and never join a fraternity.

Jeffrey loved women, true enough. But like he'd said to Sarah, he wasn't a dog. During his marriage to Mariette, he'd been tempted to stray dozens of times—certainly dozens more than he'd given in to. And she'd had at least one affair of her own.

But this thing with Sarah was different. He knew as he watched her walk out of that restaurant it was only a matter of time, and not a very long time at that, before he would be with her. And now he had only to recall the feel of her fingers on the side of his neck, and he was suddenly fighting an erection.

What he wanted to do was stay with Sarah all night, waste himself inside her, sleep with her coiled around him. It rankled that he couldn't. He'd have to get going in an hour or so, go home. *Sorry, babe. I had a really late night at so-and-so's office. Deposition was a million pages long.* He could make that one fly with Mariette any day of the week. But she would have his ass if he didn't come home at all.

He rooted around in the cabinet and found the tea that Sarah said she liked. He'd bring her a cup of that and then he'd shower and say his goodbyes for the night.

Jeffrey walked slowly as he headed for the bedroom, his head down. Cop to it, fella, he told himself. You want to put your dick in Sarah and never let her out of your sight. You don't want her to be with anybody but you. *And* you want to keep your kids. *And* you want to keep Mariette.

You are a dog.

## CHAPTER 8

# Lower Broadway, 2000

Kofi looked out of the tall window of the Internet café off Lafayette Street.

"I used to come down around here when I was a kid, acting up with my friends. This part of the Village was kind of a no-man's-land. Mostly old winos stumbling over to the Bowery."

"That gentrification is a bitch, ain't it?" Yvonne said. "I don't know how you Manhattan folks afford the rents."

"My nephew Bean lives on the Bowery. He lucked out; he got an old loft over one of those kitchen-supply places. The Bowery is one of the hippest nabes in the city these days."

"That's his name—Bean?"

"His name's Benjamin. We call him Bean. He's a good kid. He's a real boho type. You know—arty, smokes a little too much weed, and he's sometimes not too good at listening to his elders.

He should be here in a couple of minutes. He wants to meet you, so I told him to come over and we'd walk you to work."

When young Benjamin Collins arrived, Yvonne understood at once why they called him Bean. As in string bean. He was a six-footer-plus, with long dreadlocks, delicate shoulders and waist, and no ass to speak of. Under his jacket he wore a form-fitting orange tee shirt, and on those endless legs, faded cargo pants. He broke into a sly grin when he caught sight of his uncle. Yvonne watched in amusement as they embraced and then gripped hands, entwined thumbs, banged knuckles, and more.

"Yvonne Howard, this is my home slice," Kofi said. "He's gonna be the next Gordon Parks."

She looked blankly at him.

"Famous photographer," Kofi said. "I'll show you his stuff sometime."

She took stock of the young man. "You in school while you waiting to get famous?"

"I'm going to Parsons."

"Yvonne's a chef," said Kofi. "Over at a new place on Greenwich."

"Cool," Bean said.

"I'm not exactly the chef."

Kofi excused himself a few minutes later. He was running across the street to turn in a review at the *Village Voice* office. That left Yvonne and Bean alone at the table.

"Wow," the young man said softly. "He is so into you."

"Say what?"

"My uncle. No wonder he sounded kind of dorky on the phone. I didn't realize he had a new lady."

"He doesn't. Who was the old one?"

"Oh, the usual. A brain. My uncle always goes for the brains. You're not what I expected. No, wait a minute. That didn't come out the way I meant."

"That's okay. I know I ain't no professor. But I can dress myself, sign my name, and everything."

Kofi watched them as he walked back into the café. Yvonne was laughing. It made her look younger. He guessed she was fortysomething. Tough woman, Yvonne. Strong. She had probably had a hard life, but she didn't look beaten down. He might even be a little scared of her.

He'd often had that reaction to other black people: ones who'd had it rough in life, growing up poor, everything a struggle, and yet they had come out right. Resourceful. Resilient. They never failed to inspire his admiration, and they never failed to intimidate him.

Yvonne was physically different from the women he was usually attracted to. She straightened her hair, for one thing. He thought back over the last four women he'd gone out with: two with braids, one with a nearly shaved head, and a white woman. All had been conventionally pretty, slender, feminist, intellectuals. Yvonne was solidly built, not heavy but with strong, wide shoulders and a real colored woman's butt. She was quick and funny but had had little schooling. And it seemed he was offending her every ten minutes with one of his dumb cultural assumptions or some other kind of blunder. He was usually a social smoothie, but he was constantly stepping on her toes. She was just so hard to read.

His late mother would have been baffled by his attraction to Yvonne, as Kofi himself was, in a way. Mimi Collins, an avowed social snob, had been a powerful presence, a deeply intelligent woman who had owned a travel agency and run an art gallery for a European investor. She was ambitious for her children—especially in her hopes that they should make "good marriages"—and would wonder what he had in common with an ordinary-looking, working-class woman who'd once made her living as a prison guard. Kofi recognized that much of what he had accomplished in life was due solely to his determination not to disappoint her. He knew just as surely that he still had some miles to go before her ambitions for him would be completely satisfied.

Bean, always a joker, appeared to be teasing Yvonne now, or maybe it was the other way round. In any case, the two of them had their heads together. Kofi had loved his sister fiercely, and once she was gone, his affection for her child seemed to double.

"What kind of nonsense are you telling this lady, Bean?"

"Nothing. I just said your cap kinda makes you look like Marvin Gaye."

"Nothing wrong with that," Yvonne said merrily. "But we better hit the road now. If y'all are going to walk me to Sea Grass, you better get to it."

When she got in to work she changed into her white apron. Then she put up water for a cup of tea before starting the pie dough. Three other kitchen employees were milling about. Someone had stuck a Post-it note with her name on it on the stand mixer: *BITTY CALLED*, the note read, *PLEASE CALL BACK ASAP.*

Nobody could figure out why Yvonne suddenly started cussing.

## CHAPTER 9

# Midtown Manhattan, 2000

After Jeffrey left, Sarah fell off again. A drunken, drowning sort of sleep. She went under the heavy waves and then resurfaced time and again, like a sea animal feeding and dying at the same time. It was three in the morning when she awoke.

Life had suddenly taken on a propulsive forward motion. The wracking, exhilarating sex alone was enough of a change. But it didn't stop there. Jeff apparently wanted more; he talked as if he saw some sort of future for them—that word that meant everything and nothing when applied to human interactions: a relationship.

Part of her said she'd better take control of herself, put the brakes on the affair. Yet, another part of her was eager for the next step, no matter what that step would be. Watch yourself, said half her brain. Let go, said the other.

She put on her warm robe. In the closet were the cartons she had mailed to herself from Wilmington. After the Salvation Army came to pick up all the clothing, dishes, and furniture, Sarah had hurriedly packed up everything that was left. She retrieved the boxes now, then sat on the bed and slit the first one open.

It contained some tea towels that clearly had never been used, several fragile-looking lace hankies and curtains, and a beautiful old silver service, not sterling, but still striking. In the next box were a couple of fur hats and half a dozen pairs of ladies' gloves, vintage ones from the 1940s, Sarah guessed. A smaller box inside the carton held a few good pieces of costume jewelry and a winder watch with a mother-of-pearl face. There was also a crystal cigarette box with a matching lighter. With no memory of seeing most of those things growing up in the Wilmington apartment, Sarah decided they must have belonged to her mother's mother.

In the third carton, the largest, were some small pillows her mother had embroidered, a warm afghan, and miscellaneous bedding. Sarah began to tug at the tightly packed items.

She was astonished when she unfolded one of the faded quilts and saw the figure stitched at the middle of it: the likeness of a forbidding-looking black man with wild tufts of hair made of black wool. Actually, when Sarah examined the quilt more closely, she could see that the untamed coils on his head were shaped like sea horses; it was as if they were devouring one another. The man's huge eyes were sewn in white, the eyeballs red, and fairly popping out of their sockets. Along the borders of the quilt were carefully stitched images: weeping willows, setting suns, an arrow in flames, a figure—surely meant to suggest Satan—with a split tongue, and, most disturbing of all, a solitary white serpent.

She ran her hand over the surface of the quilt, then suddenly withdrew it when she felt a jolt like pinpricks run up her arm. She hesitated, but then placed a few fingers on it again. The same sensation occurred. She took the large square by its edge and slid it aside.

At the bottom of the carton was a Bible. When she picked it up a snapshot fluttered out. A small group of people in a park. A young version of her mother was one of them. It looked as if they were at a picnic. Could one of the two middle-aged men in the photo, holding paper plates, be her father? Not likely; she didn't look a bit like either of them, and besides, Lila as pictured was a great deal younger than the others.

She sat staring at the faded image of her mother for a long time. Then she remembered something from the last few days she had spent in Wilmington. Her mother, Lila, had been attended by the childless woman who had always lived in the apartment below. Miss Bea, who'd been as much a servant to Lila as a friendly neighbor, was crazy about little Sarah. Where Lila had an oddly remote relationship with Sarah, Bea doted on the little girl. Baby Sarah would coo and raise her little arms, and Lila would usually just look at her. Bea was the one who'd lift Sarah from the crib, babble her love at her, kiss her little forehead. It was she who picked Sarah up from kindergarten, she who babysat when Lila had to work at night, she who fussed with young Sarah's clothes, took her for ice cream as a reward for every exemplary report card, knew what toy she wanted for Christmas.

When the funeral was over, Bea and Sarah cried together for a few moments in the apartment. Bea dried her eyes, and then turned to Sarah with an odd, pained expression, clearly having trouble voicing what she wanted to. When Sarah asked why she was looking at her that way, Bea, after another minute's faltering, admitted that she'd done "something bad." Something maybe unforgivable.

"What are you talking about?" Sarah said. "You never did a wrong thing in your whole life."

"There was something she made me promise to do. But I didn't," Bea choked out. "I couldn't."

"What was it?"

"There was a notebook, like a diary. She made me promise to give it to you after she was gone."

"Where is it?"

Bea shook her head.

"What did you do with it?"

"I burned it, child."

"What?"

"Yes. I tore it up and burned it."

"Why would you do that?"

"I read it, that's why. I know it was wicked of me, but I read it. I know I had no right, it wasn't none of my business, but I had a feeling about what was in it, and sure enough . . . I wasn't gone let you see that crazy nonsense, Sarah. It was only going to make you more unhappy. Fearful. The last thing in the world you needed. And it just wasn't right. It wasn't fair! You deserve better, you deserve to be happy.

"Lila wasn't right, honey. I mean right in her mind. Not for a long time. I knew it. Her pastor knew it. Some of the things she said—even when she was young—things about putting herself out of her misery, and you along with her. I was scared, I swear to Jesus I was scared of what might happen to her, but mostly I was fearing for you.

"I came to realize she couldn't hurt you. She loved you, baby, in her way she did, and she did her best for you. But, Sarah, I think she did hurry her dying along, at the least she let herself sicken and die. She had a sadness that was beyond help, even God's. That's what she thought, anyway. Such a heavy, heavy stone on that girl's soul. I wasn't going to let it be something that you'd have to carry. I made up my mind that crazy talk was not gonna ruin your life too. You got every right to be angry with me for what I did, but I stand by it."

"I'm not angry, Bea. But how was a diary going to ruin my life? Were there things in it about my father? Something terrible about him?"

"No! No, far as I know there wasn't nothing wrong with your father. I believe your father was a nice young man, a good man who loved Lila. Please, child, don't ask me no more. Just go back home now. Live your life and know your Nanny Bea's thinking of you, pulling for you to be happy. Like I always have. Find somebody, live your life, and be happy."

Bea kissed Sarah goodbye and told her to be sure and call when she was safely back in New York.

———

Now, staring at her pretty, expressionless mother in the old snapshot, Sarah felt an odd but somehow familiar ticking in her ears. She suddenly placed both hands on the quilt with the old man's face and once again felt the prickling shoot up her arms and heat up her core. Fierce, scalding heat.

She looked over at the radio alarm clock. It was six in the morning now, and barely light out. She dressed for the street and took the elevator down to the lobby, then out through the heavy glass doors. She began to hurry west, toward the nearest subway.

She had no idea where she was going.

## CHAPTER 10

### *The Georgia Backwoods, 1865*

Nightfall.

Something was wrong.

Ruben and Henry had been walking up ahead. Monroe, Abner, and Preacher Jack trailed behind because the boy, Abner, had cut his foot on a stone, and Jack and Monroe had stopped to wrap the foot in rags.

Now there was no sign of Ruben and Henry.

Something was wrong. Monroe knew it. He used his shirt-sleeve to wipe at the sweat dripping from his forehead, all the while searching the leafy wilderness.

From not far away came the faint whinnying of a horse. Then the smell of fire reached them. The three stragglers stopped, halted their breathing along with their footsteps. When they heard the sudden cry of agony, they all hit the ground and began to crawl on their bellies.

There must have been four or five of them—in dirty gray uniforms rotting on their flesh. They had Henry hanging upside down over the flames, hands tied behind his back, one foot dangling from the rope swung across a huge oak. The fire was eating at his face. Abner tried to spring up, go to his father, but Monroe held him fast while Jack used one hand to cover the boy's mouth and used the other hand to cover his eyes.

The three black sojourners lay pinned to the ground while Ruben was led to a tree stump where one of his captors chopped his head off with a dirty saber.

## *Chelsea, 2000*

Tuesday was Yvonne's day off. Ordinarily she used the day to clean the apartment, catch up on the newspapers, pay bills, do the shopping. But today she had not one but two appointments. She had agreed to meet Kofi and his nephew in the afternoon, and then, late that night, she was going to make the trip up to the after-hours place where Bitty worked.

Yvonne had a buddy, Sheila Morton, who left the prison guard scene even before Yvonne did. Sheila, who had married and divorced before she was thirty, met a cop, a white guy named Richard, and they fell in love. They married and Sheila quit to have his baby. She now had a low-stress job as a receptionist in a law office. She and Yvonne didn't spend much time together anymore, but they remained friendly—a dinner invitation from

Sheila a couple of times a year, going to a show together once in a blue moon.

Yvonne had been meaning to invite Sheila and Richard to have dinner at Sea Grass, but had not yet managed to get around to it. She phoned Sheila at the office and told her she needed to call Richard's closest friend, an NYPD homicide detective. Did Sheila have his phone number?

———

Detective Kyle Sansom wasn't so easy to reach that day. Yvonne had to place three calls before she caught up with him. He was busy but seemed pleased enough to hear from her.

"Yvonne? Sure, I remember you. We were at the same table at the wedding. And that barbecue Sheila and Richard had last summer; you brought that incredible lemon pie. What can I do you?"

"Well, remember what happened a couple of weeks ago at that hotel on Fifty-Sixth Street?"

Of course he knew about the jumper. It was the damnedest thing. They were calling it a suicide for now, but the books were far from closed. "What in hell," Sansom asked, "does that have to do with you, Yvonne?"

She outlined the problem, Bitty's problem, and asked if there was any way he could get some inside dope on the case.

For a full thirty seconds, he didn't answer, then he said, "Let me get back to you."

———

"I feel like a lady of leisure again," Yvonne told Bean.

"What do you mean, 'again'?"

"When I didn't have a job, I spent a lot of days like this—just taking walks, going to see movies and stuff. I was trying to get my head straight after all that time in the system."

"Did you ever go to any galleries?" Bean asked.

"No. The ones we got in Queens didn't have a handsome young man like you to give people lectures."

Bean and Yvonne were walking along Tenth Avenue. They were due to meet up with Kofi, who had phoned to say he was delayed, so Bean and Yvonne were passing the time by looking at art in the busy gallery district.

"You have a good way of explaining things," she told him. "You know how to help the other person understand what they looking at. Planning on being a teacher?"

"Not me. I'd rather be the guy the teachers teach about."

"I hear that. What kind of photographs you take?"

"I don't know—lots of different things. I'm kinda into clocks right now. Big ones, little ones, antiques . . . whatever."

"What's so interesting about them?"

"I don't ask myself that. I just do it. I figure someday they'll be looking at my work and calling it my 'Time' period."

"Well," Yvonne said, "time is important, isn't it? And you never know when yours is gonna stop."

"That's kind of deep, Aunt Yvonne."

"*Aunt?* Hold your horses, boy. You way ahead of yourself. I haven't even had lunch with the man, and you already got us married."

"Tell me about what you used to do, would you? Kofi says you were a prison guard. How'd you get into that?"

"No mystery to it. The pay was good for somebody with no education to speak of. I was telling myself I was going to help make a bad situation a little better. They say everybody deserves a second chance. Guess I was also thinking maybe I'd learn a little more about life myself."

"But . . . ?"

She shook her head. "I had to get out of there before it drove me crazy. And now, as much as I want to put some distance between me and that place, here I am in contact with one of the old inmates—at least, she's in contact with me."

"Like, as a friend?"

"We not friends. She had a brother who died a few weeks ago. She's bugging me to look into it for her, and I'm gonna do what I can."

Yvonne picked up her pace, but Bean suddenly stayed her with his hand. "Hang on a sec," he said. "I want to get a shot of you with those old rail tracks in the background."

"Help yourself," she said, striking a pose. "But don't blame me if it breaks your camera."

Who in the world would've thought I'd be traipsing my ass around 141st Street at one in the morning?

Yvonne peered into the bar through the smoky front windows.

Not me, that's for damn sure. And I'm so stupid to be doing it, I deserve whatever I get.

She opened the ornately carved front door and walked in.

Shiny red-leather booths and a long bar with a polished brass rail. On the shelves were some fairly high-end bottles, with Courvoisier given a show-off spot in the front row. Okay, Yvonne thought, okay, not too shabby.

Yvonne saw Bitty at the computerized cash register. "I thought you said you were doing so great up here. Don't look like business is exactly booming tonight," she said. "Where is everybody?"

"This was a real off night," Bitty said. "It happens. We gone go ahead and close a few hours early. I'm just about to lock up." She dropped her voice a bit then. "There's a little meeting—I mean a game—going on upstairs. My partner and some friends of his."

"A game, huh?"

"You got something for me?"

"In a way. But you're not going to like it."

"What you mean?"

"I mean, the cops say they have no reason to think your brother was murdered—even though there's a few things don't make sense about the case."

"See there?" said Bitty. "What kind of things?"

"Did Crawford have a heart condition?"

"No. He never said nothing about that."

"Any other health problems, like stomach troubles, maybe food allergies or something?"

"No. Why you asking that?"

"Because it looks like he went into cardiac arrest before he went out that window. Healthy man just had his heart seize up on him. Doesn't sound right."

"Damn straight, it don't. What else?"

"The medical people say they had a hard time with the body because it was so smashed up, but there were traces of something nasty on his arms and legs, like pus, along with some indications he was choking on something."

"Choking on food?"

"Well, maybe. There was some food in his stomach, but no sign he gagged on anything."

"That's some crazy shit," Bitty said. "Go ahead."

"I know what you said about your brother hating prostitutes. But it looks like he was with one. The waiter in the lounge of the hotel told the police all about the pickup. Crawford and this gal left the bar together and went upstairs, most likely to his room. Security camera didn't catch them actually going in. That was the last time anybody at the hotel saw him alive."

"That's it then," Bitty said. "That goddamn whore must have killed him. She must have poisoned him and pushed him out that window."

"No evidence of that, Bitty. None. Maybe they had sex and the woman left. Because Crawford was naked when he hit the ground, and when they went into his room, it looked like he had recently taken a shower or a bath. The shower stall was still damp. He could have slept with this hooker and after she left he washed up. I don't know. But they can't locate hide nor hair of her. There were a few fingerprints left behind besides Crawford's, but they don't match any prostitute on the records."

The door to the bar opened just then and a well-groomed, dewy-skinned woman in her thirties walked in—pampered-looking, fine hairdo right out of a Madison Avenue salon. She sat at the front of the bar and looked expectantly at Bitty, who excused herself long enough to serve the woman. In the dim light, Yvonne looked at the newcomer's delicate profile. She was lovely.

Chick who looks like that strolling into this joint all by her-self at one in the morning? Had to be a story behind that. Speaking of stories, Yvonne decided, there's no way to know if this really was ordinarily a thriving bar, as Bitty had claimed, or some kind of shadow operation meant to insulate whatever the people upstairs were doing. She looked back over at the bar.

The new arrival ordered a martini. Bitty hurriedly made the drink and handed it to the woman, explaining that they were just about to close, so she'd better make it a quick one.

Bitty picked up where she and Yvonne had left off. "Damn them. There's gotta be some better answers than what you just told me," Bitty said.

"Maybe there are."

"What do that mean?"

"My source says everything I told you was in the files on the case. But there's some other medical findings they're keeping to themselves. He can't get access to the whole story. Nobody can."

"*I'm* gonna get it, one way or another," Bitty said. "Fuck them. I told you, I'm not asking for favors. Take the money I tried to give you in the restaurant. Keep on them about Crawford."

"No! No to both things, Bitty. I don't want your money. And I'm not going to get pulled in any further with this thing. I know you're hurting, but there's only so much I can do."

Yvonne had seen Bitty contentious, sullen, high. But she had never seen her look so helpless before, bereft.

"He was my brother, Yvonne. I got nothing left. Nobody. Don't you understand that? Ain't you got any kind of family you need to love and protect?"

Yvonne sighed, watched the other woman weep silently. In a minute, Bitty took a brightly colored paper napkin and blew her nose.

"Just stop it, okay?" Yvonne said at last. "We'll see what else we can find out. I'll think of something. Just stop that crying, girl. I can't stand it."

Bitty pulled herself together, nodded. "I gotta go to the bathroom," she said, "and then Ima tell this bitch she got to leave."

Yvonne poured herself a glass of water after Bitty left, and as she drank she stole another glance at the beautiful woman, who was now standing down from her high bar seat. She walked past Yvonne and into the ladies' room.

A few minutes later Bitty came back to the bar. She was ashen and sweaty, and seemed to be having trouble seating herself on the stool. She was also giving off a queer rancid odor that was utterly unlike anything Yvonne had ever smelled.

"What's the matter?" Yvonne said, even more alarmed when she saw the foam on Bitty's lips. "What is it, girl? Were you sick in there?"

Bitty didn't answer. She struggled for a few seconds, her head turning this way and that on her neck. When at last she opened her mouth, dark, stinking blood poured from it in a torrent.

Yvonne jumped back with a shriek.

Bitty was on the floor now, spinning crazily, as her flesh began to rip open, her body spewing gore like the pulsing head of a lawn sprinkler.

Yvonne stared in disbelief for a minute, and then she knelt and began to call Bitty's name, over and over.

Then a thought broke through her panic—the refined lady. The refined lady—what about her? Oh my God, is she in there rolling around in gore too? Is she dead? Yvonne ran into the powder room, and found it empty. She kicked open all the stall doors but there was no sign of the woman.

By the time Yvonne returned to the bar, Bitty was all but finished. Yvonne knelt again and watched helplessly as she spasmed on the red-tiled floor, then finally went still. Then she heard thundering footsteps overhead.

Yvonne looked up toward the sound.

From that second on, there was a black hole in the episode. All she knew was that a powerful blow came out of nowhere—

a slap of unimaginable force. That, and the sensation of a slimy wetness. She was knocked clear back to the area with the tables and banquettes, and she was now on all fours, groveling, dopey.

There were men in the bar now, shouting, running around; no doubt, they were the players Bitty meant when she'd said there was some kind of "game" going on upstairs.

One of them was leaning over her. She read his lips: *What happened?* Yvonne wanted to tell him what had happened. But she could not find her tongue. She wanted to understand it for herself. But she could not think in words.

## CHAPTER 12

# Wilmington, Delaware, 1969

Lila Toomey was taking a drifting kind of walk along the scarred avenue several blocks from the nicer part of the neighborhood, where she lived. She was in no hurry. It was her day off, and she had spent the free time tidying the apartment, doing laundry, and chatting for a few minutes with Miss Bea, the downstairs neighbor who'd been her mother's good friend, and was now like a favored maiden aunt to Lila.

A group of young men were shooting hoops in a trash-littered lot, fit bodies colliding and caroming off one another in the dusky light. Lila stood watching them as they leapt up, took off running in one direction and then the other, talking all the while, trading insults, joking, slapping palms. She followed the movements of the thinnest of them. The one with the modest-length Afro. When he shot up and palmed the ball in midair, his long fingers seemed to scratch the sky. It seemed to her that he might just take flight, ascend straight on up to the heavens. The next time he rises up off the ground like that, Lila thought, his jeans are going to slide off his bony hips.

The game was breaking up now and Lila turned away from the lot.

"Wait a minute. Where you going?"

She was face-to-face with the young man who had spoken. It was the skinny, skyward-bound one. "I'm going home," she said.

"You don't have to leave right now. I mean, do you? Have to?"

She looked at him closely. He was young, but no teenager. Somewhere in his early twenties, she estimated.

He wiped the film of sweat from his forehead. "Come on, let me walk you home," he said. "Sorry, I'm kind of a mess."

Neither of them talked as they picked their way along the ugly street with its sagging, black-eyed buildings, its shards of glass on the pavement, burnt-out cars here and there at the curbs. He felt around in the pocket of his tee shirt, finally extracting a battered-looking cigarette and matches. He lit it, drew in noisily, then offered it to her.

She shook her head.

"Oh man. You don't like weed?"

"Not really. But you go ahead and enjoy it."

No more words were exchanged for a long time. The thin young man walked close to her, near enough to brush the back of her hand with every step. She did not pull away from him.

When they turned down her street, the supermarket manager was locking the iron grate at the front of the store. The neon of the liquor store sign blinked watery Christmas colors at them. From somewhere, dimly, came the insinuating bass growl of Sly Stone. "Hot Fun in the Summertime."

The thin young man had begun to sing along with the record, but then he stopped abruptly, stiffening as he took note of the uniformed cop at the wheel of a patrol car, just sitting there at the curb. The officer returned the look, eyes lingering on the boy.

"We close to where you live at?" the young man said. Another quick glance at the cop car.

Lila nodded.

He looked in through the window of the diner in the middle of the block. A few couples sat talking over coffee or burgers, and at the counter an older man laughed with the waitress between bites of his pie.

"You go here to eat sometimes?" he said.

"Sometimes."

"I'd take you in there and we could have—" he said, and rather than finish the sentence, he chuckled. "But I'm kind of short."

"Short?"

"You know—money."

"Oh."

"I guess I should just finish walking you home."

"All right."

"You know something?" he said a minute later. "You about the best-looking girl I ever talked to in person."

"You're nice to say that. You stared at the coffee shop. Are you hungry?"

"Yeah . . . ?" Puzzled. Suspicious.

"I can make you something. I know how to cook."

"Hey, listen," he said. "Is it just me, or do other folks tell you you're— Wow, this is weird, man. You really gone just take me to your house and make me something to eat? I mean, I can't tell if you just fucking with my head."

"It's this way, at the other end of the block."

"Wait a minute, Crazy. I don't know your name."

"It's Lila."

"Lila. Okay. My name's Eugene."

———————

"You live by yourself?"

"Yes. Since my mother passed away."

"You don't have a man?"

She shook her head.

"I don't believe that. You. Don't have no man."

"I don't."

She rose from her chair and picked up his empty plate, headed for the kitchen. "There's coffee if you want. I don't have any beer or anything."

When she came back to join him, he was holding another joint. "Okay to smoke?"

"Yes."

"Why don't you smoke some with me? Come on."

"If you want," she said. "You seem to smoke quite a lot of marijuana."

"It cools me out, keeps me from worrying all the time."

"Yes, I can see how it might do that. What are you worrying about?"

"What don't I have to worry about? Anything you can name. Being broke. All the time. Being black. All the time. Being ignorant. And mad as fuck about—everything. Just—you know."

She nodded.

"I guess," he said, "I could just as well be what my grandmother calls 'one a those awful street niggers.' But she says I'm all she got left, and if that's gone be me, she rather I just kill her in her sleep."

"You wouldn't ever be an awful street . . . you wouldn't be that, no matter what. Any more than you'd kill your grandmother. I don't see you hurting anyone."

"Whatever. Long as you know I'm not out to hurt you. 'Cause I'm not. I swear."

"I believe you."

When he asked if she wanted him to leave, she said no.

"Good," he said. "'Cause I don't want to. Even if there's a chance all this ain't real, I'm just stupid high and this not really happening."

He followed her into the kitchen and stood near her while, with amazing efficiency, almost without looking, she made a batch of brownies and slid the pan into the oven.

"Remember what I said, I'm not gonna make no kind of move on you. But . . . I'm dying to kiss you. I won't lie about it. You think I could do that?"

Lila placed her dish towel down on the counter and then stepped to him.

"Damn." He grinned. "You not afraid of nothing, are you?"

Eugene did not go home that night.

"I'm kind of dirty," he said at the doorway of her small bedroom. "Sweaty and stuff."

She nodded toward the bathroom. "There're towels in there."

His heart soared five minutes later, when Lila stepped into the shower stall. He reached out timidly, smoothed her wet shoulders. "Damn. Look at your skin, girl. I don't believe this."

After they made love, they sat in the dark talking. He didn't believe she was from down South—she didn't talk like anybody from down South that he ever knew. She sounded more like a white girl.

"Actually, it's my mother who was from there. We came up here when I was quite young. She worked like mad, sent me to private school from the time I was nine. I think she was secretly happy to not have me around so much. Anyway, is that what you mean by 'white'? You mean educated?"

"Yep," he said.

"Is that a problem for you?"

"Naw. I don't have one single problem with you."

Half an hour later he got out of bed and made his second trip to the kitchen for more brownies.

"We do have one or two things in common," he said. "Your mama's dead and so is mine."

"And not knowing much about our fathers," Lila added.

"Mine was always in jail somewhere. I used to hate him, you know? But what did that get me? Anyway, so Gem—that's what we call my grandmama—she raised my brother, Holly, and me. She kinda had to. Lest the state was gonna take us."

"I never met my grandmother," Lila said. She stopped there and reached past him to pick up the stub of a joint from the ashtray. She lit it. "What did you do when the riots broke out? Did you and your brother take part in the looting?"

"Naw, I gotta stay by Gem. What if the building caught on fire or something, she never get out by herself." And, he added, he had to make runs some days to the stores on the other side of the city, "to get food and shit, and she gotta have her medicine."

He'd pick his way around the tanks of the National Guardsmen who remained a hulking presence in the ruined streets for almost a year after the murder of Dr. King. "It wasn't even funny, man. You go out for milk or something, some army clown got a rifle on you."

And as for his younger brother: "Holly too busy to be looting shit."

"Busy?" Lila asked.

"Right. Busy in 'Nam."

———

Lila had to dress and get to work, so she woke Eugene early and told him he'd have to go. He gave her a stormy look when she ushered him to the door.

"And so this is it, right?" he said. "My groovy acid trip is finished and I'll never see you again. Maybe except in my dreams."

She laughed, but said nothing.

"No shit though. I'm serious. Can I see you tonight?"

"Yes."

He bent down, clumsily, and kissed her.

She waited until she heard the street door close behind him. She hid her face in her hands, and stood there like that for a long time.

———

Eugene became enough of a fixture at Lila's apartment building that the other tenants were wishing him good evening when they passed him on the stairs.

He was waiting for her one Sunday when church let out. On the sidewalk, he watched as she approached him. He noticed someone else looking at her too. A small man in purple robes standing in the church doorway.

"Who is that?" he said when she was by his side.

Lila turned and exchanged a long glance with the robed man. "My minister. I mean *the* minister. It isn't as if he's only mine."

"How come you go to church anyway? You don't have religion. I mean, not like my grandmother and all the old people."

"You're right, I'm not religious. I really don't care about the services. It's just—my mother went there and she was devoted to the minister. She depended on him."

"But you don't need him, do you? What's so great about him?"

"He's someone to talk to. I need to talk to him sometimes."

"You can't talk to me?"

"Stop, Eugene," she said. "Let it go."

So this is how it is with normal people, she thought. Needling. Little jealousies. Things you said between tight teeth. Lila looked back at the empty doorway. "Please, Eugene. No more questions."

———————

"I got something to tell you," he announced one evening. "Don't look like that. It's nothing bad."

"Tell me."

"You no longer with a loser sponging off his grandmama. I got a job. Kind of. This dude who runs a car service says he'll put me on a few days a week."

"That's wonderful, Eugene."

"Yeah. He's cool, for a old dude. You should meet him sometime, and Gem too. I want her to know you."

"Oh, sometime," Lila said. "I'll meet her sometime."

*Meet his people or don't meet them. It doesn't matter. But the other thing . . . that* has *to happen, doesn't it?* Lila would think, laying close to him as he slept. *But why? And when? All I know is, I'm not the one who decides.*

She never expected to have these feelings, ever, for anyone, but then came the surprise of sweet Eugene, and she did not know what to do. Except to play it out. She had located him two weeks before he noticed her in the lot where she allowed him to pick her up. But, again and again, she'd put off actually approaching him. You can't know about a person's gentleness, his essential goodness, before you even speak to him for the first time. But somehow, she did know. That first night they were together, he'd turned to her sheepishly after the sex. "You all right?"

"I'm more than all right," she said.

"Okay. 'Cause I don't want you thinking I look at myself like some kind of stud. I know I'm nothing special in the sack," he said.

"Nor me, Eugene," she answered, "but you are tender. You don't realize how much that's worth."

*The funny, horrible part of it—feeling like I should, or could, protect him, shield him. I should have told him he'd be better off in Vietnam. I should have said run a thousand miles away from me, but he wouldn't have listened. I should have run those thousand miles away from him, but I couldn't, I can't. So when it comes, it'll be the worst thing in the world for both of us. Like evil itself is laughing at us.*

Her restlessness had awakened him. He was yawning now. "What's wrong?" he said. "You shaking like a leaf. You crying, Lila?"

"No."

He moved closer. "Lila," he said, "you know what I figured out?"

She waited.

"I'm better than I thought I was. And I don't feel like I'm just ordinary no more. And that's on you, Lila. That's what you doing for me."

"It isn't me, Eugene."

"Yeah, yeah it is. You look at me full-on with those eyes, I see you liking me, respecting me. You looking straight into my soul, girl. I can't even tell you how damn glad about it I am."

She sobbed once, a bottomless sound.

"What? Tell me what's wrong."

"It doesn't matter," she said when she could speak again. "I want to stay with you for a long time. I love you."

"Then why you keep getting sadder, baby?"

She turned toward him and kissed his mouth. "Just hold me for a while. I'm cold."

He wrapped his long arms around her. "Here you go, Crazy. Go back to sleep."

## CHAPTER 13

# Kew Gardens, Queens, 2000

Yvonne walked back from the kitchen and crawled into bed with the ice pack. Her head was pounding something fierce.

The police had questioned her for hours after it happened, letting her know she was about the shittiest witness they'd ever encountered.

And why wouldn't they think that? The story she told about Bitty's freak show—where she acted like the child in *The Exorcist*—and the gorgeous martini-drinking woman who could make herself invisible would have made anybody think she was nuts. Or drunk.

After the EMS people brought her around with smelling salts, the only believable thing she said was the name of her police department acquaintance, Kyle Sansom. That got the cops' attention. Sansom, thank God, got out of his bed, drove over to the club, and convinced them to let her go.

He bundled Yvonne into his car and took her to her place, where he questioned her in a gentler fashion, and finally left her to her bed. She'd been there ever since.

She finally fell asleep. Her dreams had her back in the hell of the club where Bitty had met her terrible end. She awoke only when she heard the insistent ringing of the doorbell. Sansom had promised to leave her be for at least a day, but apparently he wasn't a man of his word. That had to be him at the door. She dragged herself up and through the apartment.

It wasn't Detective Sansom at the door. It was Kofi.

"Yvonne. Are you all right?"

She felt too weary to answer.

"They said you didn't show up for work, and your phone's off the hook, and you look awful. *Are you all right?*"

***

Kofi made the coffee and scrambled eggs while she explained.

He let her complete the whole story before speaking: "I don't believe it," he said.

"Believe it, man. I told you exactly what I saw."

"I'm not saying I don't believe you. I just meant, maybe you were so upset by the whole thing that you imagined . . . The way you told it . . . Look, there has to be some rational explanation for what happened."

"What you saying? I'm not rational? I know what happened, Kofi. I'm not in a daze no more."

He held up a placating hand. "Okay, okay. What did the cop say, this Sansom?"

"He doesn't know what to make of it either. But he says he thinks *something funny's* going on. Hmmm—ya think? Two healthy people just dropping dead, their hearts exploding and shit, and both with this untraceable stuff on their skin—and both of them black. And they're sister and brother!"

"He ought to take it easy, and you too, Yvonne. Don't go seeing a conspiracy yet. Bitty and the dude in the hotel were brother and sister, right?"

"Yeah."

"So, look at all the health troubles that run in families: diabetes, high blood pressure, even schizophrenia, not to mention *heart disease.* I ought to know. My mother and my sister both died way ahead of their time from it. You inherit that kind of stuff from your parents and their parents, and so on. Say everything you described to me really happened just the way you said. Okay. It was just something crazy in their DNA. Make sense?"

"You weren't there, man. You didn't see what I saw."

"What I said makes more sense than somebody covering folks with slime and killing 'em for absolutely no reason. Doesn't it? . . . Doesn't it make more sense?" When he got no answer, he said, "Let's leave it alone for a minute. You have a drink in the house? I know I could use one."

Yvonne pointed at the cabinet over the microwave.

He took down the glasses and poured two overgenerous bourbons.

"You know, you're not the only one who had a scare today," Kofi said.

"What do you mean?"

"We were supposed to speak in the afternoon. Remember,

we were going to make a date? And then when they told me at the restaurant that you didn't show and hadn't called in—and when I kept calling you at home and couldn't get through, I thought something terrible had happened to you."

She snorted.

"Yes, I know. Something terrible did. But you're still here, and you're okay. I'd be devastated if something happened to you, Yvonne."

"I'm glad to hear it," she said. "Let's drink to my health, why don't we? I was sho nuff worried about it last night."

He took a long gulp. A minute later he said, "Promise not to get mad if I ask something else about what happened."

Yvonne sighed.

"That woman," he said.

"Yes. That blond heifer."

"You said she must've been the one who knocked you out— literally knocked you out. Because there was no one else there all night."

"Damn right."

"Right. But you were hit over by the bar. And you kind of woke up on the other side of the room."

"That's right."

"How could that be?"

"I don't know, baby. But it do be. And you know what else? I thought there was something wet on me. Something slimy. And I—" She stopped there.

"You what?"

"Classy looking. She was fair skinned, with a beautiful slim figure, the bartender said."

"What bartender?"

"The witness at the—"

"The witness at the hotel where Bitty's brother died."

"Yeah, we ain't too stupid, are we? He said she was a fine sister, a *re*fined sister, that it was hard to believe she was a prostitute."

"Don't let yourself leap too far ahead, Yvonne. New York is full of good-looking, light-skinned black women. Ever hear of the fashion industry? Or show business?"

"Yes, I have, Kofi. And there's pretty, fair-skinned school-teachers and waitresses and nurses too. I get it. But don't you think it's one coincidence too many? You gonna sit there and tell me it's not more than likely we talking about the same woman who was with Bitty's brother?"

"I'll admit it's not a crazy assumption, okay? I'm admitting it's possible. When do you see the homicide detective again?"

"Tomorrow, I guess. And speaking of tomorrow, I better call in to work." She rose quickly. "I'll be right back."

He was staring at her when she returned and resettled herself in the chair. "What?" she said.

"Listen, Yvonne. I wish you'd be more careful. About everything."

"I guess that means you believe me now."

He continued to look at her, hard, and while he was looking Yvonne realized she had answered the door wearing nothing but her slip, and had been sitting across from him all this time without a stitch on underneath it.

Kofi stood behind her chair. "Believe, don't believe," he finally said. "It doesn't much matter. The main thing is, I'm with you." He placed his hands on her shoulders. "Are you getting cold?"

"Not hardly."

He brought her to her feet and they kissed.

"You're lovely, Yvonne."

"Naw," she said. "I have a good ass is all."

She waited for him while he undressed in the bathroom.

"You know what your nephew asked me?" Yvonne said when he joined her on the bed.

"What?"

"He wanted to know when we were getting married."

Kofi froze, the color draining from his face.

"Take it easy. He was kidding. Come on in, niggah."

Oh good, he thought. That's a good thing, I think—she called me nigger. He smiled then. Mom is turning over in her grave.

## CHAPTER 14

# Midtown Manhattan, 2000

Sarah slept late. It was nearly eleven when she woke. She swung her legs over the side of the bed, and then looked down quizzically at her lap. She was wearing a nightgown she had no memory of buying, a white satin one with a plunging back.

Then she remembered. Jeff gave it to her the last time he was over. The thought of him made her happy, and she realized there was salaciousness in her smile. She wanted him now, wished he were there with her. She summoned up the sensation of his hands on the small of her back as he pulled her to him. She rode that feeling for a long moment. Repressed little Sarah Toomey waking up with sex on her mind. Sex. Jeff didn't say *sex*; he always said *fucking*.

"You still feel broken?" he had asked as they sat naked drinking ice water, Sarah still vibrating from the orgasm.

"Maybe not quite so much anymore."

"See? I told you. We're going to get you straight. Even if you're broken in a hundred pieces."

"You can do that?"

"You bet your ass I can. I must. You know why?"

"No."

"Because, number one, I love you." Then he spoke into her ear: "And two, because Sarah Toomey is a great fuck."

She clamped both hands across her mouth, abashed.

"Say it after me. Sarah Toomey is a great fuck."

"Sarah Toomey," she said, barely audible, "is a great fuck."

———

She made coffee for herself. Back in the bedroom, she sat down on the padded bench and began to pick through the selection of lipsticks in the porcelain saucer she kept on the vanity. On the edge of the table was something she'd completely forgotten about: a cameo that had been in the box with the other things from her mother's apartment.

She set her cup down and picked up the brooch, sliding her finger along its raised surface. I think this was Mom's, she thought, I kind of remember her wearing this. I'll put it on my gold chain, wear it in her honor.

Now she had the same sense of urgency that she'd felt when she unpacked the quilt. Most of what had happened that day was fast vanishing in the rising mist in her mind. She just knew that she rode the trains and wandered the streets for hours. Had she stopped anywhere along the way? Met other people? No idea.

Today, again, she had no idea where she was going, or why. She just knew that she must get dressed and leave.

She got out of her night things and turned on the tap in the shower stall, but before she could step inside, the doorbell rang. That had to be Jeffrey. She wrapped herself in a towel and answered the door.

At the sight of her: "Wow, it's Dorothy Dandridge."

"I thought I was Myrna Loy."

"That was last time, when I was studying your forehead. My dad always said Dorothy Dandridge was the sexiest woman in the world. All I can think about now is what's under that towel."

"What are you doing here so early? Why aren't you at work? I'm the one on leave from the office, not you."

"I had a breakfast meeting on Eighth Avenue. Thought I'd stop by."

"I don't know if I believe you. But I don't care. I'm glad you're here. Can I give you some coffee?"

He didn't answer, just loosened his tie.

She let him undo the towel, stepped closer to him, and ran her hand over the bump in his trousers.

"Tell me what you're going to do with me," she said.

"Uhn uhn. I like it when you tell me."

---

"You keep asking me things," Sarah said. "Things about my childhood and my mother. But, do you want to hear something strange?"

"Sure."

"I don't remember most of it. I'm being literal; it's as if some-one's wiping my hard drive a little more every day, and it's tak-ing bigger and bigger chunks now. We had a neighbor, an older woman named Bea who never had any children of her own. She was wonderful to me. I guess you could technically call her a nanny or a babysitter. But she was more of a mother to me than my own. I don't think Mom ever wanted me. I don't really know. But childhood in general," she shook her head, "very little of it comes back to me. And even things that happened later, they're gradually slipping away too. I do remember Mom was always telling me I had to be good. *Be a good girl,* she'd say. *Promise to be good.* I thought she was talking about minding Miss Bea, and also getting good grades at school. And I did. I always got As."

"Maybe she meant you should be good in the other way. You know. Sexually. Like, don't let the boys take advantage of you, don't dress too flashily."

"She didn't have to worry about it. Nobody was interested in me. Not that way."

"Yeah, there's that clueless thing about you and men."

"What men?"

"All kinds. Am I dumb enough to point them out to you? Anyway, get back to your mother, your father."

"I don't remember my father at all, don't know if I ever saw him. I never pushed Mom on it, but I figured out long ago that she was probably never married to him, or anybody. I think she made that up because she was ashamed. Instead of this wonder-ful husband she talked about, some man just got her pregnant and she never saw him again. I had a lot of bizarre dreams as a child, and maybe he was a presence in them, like a big shadow."

"You think he was black or white?"

"I don't know. It's a good question. I mean, if he was white, it would explain a lot, wouldn't it, like why it was all so secret, like why he wouldn't marry her."

"It would. 'Specially given where you're from. Delaware. Practically the South. Kind of like Boston. And it would go a long way in explaining why you look . . . why you look the way you do."

"Paper Bag. A kid in the neighborhood called me that."

"Yeah, I've heard that one: if you're darker than a grocery bag, you're not acceptable in certain parts of black society. Do you ever think how it might be better, or worse, if you were darker?"

"Yes. My being darker would end a certain amount of unwanted attention, sometimes astonishingly rude questions. But I also see how the way I am makes a lot of white people more comfortable. I don't know—maybe they look at me again, and when they figure it out it makes them even more *un*comfortable."

"Not too often people discuss colorism in the black diaspora while they're naked, don't you think? But I gotta say, I wouldn't mind if you were browner. You know, walnut, English walnut, pecan . . . burnt toast."

"Why?"

"Well, I'd be Mister Cool on the street with my fine black girlfriend. And then at night, oh, it would turn into *Gone with the Wind* up in here. I'd rip off your cheap muslin frock and I'd twist my fingers around a mass of your wild, curly-kinky hair. Pull it back real hard and expose that neck of yours that I love, and I'd fuck the hell out of you, and then make you cook black-eyed peas. Or whatever that shit is they eat down there. I'm making you laugh, right?"

She nodded.

"You've got a goofy laugh. It's so great. I'm making you hot too, right?"

She nodded, pushed the coverlet down.

"I'm not going to work today."

"Yes, you are. But not yet."

———————

"Did you ever see your birth certificate?"

"I'm not sure." She stopped there for a long minute. "I'm beginning to think of myself as the woman who never was."

"No friends, other girls, women, you could talk to about—about anything, everything?"

"That might have been nice, but I don't think so."

"Did your mother ever have a boyfriend? Did she go out with anybody? Maybe a man was living with you two?"

"I don't think so. Why do you ask?"

"Because I just know somebody took something from you. A lot of women get abused when they're little—and they repress it. It happens to boys too. Kids just push it out of their mind in order to survive, and probably a lot of the rest of the past gets buried along with it."

"That makes sense. But I don't think it happened to me. Maybe nothing happened. But even if it did, I don't know that understanding it is going to fix what's wrong with me now."

"Okay. But how about we stop thinking of it as something being 'wrong'? It's like, you know how you said that sometimes you feel like what's going on with us is so . . . so powerful, it makes you scared."

"Yes."

"Well, I'm astounded by it too. Sometimes I can't concentrate on what I'm reading because all I can think about is licking you, right *there*. I actually resent that I'm not with you. I think we can be blown away by how strong it is, how big it feels, but that doesn't mean we have to be afraid of it. I don't want you to be locked in anymore, my beautiful Sarah. I gotta help you break out."

"Aiding and abetting. There's a price to be paid for that."

"Well, even my own mother said I was messianic."

———

"Why don't you let me take you to lunch before I go in to the office," he said.

"I'm not hungry. I'll get something this afternoon."

"Make sure you do, Slim. And call me later," he said as he picked up his coat.

She took his hand, stood there with it in hers.

"What, sweetheart?"

"You can say things very easily, but I never—"

"You never told a guy you loved him, right?"

"Right. I mean, not as far as I know."

## CHAPTER 15

## *Mesa, Arizona, 1998*

Sarah sat alone in the hotel's lobby café. She picked up the wedge of lime balanced on the tiny saucer under her ginger ale and squeezed it into the tall glass. The colleague at the firm who was scheduled to attend this 40 Act conference had come down with the flu. One of the partners asked Jeff if the young associate Sarah Toomey could go to the annual confab in his place and come back with a report; it didn't have to amount to much, just a recap of the greatest hits in the world of financial regulation.

This year's meeting was in Mesa, Arizona. Sarah was no investment specialist, but she calculated she had little to lose. If nothing else, it would be a break from office routine. And guaranteed good weather.

The yearly boondoggle fell under the firm's umbrella of "continuing education." Droning rundowns of the latest SEC rulings;

chilly conference rooms in one of the giant look-alike hotels; buffets with awful food; too much free alcohol. But even with all that, many of the attendees were happy to be there, glad for the chance to catch up with friendly acquaintances or former colleagues they saw only once a year. Not Sarah, of course. She didn't know a soul.

"I hope you don't mind."

The woman speaking those words was pulling out a chair and descending into it as she spoke.

"No," Sarah said. "Please sit down."

"Thanks. I'm Nadine Henderson and I usually have nicer manners, but, one, I'm exhausted, and two, I'm kinda reverting to tribalism here—we're the only Negroes for miles around."

"I do believe you're right," Sarah said. "I'm Sarah Toomey."

"New York, right?"

"Yes."

"I'm from Oregon. I don't mean I was born there. I practice there. I more or less make it rain there." She caught the eye of a waiter just then. "Scotch, rocks," she called to him.

Nadine was dressed casually, jeans and a hooded sweater. Sarah looked down and caught sight of her celebrity-branded sneakers.

"Yeah, just finished a workout," Nadine said. "I'm probably a fright."

"No, you're not. And you're awfully disciplined to be working out when you could be—well, I don't know what bad things you might be doing. What do our peers get up to at places like this?"

"Playing golf. Yawn." Her drink arrived and she nodded her thanks to the waiter. "Then of course there's always this," she said, stirred the ice in her glass, and took a healthy sip. "You don't drink?"

"Not really."

"You know, I was kidding earlier, what I said about us being the only black people around. But, have you noticed we're the only black people around?"

"I had. It's not a novel situation though. Considering what we do, what kind of places it takes us. And besides, I usually see a sprinkling of black men at things like this. I imagine some'll show up before the conference is over."

"You know what you sound like?"

"What I sound like? What do you mean?"

"You sound like Richard Pryor making fun of white people. Folks would be laughing their asses off."

"Oh."

"Let's put our little backstories in a nutshell, shall we? Me: Upper Marion Country Day School, Bryn Mawr. Yale Law. You?"

"Washburne Friends Academy, Mills College, Columbia."

"My sistah! To continue, I'm an only child. Are you?"

"I am."

"Parents big on uplifting The Race. On the board of this, on the committee of that. Had you fairly late in life."

"No."

"Oh. Okay, I missed that one. Let's continue. Place of birth. Choose one: (a) outskirts of Philadelphia, near some hall or something where Frederick Douglass used to lecture; (b) one of the Carolinas, cotillions and horse shit; (c) tony town house in maybe a gated community in Atlanta—or Connecticut?"

"No again."

"Hmmm. So I guess your dad's older brother wasn't a world-famous chemist. Younger brother the head of a justice project in Alabama. His wife wrote two books and committed suicide when their brilliant doctor son's plane went down on the way back to Nigeria."

"All those are your family statistics?"

"Yeah, they are. There must be some counterparts in your family tree."

"Nothing anywhere near that. We don't have any high achievers in the family. There isn't any family, actually. I'm from a poorish neighborhood in Wilmington. My mother had me young. Really young. But she was smart enough to get me into the right high school. She's probably been clinically depressed all of her life. And all of mine. From day one, I think. Father—who knows where, who knows who. A very short résumé, I'm afraid."

"Wow." Nadine snorted. "You've done some impressive bootstrapping, Miss Toomey. Good show. We're real hot stuff, me and you. Shining exemplars of how far a good little black girl can go. Awful lot of our people still up to the neck in shit, though. Killing each other. Living like rats. Shame about all that."

They fell silent for a moment.

"I'm going to finish my drinkie and then go clean up," Nadine said. "Maybe catch a few minutes of one of those fascinating panel discussions we should be attending."

"I should do the same thing," Sarah said.

"Listen, that sprinkling of black guys—not just them, I mean all kinds of guys—I guess they hit on you with dizzying frequency."

"Sometimes."

"Sometimes, eh? Well, Sarah. If you aren't occupied with some gentleman yet to appear, wanna have drinks later, maybe go to a place for dinner with some actual food?"

"That sounds nice."

"Great. And just to set your mind at ease, yes, I'm that brittle gal with good taste and a biting sense of humor, but I'm not going to hit on you. I'm not gay."

"All right. It still sounds nice."

"Fabulous. You'll have at least *this* much wine with dinner, right? Don't make me drink alone."

"So, you're not Wall Street, not obsessed with money, but you're at a heavyweight firm. Just out of your twenties but you've got a few bucks."

"I make enough to live comfortably, help my mother."

Nadine smiled. "Of course you do. I know it's rude to talk about money, and I'll stop in a minute. I'm rich, you know."

"How lovely for you," Sarah said.

"Yeah, I guess. And it's almost as if I should apologize for it. Some people are suspicious of any black person with bucks. They think you do underhanded things, they think they know who you are, but . . . Oh, who cares? On the one hand, I don't give a shit what they think. On the other, I sometimes do catch myself feeling guilty about it." She pushed her plate aside and refilled her wineglass. "It's fucked-up, isn't it? Trying to be normal, just a normal person."

"I don't have a great deal of money," Sarah said, "but I sometimes feel like that—judged, dismissed, guilty. And I don't even know why."

"I'll tell you why. It's the goddamn black washing machine."

"What is a black washing machine?"

"It's the one you have to run everything through before you do or say or get anything. It's got these cycles, these settings, like all washers do. *Remember you're black—Mustn't Do This. Remember you're black—Have to Do That. You Have No Right to Be in a Rage. Interrogate Yourself. They All Know Better. You've Had It Too Easy.* And don't get me started on the spin cycle and softener metaphors."

"Plenty of them to be made," Sarah said. "Not to mention drying and folding."

"You made a joke! What can't you do, girl? But back to bitching: the machine starts working on you as soon as you're sentient; it's got to ensure you never have a natural, unguarded moment. In a word, it's fucked up. Well, wait, that's two words, isn't it? And anyway, you probably have a whole 'nother set of crap to make you feel bad. People may take a look at you and project a lot of their own shit onto you. Maybe some figure you always get off easy: you kinda look white, so you don't have to deal with race if you choose not to. And then there's that jar of haunting beauty that you've been dipping into and leaving so little for the rest of us. We kind of resent that. And you're smart. And, by all appearances, a lovely person."

"You're attractive too, and obviously very smart."

"Please. I'm disciplined, like you said, and I've got a damn good colorist, an Eastern European skin lady, and a personal shopper."

"And, as you pointed out, you're wealthy. Since when is that not a point in one's favor?"

"True enough," Nadine said. "I'm a force to be reckoned with. So how come I'm alone?"

"I don't have an answer for that," Sarah said, "but I'm alone too."

"Like fun you are."

"No, it's true."

"And that's just fine with you?"

"I don't know. Not exactly. But I don't feel aloneness as acutely as you and a lot of others seem to."

"Well, good for you, Miss Thing. I know I have a lot of nerve complaining about anything. I get love and support from friends, I'm passably attractive, all kinds of rewards from work, I can go anywhere, buy anything. But nobody's ever been wild about me. I wouldn't mind a bit of that old-fashioned bullshit. Shameful of me, isn't it? Retro. Un-feminist."

"I don't know. As my colleague Jeffrey says, it is what it is."

"Jeffrey who?"

"Bender. He's a partner."

"And he's your boss?"

"Um."

"Is he white?"

"Yes."

"You sleeping with him?"

"Certainly not."

"Don't look so scandalized. You do date white men, don't you?"

"I don't have that much of a dating history. But yes, I have. Do you?"

"No." Nadine shrugged. "Truth be told, they never asked. There've been a few of those attorneys you mentioned earlier. Colored 'sprinkles.' Lord Amighty. I thought I was fucked up. What the soul—the washing machine—of the bourgeois black man must be like. Poor babies. They probably *are* better off marrying white girls. Once in a while I'd go to bed with a guy from the deep end of the pool. Working class. They can get so defensive, though, you know? Like I'm a snobby bitch and I need to be put in my place after I give them a blow job.

"You're laughing, Sarah. And you should be. If I was honest, I'd admit I couldn't care less about somebody being mad for me. Or even vice versa. Big love won't make me feel whole, won't make me feel free, and won't make me feel hopeful. Nothing's going to make me believe we really are going to overcome—oh, wait, except for rap. Rap is going to be the salvation of every kid in every housing project. The way I make my money is filthy enough, but the guys making a fortune off that . . .

"Oh, well, Doctor and Missus hate it that I'm cynical, don't have faith in nothing and nobody. No husband, no children.

God, I am depriving those poor people of what they think of as rightfully theirs: grandchildren. I've done nothing but make a shitload of money with, and for, a bunch of white men. Doctor and Missus are embarrassed and disappointed in me. Well, quiet as it's kept, I'm not that fucking keen on them either. That's an awful thing to say, isn't it?"

"I don't know. Sounds like the disappointment is mutual; maybe they've let you down too. What is it worth if someone loves you only when you do what they want you to do?"

"Sarah, lesbian or no, I think I love you, kid. And I have to wonder where all this equanimity . . . this balance is coming from. You're like some enchanted Zen child. Tell us, Ms. Toomey, have you been through the fire, lived to tell the tale?"

Sarah picked up her half-full glass. "My 'tale' would probably bore you to death."

"Bullshit. You're a mulatto sphinx. Mother's nuts. Daddy could be Colonel Sanders for all you know. You got a story all right. Which of us strong black women doesn't? Or, in your case, a strong semi-black woman. You've got a tale to tell, but you don't tell it. I suspect you ain't told it to nobody. Not yet."

Sarah smiled a bit.

"But when you do, it's going to blow up like Vesuvius. It's gonna change the course of mighty rivers."

## CHAPTER 16

## The Georgia Backwoods, 1865

The white killers were gone by morning.

Jack, Monroe, and the boy moved slowly into the abandoned campsite. The ground was littered with refuse.

Henry, charred beyond recognition, still dangled by one leg from the oak at the north edge of the clearing.

Ruben's fast-withering torso had been kicked out of the clearing, but his severed head was stuck on the top of a broken saber that had been thrust into the ground. His eyes seemed to have vanished.

The trio stood mute for the longest time, surveying the scene. There was a strangulating smell in the air: dropped petals, feces, death.

Holding fast to Abner's hand, Monroe looked to Preacher Jack for instruction. But Jack did not speak.

Finally the silence was broken. "Why they take his head?" Abner said.

"You hush now," Monroe whispered. He turned to Jack. "We gone put them in the ground?"

The preacher looked at Monroe but still did not speak.

Abner broke free, walked over to the impaled head. He began to circle it, moving closer and closer as curiosity overcame fear. He had not yet looked at his father's body.

"I'm cutting Henry down," Monroe suddenly declared. "Help me." And he started toward Henry's twisting corpse. When he looked back, Jack was not following. He was still standing in place.

Abner suddenly kicked the broken saber and Ruben's head rolled away. Then, his mouth agape, the boy ran toward his father. But Monroe intercepted him and flung him to the ground where Abner lay motionless, his face in the dirt.

As he began to chop at the rope, Monroe could see wounds on Henry's body other than the horrendous burns. They had cut off his private parts. Monroe tried not to touch the body as it swung and hawed, but as he hacked at the rope the black meat kept moving against him. For a few minutes, he was close to hysterical laughter. *Law says we ain't slaves no more. What are we then, Jesus?*

At last Henry fell to earth with a thud. Monroe looked around and found a discarded iron cup. About ten feet from it lay a splintered wooden cartridge box. He picked up the cup and flung it to Abner. "Start digging a grave for Ruben," he called to the child. Then he barked at Jack: "You gone stand there or you gone help me get him in the ground?"

Nothing moved the preacher. He was staring straight ahead, calm, hearing nothing but his own thoughts.

*Young Jack lay face down in the moving wagon. Going places. He could see the dirt road through the slats on the wagon's floor.*

*When the wagon rolled steadily along, when he felt the wind on his cheek, those were the times he felt the most alive in his black body, felt the nearest to hope. He was eleven years old, and along with two white men he was taken once a week to the Spurlock place, on loan to Master David Spurlock, the wheelwright. My little apprentice, Spurlock called him. His wife, Carrie, picked up on it as well. How's your little apprentice working out? she'd ask with a laugh when she saw them together in the yard. Jack once saw her kiss Master on the mouth before she swept out of their way. Nearly dropping the razor-like strip of metal in his hands, Jack regarded them wide-eyed. He had never before seen the exchange of such a kiss.*

*There was a discarded paper calendar in the corner of the barn. One day, Master David noticed Jack staring at it. On Jack's next assignment to the Spurlocks, a Bible was tucked underneath the old calendar. It was David Spurlock who, at some risk to himself, let alone the possible consequences for Jack, taught the little black apprentice how to read a few words every week. At the end of Jack's second year as helper at the wheelwright's, his tenure there ended abruptly. Week after week, Tuesday came around and Jack was sent out into the fields with the others, no mention of the wagon and the journey to Master Spurlock's. Jack went numb when he came to understand that this singular episode, partaking as it had of a different, almost imaginary world, had come to an end. He would never see the Spurlocks again. He would never again be transported in a wagon, nor be given a warm biscuit at the noon hour, when the white men were fed, nor feel the wind and sun on his skin in that blessing way. He never learned why.*

Monroe began to dig alone. Using the edge of the wooden box, he cut into the soft earth. It was not easy to dig. Buried vines had to be chopped away.

Monroe and Abner worked for hours. The graves they fashioned were shallow, barely deep enough to hide the bodies. Monroe covered Henry's grave with a tattered horse blanket he found. There was nothing for Ruben's grave. Finally, he kicked dirt and leaves on the two burial sites. It was over.

Monroe waited now for Preacher Jack to say some words. Somebody was married or baptized or buried—Jack always spoke those pretty words. But not this time. All he did was turn around and walk quickly out of the clearing, back onto the trail, signaling with one arm that the other two should follow.

So they were to leave the graves unblessed. Monroe could hardly believe it. He hesitated, trembled. But he followed.

## CHAPTER 17

## Greenwich Village, 2000

Kyle Sansom, lending support, sat in on the questioning when the homicide detectives on Bitty's case called Yvonne to the station. She had repeated her story numberless times by now, and was sick of it. In fact she was sick of all the pothering and the head-scratching and the secrecy going on. It was time for somebody to do something. Bitty was owed, and so was her brother. But nobody *did* anything.

Kofi knew how badly it had gone with the police this last time, and he felt terrible for Yvonne. More or less terrible. Absolutely not terrible. He wanted her to back off from the thing, wanted her out of it altogether.

Kofi had great faith in the power of aimless strolls. He usually found a walk to be the best cure for one of his own gruesome moods. Maybe—just maybe—a twilight walk would work for Yvonne too.

He touched her arm as they crossed Hudson Street. She was no longer cussing, in fact she wasn't talking at all now. He wanted to say something comforting. But he couldn't predict what would comfort her and what might set her off again, so he figured it was best to keep his mouth shut—for once. Like Bean said: "Man, you throw words at a problem instead of getting up and fixing shit."

Bean was so like his mother, Laura. She was where he got that habit of forming and announcing instant judgments of people, usually harsh ones, and usually because she wasn't getting her way. And Bean's impatience had come from Laura as well, along with some measure of arrogance. Headstrong, as their mother, Mimi, would say. But all those traits had clearly passed down to Bean through osmosis, as he was an adopted child. Laura, a committed enemy of conformity, a committed enemy of marriage, of monogamy, and as it so often appeared, a committed enemy of her mother. She had fastened on the idea of adopting a kid and raising it on her own. She not so much announced it as hurled it into Mimi's face.

*"Oh, I see. You think you're going to be somebody's mama? You manage to get to twenty-one without getting yourself pregnant and ruining your own life, but now you're going to raise somebody else's mistake?"* Mimi laughed in that bitter, whinnying way that never failed to kick Laura's fury up another notch.

Kofi saw his younger self lying on his back, listening intently as the two of them screeched and accused each other, Mimi trailing her up and down the corridor. *"Out all night smoking dope with some trifling niggers . . . When are you going to develop some maturity . . . Oh, darling, listen . . . Where the hell do you think you're going . . . Don't you walk away from me while I'm talking to you . . . "*

Kofi's room in the spacious flat on Riverside had been his sanctuary. His records, his skates, his massive wardrobe of tee shirts, all put away so neatly, his posters framed in plexiglass, his treasured back issues of the *Village Voice* and the *Black Scholar* piled neatly atop his bookcases, the shelves of which held the fierce, illimitable wisdom of James Baldwin and Albert Murray and Régis Debray and Audre Lorde.

*"Fuck you, Mimi."*

Laura refused to call her mother anything else. No Mom, no Mama, no Mother, just her first name, and the occasional "bitch."

*"And by the way, Mimi, I'm gay. Deal, bitch."*

The door slams shut. End of Act 1, he thought.

Kofi lay there, ramrod straight. Damn it, damn it, goddammit. She'd told him she wasn't going to come out to Mimi yet. She said she'd wait until he graduated and left home. Cat out of the bag now, Laura's going to split, sooner rather than later. Mimi's gonna be my problem now, mine alone.

"Nice neighborhood," Yvonne said.

He halted the private slideshow of his memories, turned toward her.

"I always liked it around here," she added. "So quiet in the daytime."

So it appeared his instincts were right. Just let her come down on her own. He'd been wise not to try talking her out of her mood.

"Yeah, I love the Village too. When I was a kid, I'd take the bus down here every chance I got. I got to know every nook and alley. How do you get to Gansevoort Street? How old is the White Horse? Where's James Baldwin's apartment? What famous people went to Little Red Schoolhouse? Ask me any question about the Village and see if I don't know the answer."

"I don't need to. I know you got the answers."

Damn. Busted for showing off. Again. When am I going to learn?

He took Yvonne's hand and they were quiet for a while, but then she said, "I know something you don't have no answer for."

He didn't have to ask what that was. "Your girl, Bitty. And her brother. Well, you're right. I've got no answers. All I can suggest right now is, we get drunk."

"We what?"

"Drunk. When you apply a couple of bottles of good wine to a problem, things tend to get clearer."

"That sounds like bullshit, Kofi."

"Yeah. But that doesn't mean we shouldn't have a nice meal and get tight."

They had a splendid dinner at an Austrian restaurant on West Eleventh, not five minutes' walk from Sea Grass. And it was as if Kofi really did believe in his theory about drunkenness and clear thinking. They had predinner cocktails and two bottles with their lingering meal. A fine minerally white and a somber red.

"Food's pretty wonderful here, isn't it?" he said as the waiter handed out the dessert menus.

Yvonne watched him as he divided what was left in the bottle between their two glasses.

"Something just crossed my mind, Yvonne."

"What?"

"I was thinking, what if someone had murdered my sister in some horrible way, and then the same thing happened to me. Who would there be to care enough to want to catch the killer?"

He went on before she could say anything: "I guess I'd want someone like you to make noise, not give up until there was some kind of justice done."

"From what you told me about your sister, I wouldn't be surprised somebody wanted her gone."

"Aha! Get a bit of liquor in you, and come to find out you're not Joan of Arc. You have a little snark in you after all."

She looked around and noticed they were the lone diners. "We're closing the place, looks like," she said.

"Won't be the first time."

Their kingly meal was over at last. Kofi said good night to the staff as he held the door open for Yvonne.

"I think a lot of you, Kofi," she stated.

"Well, thank you. However you mean that."

———

"You don't fall out of that thing?"

She was looking up toward the ceiling, at the loft bed he and Bean had built three years ago.

He spoke over his shoulder as he rinsed out the brushed aluminum espresso pot. "It was the only way I could think of to get a few more feet of room in here."

Yvonne hung up her jacket and then sank into the brown leather armchair, letting out a sigh of relief. "Oh, Lord, this feels good. Think I'll stay here awhile."

Kofi slipped her shoes off and gave her feet a quick massage.

"You sure that's decaf?" she said.

"Yes, I get it at McNulty's. They wouldn't lie."

"You got something I can sleep in?"

"Absolutely."

"I gotta climb up on that ladder?"

"Yes. But I won't let you fall."

A few hours later he turned over in his sleep, reached for Yvonne. Sensing her movement toward the ladder, he was suddenly wide awake. "What are you doing? You're not going home, are you?"

"No," she said. "Just taking a pee. You go back to sleep."

"Okay."

He didn't though.

God, for a minute there, she sounded like Mimi—Mom.

What is it with you, man? Well, okay, you kind of know what it's about, don't you? You're a big mama's boy. But, so what? We're not about disparaging mothers. Remember, when both Laura and Mimi passed, somebody had to step up for Bean. You got elected Mother by default. A good motto for today's males: Man up and be a mother!

Kofi often thought of how unfair it was, the things mothers never get in return for the sturdy arms, the good night kisses, the sacrifices. If only he could make up for all the losses, all the bad shit that befalls so many black mothers. Not just mothers. In fact, all the colored women, young and old, past and present, known and unknown, who have the roof fall in on them, son in some murderous gang, daughter knocked up at sixteen. Who get underpaid and disrespected and fucked around on and beat on and buried too soon.

After she came out of the bathroom, Yvonne took a glass of water and sat with it in the comfortable nook beneath the loft bed. It was the kind of thing she was used to doing at home, being such a bad sleeper. Getting out of bed in the middle of the night, staring into the darkness, her thoughts as black as the shadowless room. She curled up under the red mohair throw that had been lying across the back of the chair.

His voice startled her: "If you're sitting down there in the dark planning something crazy, forget it."

She looked up to see Kofi leaning over the edge of the mattress.

"I mean it, Yvonne. You could get in real trouble."

"Kofi. Where would we be if all people ever thought about was getting in trouble? You said yourself—"

"You know what I mean, damn it. I'm not going to let you do any stupid stuff, and I sure as hell won't help you do it."

"Okay. I hear that."

*All we did was exchange little bits of information. So now I understand part of your past and you know a few things about me. Don't blame you for wanting to know more. But maybe you not as smart as you think, Kofi. Only been in my life a hot minute and already you figure you got me pegged. Huh. You'd go running off like a scared puppy if you knew who I am—if you caught so much as a glimpse.*

"What if you can't find out the truth?" he called down. "What if you never find out who did what to who? Did you hear me, Yvonne?"

"Yeah. I heard you."

———

Back at work the next day, things were proceeding as usual. Finished with her prep work, Yvonne was drinking coffee and paging through an old recipe book when a uniformed cop swung through the kitchen doors. He was walking purposefully toward her.

*Oh shit.*

She thought those two words were only in her own head, but apparently she'd said them out loud, loud enough for him to hear.

Oh. Wait. How terrible could it be? He was laughing.

"No bad news," the officer said. "I brought something for you." He pushed a plastic shopping bag at her. "From Detective Sansom. He said to say sorry it took this long, he's been meaning to return it but it always slips his mind 'cause he threw it in the trunk of his car that night."

"Huh?"

"You know, that night in the bar. Uptown. The Willetts killing. I thought he said you were there."

"I was there all right."

"Okay. So you forgot your purse. He picked it up in the bar and he kept it for you."

She wasn't sure if she thanked the officer, but she did know enough to simply take what was being proffered and not mention that she'd carried no bag that night.

She opened the shopping bag. Inside was a stunning, satchel-style red bag. Yvonne picked it up. Good God, was this leather or a cloud fallen to earth? She was no fashionista, but it was clear, even to a Kmart shopper, this was a high-ticket item; they probably got a thousand bucks for things like this. She held the bag for several minutes, thinking.

Oh yeah, it had to be.

She undid the clasp and reached inside. Apartment keys. Cash. American Express. Lipstick. Comb. Mirror. American Bar Association ID. Driver's license.

Sarah Toomey.

So that was the name of the woman who came unaccompanied into the club where Bitty worked. The one who followed

Bitty into the ladies' room and then split while Bitty writhed in agony and finally died. By default, as nobody else came in or out, the one who knocked Yvonne into the next dimension.

And there was every reason to believe she was the same woman who had had drinks with Bitty's brother; the last person to see him alive.

Yvonne tapped the driver's license against the stainless-steel counter. Oh hell yes, that was her all right. When you're that pretty, you couldn't take a bad picture even if you wanted to.

## CHAPTER 18

# Georgia, 1865

Late afternoon. They saw the shed at the top of a drained hillock. Jutting out from the pinewood structure were several sturdy pens. Maybe these were where, once, somebody had raised chickens for market. Must have been a long time since there were any warm-blooded critters hereabouts, Monroe calculated. No sign of skat or leftover feed. Even the smell of animal life was gone.

"Ain't nothing to eat in them there," young Abner said.

Monroe caught him roughly by the shoulder. "Be quiet, boy. Suppose somebody nearbouts and hear you."

But he persisted. "Nobody 'round here. I'm hungry."

"Hush, I say," Monroe warned.

Abner twisted away, lowered his voice to a belligerent whisper: "I'm hungry."

Monroe looked to the preacher, wondering why Jack didn't quiet the boy, make him mind. After all, Jack had always been the final word in any conflict among the slaves at the Clarkson spread. But Jack was saying nothing. Doing nothing. He had become a regular old turtle, head down in his shell. Since they'd found and buried Henry and Ruben in the clearing, the preacher had hardly spoken a word. *He don't talk no more,* Monroe thought. *Don't boss us no more. And sho nuff don't preach no more.*

No, mostly he just stared ahead, often with his lips moving. Then, when the dumb show ended, he'd act like he was listening to something, listening hard.

Abner had begun to inch forward again. Monroe caught him up. "Where you think you going?"

"May be something to eat up in there," the boy said, pointing.

Monroe looked at the shed and then back at Abner. "Maybe they is. But don't you be so mannish. You do what grown folks say, less you want the same thing happened to your daddy to come to us. Just wait here."

Monroe sank low to the ground and noiselessly approached the shed. The bolt on the thin door was undone. He eased the door open and took a long look inside. Traps of all sizes lay on a table, along with assorted skinning and butchering knives and a short-handled ax. And there, against one wall, were burlap sacks, one half full of beans and another with rice. A small crock with salt rested on top of an empty barrel, and hanging above it were six long strings of jerky.

Monroe signaled to Jack and Abner to come.

Inside the shed now, Abner ran directly to the array of knives. Jack snatched them out of the boy's hand and quickly rolled them up in a rag along with the ax. Monroe tore down the jerky, forcing one greedily into his mouth while he passed some to the others. Then he filled empty flour sacks with as much rice and beans as they would hold.

"We best go," he said, his voice low. And he propelled Abner toward the shed door.

They lit out, heading for the tree line in the swamp. But Abner stopped in his tracks. "What that? I hear something."

"What you hear?" Monroe said. "Somebody after us? *Run.*"

"Naw. Ain't a body talking or nothing like that."

"What you hear then?"

The three remained frozen in the moment.

"I hear it," Jack said.

Monroe looked at him in alarm. "What you talking about? I don't—"

"Up there," Jack said. "In that other pen."

Before Monroe could grab him, Abner took off, back up the hill. By the time Jack and Monroe reached him, Abner was bent over one of the pens, peering through the slats. Monroe turned his eyes to the perimeter of the hillock, trying to spot the doom he knew would be coming at them any minute now.

"I see it in there," Abner cried out. "It real big."

Meat!

Monroe and Jack dropped their bags and hit their knees next to Abner, who was fiddling with the thick rope that kept the pen's gate closed.

"I can't see nothing," Monroe said just as Abner got the gnarled knot undone.

Abner laughed. "Here it come," he said, and the pen door swung open.

The crude cage shook as though the earth beneath it were rumbling, and the creature they had wakened burst forth.

The huge, lumbering thing—a bear dog, as they were called—looked starved, demented. Swamp people had developed the powerful breed, a cross between the scent hound and the English mastiff, to track and kill bear.

With a strangled growl coming up from its belly and through its lethal slobbering mouth, the dog charged, launching itself at Abner, whose legs wobbled in terror but refused to let him move.

Preacher Jack sprang up and knocked the boy off his feet, taking the assault upon himself full-on. The impact set the preacher reeling, but he did not fall.

The dog bit deep into Jack's arm, held on.

The animal's teeth still embedded in his right arm, Jack brought his left down with enormous force on the dog's spine. Again and again he hammered. With the final blow the ugly black thing whimpered and released its hold. It went writhing onto its back.

Abner picked up a stone and smashed at the creature's head until it was no more than pulp.

Jack's arm was ripped open from elbow to wrist.

"Lord have mercy," Monroe kept repeating as he snatched up mossy grass and packed the preacher's bloody wound with one fistful after another. "Lord have mercy." When he was done he covered Jack's arm with mud, then he emptied a sack and used it to wrap the hanging flesh as tightly as he could. "Fetch that rope," he barked at the sobbing Abner, who then ran to the dog's old lair and tore the dirty rope free.

Jack had never once moved during Monroe's ministrations. No whining, no flinching, no words.

Monroe spoke through the clotted tears in his throat: "You

hurt bad, Brother Jack. You oughta rest. But we cain't stop here. *We cain't.*"

The preacher nodded. He wore the strangest expression now, but it signaled neither pain nor fear. Instead his features were alive, his eyes were full of light, and he almost seemed to be smiling.

## CHAPTER 19

# *Midtown Manhattan, 2000*

Yvonne used the public phone on the corner of Fifty-Seventh and Eighth to call Sarah Toomey at home. Luckily, there was no answer. But that was to be expected. Sarah Toomey was a big-shot lawyer and it was a workday. If her luck held, Yvonne would be long gone before the crazy woman came home from the office or the courtroom or wherever the hell she was.

And what if Sarah Toomey did come home while Yvonne was going through her apartment? There would be one hell of a battle, that's what. A girl fight to end all girl fights. Yvonne was ready for the smackdown; she had a nightstick in her tote bag along with a canister of Mace. *This Toomey bitch may be strong, but let's see her throw me across the room with a quart of this shit up her nostrils. She's owed some major pain for knocking me around in that bar, let alone the way she took out Bitty Willetts and most likely her brother Crawford too.*

The posh high-rise building where Sarah Toomey lived was forbidding, just as Yvonne had predicted. Also predictable, the doorman was black. And once Yvonne identified herself as a servant, he was even cordial. When she told the uniformed brother at the lobby desk that she was Miss Toomey's new cleaning lady and showed him her copies of the keys, he questioned her no further.

Well, that was one hurdle cleared.

"A young fella from the hardware gonna deliver the floor polisher and my cleanin' supplies," Yvonne said. As she talked, she was making a quick survey of the alphabetical tenant list behind the doorman's head. She spotted the name Toomey, but could not quite make out the apartment number before she had to pull her eyes away to meet his. "Would you please call me when he get here? Let's see, that's number 1402, right?"

"1204," he corrected her. "Don't worry about it," the doorman said. "I'll send him up."

Yvonne fitted keys into both locks with no trouble. The heavy door opened onto a long corridor with a ruby-colored kilim underfoot. She made a soundless reconnaissance of the apartment, checking the master bedroom and bath, the spotless kitchen, and the spare room/office with its hulking mahogany bookcase and tufted leather armchair. She walked back to the living room window overlooking Fifty-Seventh Street and spent a minute studying the top of the crosstown bus.

*Looks like you do want to go back to prison, after all. What the hell are you going to say if somebody gets suspicious and calls the police? How many stupid women are sitting up in a cell regretting some B&E job just like this one?*

She took a few deep breaths to still her trembling. *All right.*

*Calm down, woman. Don't lose it. There's still time to get out, not do this.*

Still time to phone her accomplice and tell him not to come, say that she had changed her mind. All she had to do was call Bean on his cell and tell him to ditch the shopping bag full of sponges and Mr. Clean and Endust, just wait for her at the coffee shop around the corner.

She had not had to twist his arm to enlist him in this escapade. Bean clearly had something of the devil in him. Even after she warned him that what they'd be doing was risky, he couldn't agree fast enough.

"I guess you wonder why I didn't ask your uncle to do this instead of you," she'd said.

"I don't wonder. Kofi would never do anything illegal. For starters, he's too proud to impersonate a delivery man. Plus," Bean added, "Uncle Kofi's got one huge problem in life."

"Just one?" Yvonne asked.

"One big one, anyway," he said. "He never grabs the beast by the balls. It's like he's scared of living."

"You calling him a coward? How do you know what he's been through? He's got almost twenty years on you, Bean. It's not on you to judge him."

"Okay, you're right. I don't mean to say he's a wuss. Look, I love the brother, but he always hesitates at the wrong time. Never gets what he really wants."

Yvonne had stopped arguing there. She knew the boy was right. That was why she had not dared tell Kofi what she was planning to do. Kofi would have found a way to stop her.

She may have been right about Kofi's timidity. But Yvonne was wrong about there being time to abort this search of Sarah Toomey's home. Someone was knocking at the apartment door—right now.

Shit. The plan had gone south already.

Yvonne's throat went utterly dry. It hurt to take a breath. *Think, girl, think fast.* But it was as if her brain had turned to strawberry jam.

Bean was half a block away, waiting for her call to tell him it was safe to come up. That had to be somebody else at the door. That goddamn doorman had not bought her story for a minute. He had played along with the scam, and then called the police. And now she was about to be busted on a housebreaking rap. Goodbye, job. Goodbye, Yvonne's Little Bakery. She would put up no argument, there would be no resisting arrest. But at least Bean would be out of it. Like she had told him: "Anything goes wrong, you in the clear. It'll all be on me. I'm the one took the woman's key. I'm the one told a lie to get up to her place."

Her heart clicking in her ears, she crept up the hall and stood behind the door but did not speak in answer to the persistent knocking.

"Delivery, ma'am. Hardware store."

Yvonne jumped away. That was Bean's voice.

She flung the door open and pulled him in. "Jesus God, man. You were supposed to wait."

"I know, I know. But the doorman was out on the sidewalk having a smoke. He saw me with the polisher, asked if I was the one you were expecting, and waved me in. What was I supposed to do?"

Yvonne let out a strangled moan and ushered him into the living room.

"Pretty nice crib," Bean said, and immediately abandoned the decoy paraphernalia he had lugged up on the service elevator. "But this woman has no real taste. You know what I mean?"

"No, I don't. And don't explain it to me. We have to get busy."

"Right. Just let me grab my stuff." He dug deep into the shopping bag and extracted his Leica and another, miniaturized, camera.

"What are you doing with that?"

"Documenting. I'm making a photographic record of the crime. Don't worry, it's cool. I'll never identify when and where it took place. No names or anything like that. I haven't come up with a title for it yet, but I think I found my senior thesis. Maybe I'll call it 'Unlawful Entry.'"

"Don't tell me nothing else, or I may hurt you, boy. Just let's go."

---

The papers and appointment books in the study yielded no information of any use. Bean and Yvonne moved into the bedroom.

Yvonne went into the walk-in closet and sorted through the neatly folded sweaters and underthings in the built-in drawers. She opened the lid of the laundry hamper. "Here," she said, lifting Sarah's soiled coral dress from the pile of clothing. "She was wearing this that night."

Bean leaned into the closet, his camera whirring in her ear. "What's in there?" he said as he pointed to the box on the floor.

Yvonne looked down. The carton had been carelessly closed. She brought it out and rifled through the cache of tea party gloves and sachet, tiny evening bags and lace.

"There's another one," Bean said.

"Go 'head and open it," she instructed him.

Bean pulled at the corner of a large piece of fabric inside the carton. After he freed it, he laid it out on the bed. They both fell silent for a long moment as they stared. Then, "Who the fuck is that?" he asked. He was looking at the ferocious black face in the center of the quilt. "Can you imagine trying to sleep with that thing on your bed?"

Yvonne used her finger to trace the stars, the trees and wagon wheels and other symbols at the edges of the quilt. But she hesitated at the figure of the spitting white serpent, almost afraid to touch it. "My God," she said. "Looks like somebody's nightmare, don't it?"

Bean busied himself again with the cameras. When Yvonne unpacked a leather-covered Bible he photographed all the documents folded into its pages—Sarah Toomey's high school diploma, a snapshot of her on a black Santa's knee, her mother Lila's driver's license, yellowing invitations and news clippings, programs from special events at a local church in Wilmington. Before he and Yvonne packed up to leave, Bean had photographed every item in the odd treasure boxes.

"What time is it?" Yvonne asked.

He barely looked up when Yvonne spoke. "Almost eleven thirty." Bean was still opening and closing drawers, searching under the bed, snapping pictures all the while.

"We best be getting out of here. Doesn't seem that likely, but I guess it's always possible she might come home for lunch."

"Does that mean we're done?"

Yvonne took a last look around. "I guess so."

"Did you find what you were looking for?"

She seemed to deflate then. "I swear, Bean, I don't know. It's like I'm beginning to think I made up everything that happened. Or that I saw it all wrong. Just like Kofi and Detective Sansom think. I don't know. I can't find a thing here to tell me why this beautiful girl, a woman who's got everything, would kill two people she never met before. I just know that she did."

Yvonne wanted nothing more than to sit down in the cushy armchair across from the vanity, but she knew she mustn't let herself rest yet.

"So," Bean said, "what now? What does it all mean?"

"No time for figuring that out now. Main business at the moment is for us to get out of here as quick and quiet as we can."

"Okay. One more shot from the living room window," he said as he hustled away.

"I said quick, fool. You take that machine down the way you came up, and I'll leave five minutes behind you. Get that thing back to the hardware store fast as you can."

"We hook up at the coffee shop around the corner?"

"No. Meet down in the subway. The sooner we put some distance between us and this neighborhood, the better."

CHAPTER 20

## Southeastern Georgia, Before the War

Some of the others thought the silent girl was possessed, insane. Some of them were afraid of her, that open stare with the unblinking green eyes. Around the time she turned fifteen, young master started arriving regularly at the drafty place where she and another youngun slept on a cotton mat. One afternoon in late spring, a white man with rotting teeth beat a field hand half to death. The green-eyed mute stood transfixed as the lash landed again and again, opening a red sluice on the black man's back. Later that day, when young master arrived at the cabin, he found the girl strafing her own flesh with a nail. He grabbed her up and shakily wrapped her bleeding arms in whatever bits of cloth he could find.

She sat unmoving while the very black cook rebandaged her.

Young master sat up late into the night watching the mysterious beauty while she slept in the ramshackle cabin.

He arrived at the cabin every day of the week save Sunday. There were nights when her silent tears would find their match in his. He, too, appeared to be ashamed and weary and on the other side of words. More than once he had gone into the woods, the deepest part, where all those years ago he and his brother were forbidden to play. He would fall to his knees, maybe praying, he was not sure, and that is where he did his confused, helpless sobbing. In time, though, both their tears ceased, and the night silence would be broken only by the sounds of their coupling. By day, the girl's mind would often drift to thoughts of suicide. The others were right to say she was mad. She must be. Her thoughts went from hanging herself to cutting the white man's heart out as he slept, and then she began waking in the dark, longing to feel his breath on her face, on her shoulder, the wanting so abject that it swept the shame aside like a stiff broom. The wishes for murder and self-annihilation returned when the other women made her understand that she was pregnant.

First chance she had, she would smash its head in with a stone.

But the child did come. And the birthing was terrible. Long and terrible. At last the deep black woman placed the tiny baby in the girl's arms, and the beautiful girl caught the scent of purple flowers rising off the crown of her untroubled baby's head. The beautiful girl began to nurse her daughter, and all the tears she had never released poured forth.

CHAPTER 21

## *The Bowery, 2000*

There was no gentleness in Kofi's eyes now. No kindness, no humor. None of the sweet things that had attracted Yvonne to him and earned Bean's undying love and loyalty.

In the kitchen of his nephew's Bowery loft, Kofi was in full rage mode, eyes bugging behind his wire-rim spectacles, face aflame. "What the fuck did you think you were playing at?" he screamed in Yvonne's direction. "Maybe you've got some kind of death wish, but how dare you try to take this child with you!"

The other two seemed to know better than to argue with him. Bean stood near the refrigerator taking swigs from a large bottle of Pellegrino, and Yvonne sat at the makeshift kitchen table with eyes downcast.

Her silence meant not only that she was wise enough to let Kofi's anger burn off before she spoke; it was also her way of acknowledging the total failure of her mission at Sarah Toomey's apartment. Kofi was right on all counts. What she had done was indefensible. She had risked so much and learned so little— learned nothing, really.

Finally, Bean spoke: "If you're through venting, I've got something to say."

"Shut up, Bean. I'm not talking to you. I don't even want to look at you right now, man. And I am *not* through 'venting.' I'm a long way from through."

Bean sighed mightily and drank more water.

"The two of you," Kofi said. "Jesus—you two morons. I feel like calling the police on you myself. This budding genius likes to posture and pontificate about his art, but he'd rather do anything other than get on with the business at hand, get the fuck out of school. And you, Yvonne, after you promised you wouldn't do anything crazy . . . after I specifically said 'Don't do anything crazy, Yvonne,' you pull something like this."

"I didn't," she mumbled.

Kofi turned on her. "What?"

At last she looked up at him. "I didn't promise you nothing, Kofi. Although I guess I should have."

He huffed in disgust.

"Look, I'm not saying you not right, Kofi. You are. But— Are you through yelling at us now?"

"No, goddamnit, not yet." Kofi, still glaring, pulled out one of the mismatched chairs and sat down heavily at the table. "But what? What were you going to say? I can't wait to hear this ridiculous explanation."

"Not an explanation," she said. "Just an apology. I did wrong."

"And stupid."

"Okay. And stupid. We finished with the yelling now?"

He took a minute. "Yes."

Kofi had finished his second bowl of soup and was slathering butter on the last bit of cornbread from the blackened cast-iron skillet. "I guess you think you can play the shit out of me," he said. "Throw a bowl of soup and a couple of homemade cookies at me and I'll be your bitch."

Yvonne couldn't tell whether he was joking, whether he had forgiven her, or not. She had sent Bean out to do a bit of grocery shopping and then made a meal for the two men.

"You may be pretty good at manipulating me, Yvonne. But you're a rank amateur compared to my dear old mom."

"I'm not trying to play you, Kofi. I'm just asking for one last favor. And like I said, if nothing comes of it, I'll leave it alone."

"Why not ask your new boyfriend? Apparently, Bean is ready to do your bidding any time."

"Bean just told you he had to keep an appointment, didn't he? Besides, I'm asking you, not him."

"You're both trying to finish what my mother left undone," Kofi said. "You're conspiring to make me your punk."

Yvonne stroked his neck softly. "You nobody's punk."

He caught her hand, trapped it. "I do this, and then you're going to tell me why getting to the bottom of these deaths is so important to you—right? I mean, you're going to start being real with me."

"Yes."

"All right. I'll do it. At least it isn't anything we could get arrested for."

"Thank you."

"Thank you," Bean echoed.

"Bean, if you're going someplace, why don't you just get the hell on the road?" Kofi said. "Where's your laptop?"

"Next to the bed," he called as he went through the door. "You all can lock up when you're finished."

Yvonne placed a huge molasses cookie and a small glass of milk next to Kofi's hand.

"First maybe I'll try some of the legal sites, since she's a lawyer."

Sarah Toomey's name turned up a number of times as counsel either for the wife or the husband in various big-ticket divorce and child-custody cases. She had also represented the interests of some of the mightiest real estate firms in the city. A couple of instances of pro bono work in housing court. Some Columbia professor had thanked her for research help in a law journal article.

"She sounds like a heavyweight," Kofi said. He looked over at Yvonne. "But strictly legit. Not the profile of your average serial killer."

"Just keep going," she said.

As to Sarah Toomey's life outside her profession, he could find nothing other than a list in a Mills College alumni newsletter of her accomplishments since leaving school and the fact that she was presently living in New York City.

"I've got an idea," Kofi said after half an hour of dead ends. "Didn't you say Bean took a shot of some kind of certificate or license you all found with a family Bible?"

"Yes."

"It didn't have Sarah's name on it, though, right? It was somebody else's."

"Yes. Lila Toomey."

"Okay. Let's try to run with that."

Not long after that, while Yvonne was heating milk for the

cocoa that he had requested, she noticed a queer expression on Kofi's face as he stared at the screen.

"Don't tell me that computer broke down."

Kofi shook his head.

"What? You found something about the mother?"

"Delaware, right?" he said.

"What about Delaware?"

"That's where Martindale-Hubbell said Sarah Toomey is from. Wilmington, wasn't it?"

"I think so."

"There's some newspaper coverage," he said, and began to paraphrase from the writing on the screen. "Thirty some years ago. A gruesome corpse. Possible homicide. Police questioned a witness who ultimately became a suspect in the case but was let go for lack of evidence."

"What suspect? You mean Sarah Toomey? She was nothing but a child thirty years ago."

"Not Sarah. Her mother."

"You're kidding."

" 'Lila Toomey, of such and such address, released on bond, blahblahblah, leaves the such and such station house accompanied by Reverend Joseph Thayer of St. Michael's Episcopal Church, into whose custody blahblahblah, she is represented by local attorney David Hofstra.' "

Kofi tapped at the keyboard for another minute. "There's more stuff listed. I'm trying to backtrack on the story," he said. "Hold on." He fell silent for a long while as he read, and then went on to yet another entry.

"Yvonne?"

"What?"

"The guy who was killed. This gruesome body. Ripped apart. They say his heart was torn open, right through the chest. The coroner couldn't explain it. But the body was 'covered in a rank and glutinous substance the police lab has not yet identified.'"

She was standing over Kofi by then, looking down at the screen, fingers tensing on the back of his chair.

"Yvonne?" he said again, in the same weak voice. "Look at the victim's name."

She followed his finger.

Yvonne spoke in a whisper. "Lord, how'd I know it?"

"Willetts," Kofi said.

She nodded. "Willetts. No way this man wasn't related some way to Bitty and Crawford Willetts. Some kinda way."

"Considering everything, it can't be just a coincidence."

"So. Now you believe Bitty's brother didn't go out that window on his own?"

"Yes."

"And Bitty herself—you believe that Toomey woman has something to do with what happened to her?"

"Yes."

"Thank you, Jesus. I ain't insane."

"Did Bean take his camera when he left?"

"Yes."

"Did he say where he was going, when he'd be back?"

"I don't think so. But I know why you asking. Those photographs he took at Sarah Toomey's place."

"That's right. We've got to get on him to develop them. You better take a closer look at them."

"Damn," she muttered. "Something told me, soon as I saw him."

"Who do you mean?"

"The man. The face on that blanket. It's like I can still feel his eyes on me. And that snake. You'll see it when those pictures get developed."

She saw Kofi close out of the window he'd been looking at and fiddle around with the keys. "What you doing now?"

"Telephone directory for Wilmington," he said. "Maybe this lawyer, Whatshisname Hofstra, is still alive."

"Kofi?"

"What?"

"The preacher who took her out of the police station. Try him too."

## CHAPTER 22

## *The Georgia Backwoods, 1865*

The owls were talking again.

But only Preacher Jack could hear them.

He looked up at the tree limb overhead and asked them to wait until Monroe and Abner were asleep.

The three sojourners were in a safe camp now, deep in the swamp. They had emptied their bags and gorged themselves on the bounty from the trapper's cabin.

At the edge of the fire, Jack cradled his ripped arm in his lap. The pain was horrific, but he knew it was a good and necessary thing. It sharpened his senses.

No talk between them, Monroe rebandaged the preacher's arm and then crawled off to lie next to the poor boy, Abner, who was sleeping all curled into himself, thumb in his mouth.

Monroe had never been so tired. He had been thinking lately

that if death came for him in the night—from marauders or wild animals, or even if his heart simply stopped—then so be it. In dying, at least he'd be free, and freedom was what this waking nightmare of flight was supposed to be all about.

Jack watched the night sky and waited for the owls to come back. In a while, a fat, luminous moon rose high above. By its light, at last, Jack spotted the flat face of the speckled bird in the cypress.

The owl laughed. *You've been all wrong.*

"I know it now," Jack said.

He did know. He began to suspect it a minute after they came upon Henry swinging upside down, his charred face like puckered fruit with teeth. And when the dog monster had ripped through his own flesh—then he knew it for sure.

*They are all branded with the mark of the beast.*

Jack looked down at his throbbing arm. "All branded," he repeated.

*Eat their flesh.*

The preacher drew back in terror.

*The angel emptied his bowl over the sea. And the sea was turned to blood.*

Jack waited.

*And so it is that the chosen are given blood to drink.*

Jack had many questions for the owl. But the bird suddenly took flight, as though it had been called away. An hour passed before it returned.

When the bird spoke this time, Jack heard the thunder in its voice, heard shrieks and whimpering agony.

*Babylon has fallen, Armageddon at hand.*

The preacher wailed. "Have mercy."

Yes. It made sense. He had heard the white preacher talk once about Armageddon. There was to be a great war between the sons of the saints and the sons of the beasts. And Babylon would fall. That was right. It was all in the Bible. The earth would be rent by blood spilled in the Lord's name and a new heaven brought forth. And who was that heaven for? For Jack and his people.

*And the sea shall be blood.*

Jack begged for guidance, but the owl only lifted its wing, screaming. *To the sea! Feast!*

"How do we feast, brother?"

*Eat their flesh!*

"Amen," Jack said.

When it was light, he gathered water from a stream. He woke Monroe and Abner by rebaptizing them.

Jack was glowing with the news. "We going to Armageddon," he announced to the astonished pair. "To kill every son of the beast, and every daughter."

Monroe sat up. "What you say?"

"But first to the sea. It's given to us."

"Kill who?" Monroe shouted.

But Jack ignored him.

"What's the sea?" Abner asked.

"It's east, child," Jack told him. "We part of the war now. We feast. And then we take heaven, cleansing this earth as we go. *Amen.*"

## CHAPTER 23

# *NoHo, 2000*

On impulse, Sarah decided to check into one of the cutting-edge downtown hotels. She had hurriedly packed things for a few days away from the apartment, hailed a taxi, and sped downtown.

She did not know the Lower East Side. All she knew was that Bowery was the downtown extension of Third Avenue. She decided to stroll a bit. Her small suitcase wasn't very heavy. It was no burden to carry it as she meandered.

She was surprised at the bustle along the avenue. The Bowery had always meant down-and-out bars, lost souls, fleabag rooming houses. This appeared to be a thriving neighborhood, though, with new luxe buildings going up on nearly every corner, a charming little faux French bakery, young mothers with their babies in strollers, pedigree dogs trotting in rhythm with them.

She turned, as if by instruction in her left ear, onto Bond Street. A few paces later she nearly collided with a tall, attractive young black man smoking in front of what appeared to be an exclusive men's clothing store. He had long braids, caught up in a neat bundle at the back of his neck, and when he turned and focused on Sarah he did a kind of comic double take.

He looked at her for a long while before speaking, and when he finally did, his eyes were shining. "Jesus," he said.

She waited.

"Sorry to stare. Jesus, you're beautiful."

She looked at the plump cigarette between his manicured brown fingers, aware at the same moment of the scent of marijuana. She stared at it long enough to prompt him to offer it to her.

"Thanks, no," she said. "You seemed to be enjoying it a lot. Is it a special blend, something like that?"

He laughed. "Not really. I'm just cooling out before work." He nodded toward the entrance to the store. "But let's talk about something much more important. Like where are you heading with that bag, and are you married."

"I'm not married."

"But you're in love with him, right? I mean, he's got you. And you're going somewhere with him."

"Yes, you could say that."

"I am hoping— Oh, by the way, what's your name?"

"Sarah Toomey."

"I'll be up front about it. I'm trying to figure, Sarah Toomey, how I'm going to take you away from him. What do you think the chances are of that happening?"

No clever retort at hand, she simply smiled.

"You're better off with me, you know. Whoever the bastard is. You think Ima have to fight him?"

"There's a good chance of that."

"How big is the brother?"

"Brother? You have a brother?"

"No, I meant 'brother' in the way— Oh. Oh, okay, never mind. I think I got it now. He's white."

"I—"

"Come inside, sit for a while, let me run down my good qualities. Here . . . I'll take that for you." He picked up the bag and she deftly took the joint out of his free hand. Before she followed him inside, she took a couple of deep pulls, let the smoke amble around in her lungs. He looked back approvingly.

The boutique was cool and dark. A pleasing scent of new leather hung in the air.

"You're alone," she said.

"Just opening for the day. Coffee? I make good coffee. We've got a machine."

"I'd like a coffee, thank you."

"Mama raised you well, Sarah. You're so polite."

This is fun, Sarah thought. I'm not the least bit scared. She unbuttoned her jacket and laid it beside her on the little wooden bench.

"No fair," he said when he handed her the cup. "You're showing off your arms. I'm not going to be able to think about anything else."

"Very well then. Don't. Don't think about anything else." She rose slowly, until she was face-to-face with him.

He moved toward her, but suddenly stopped. "Oh hell," he said, "you know what I just realized?"

She nodded. "You never told me your name."

"Right. It's Aaron. I'm so sorry."

She closed the last inch of distance between them. "A pleasure to meet you, Aaron."

After they shared a long kiss he turned the lock on the shop door and led her toward one of the dressing rooms, where he ran his hands up and down her arms as if to warm them, and after another long kiss he reached behind her to undo the zipper of her dress. "No bra?" She shook her head, laughing. He brushed her nipples with his thumbs. "Man, you are perfect."

"I suspect you are too," she said.

"Oh God, I'm doing it again," he said. "I forgot to tell you my last name."

"I know your last name."

"You what?"

"It's Willetts, yes?"

"Yeah— Wait. I know we never met before. How do you know what my name is?"

"Later. I'll tell you later, Aaron Willetts." The mocking smile never left her lovely mouth.

---

She had lost track of time. Sarah put her things back on, zipped up her dress. She had been wearing a jacket, she was fairly sure, but couldn't remember where she'd left it. She picked her way among the clothing on the nearby racks, settling on a handsome short coat. She slipped into it, but it was much too big, so she replaced it on its hanger. She tried on a cute woolen cap, but decided against that as well.

Oh, right—she suddenly remembered; jacket and suitcase, near the front door. She picked them up, undid the lock, and stepped outside.

Only a five-minute walk from Bond Street, the hotel lobby was filled with glorious light filtering down from the leaded glass cupola some ten stories above.

Sarah's aubergine blunt-toed pumps made a glamorous click-click as she walked across the tiled floor toward the concierge's desk. That happy, ten-feet-tall feeling was back.

She wanted to get settled in the suite before calling Jeffrey to tell him of her plans. He could come downtown to join her directly after work. They'd eat dinner nearby and then spend the night doing what it seemed they'd been put on earth to do: lose themselves, pour themselves into each other, soaring, drowning, holding on for dear life. Signing the guest register, her hand trembled from the now familiar sensation that started somewhere in the pit of her stomach and radiated out to her limbs. It was all she could do not to throw back her head and shout.

*We could go to Spain or we could go to the Bronx,* Jeffrey told her the other night. *We're okay anyplace as long as we're together. And it's okay to feel like you're on top of the world. Honest.*

The sitting room was wonderful. Cathedral ceilings and creamy colors and tea-stained linen pillows, and the entire suite smelling faintly of the bowl of narcissus on the console.

Sarah made the call to Jeff, then kicked out of her shoes and began to unpack her bag. That melody she was humming—it was a song she didn't recognize, didn't even know she knew—something old, with a gospel touch, but not mournful.

The bathroom was beautiful too. A tiled paradise with so many gleaming faucets and spa doodads that she decided to take a long soak in some of the pale green bath salts on the lip of the tub. She pulled a tube of ginseng cream from her cosmetics case and started to cleanse her face. Then she glanced into the oversize mirror.

And there it was again. Her living nightmare from the escalator at Bergdorf's.

She opened her mouth, began to scream. But then she blinked. And there was nothing in the mirror but her own face.

Terror stabbed at her like a crazy man with a razor. She backed away from the sink, eyes still on the mirror.

The filthy mouth with dripping fangs came back. And she could smell the death on it, the rot.

The more she backed away, the closer it seemed to come. Her head made a dull thunk as it hit the tile. She began to slide down the wall. She knew she was going out, going under, but she went willingly, grateful for the dark.

———

In the bathroom now, she was delighted by the deep grape color of the towels stacked on a glass shelf over the commode. "How wonderful," she said aloud, admiring the array of spigots and sprayers in the tub. It was nearly time for Jeffrey to arrive and she wanted to make herself lovely for him. She took her nubby wool minidress off its hanger. She began to think of having some work done on the bathroom in her own apartment. A little luxury never hurt anyone.

She unpinned her hair and placed between her breasts and on each of her wrists a few drops of the bespoke scent she'd purchased at the boutique on Lafayette Street. There! she thought, looking at herself in the mirror, that's better. And she didn't turn away when she noticed the self-satisfaction in her expression, the lust, the pride.

Maybe we won't go out for dinner, she thought as she put on her lipstick. Maybe we'll eat right here in the suite.

Jeffrey put his steak knife aside and helped himself to more french fries.

"You're not even going to taste that?" he asked, pointing to Sarah's untouched salmon.

"I can't," she said. "I'm not hungry."

"You're never hungry. You don't take in enough to keep a small grasshopper alive. Are you sure you're not anorexic?"

"I had salad."

"Lettuce, big whoop. Maybe I should've taken you out to eat, after all. There's a terrific place on Crosby where they have salads that look like the Eiffel Tower. I bet you'd go for that."

"I'm fine. Really. I'll just have some more wine. Besides, I didn't want to go out, after—" She broke off there.

"I know. We almost killed each other."

"Sometimes I feel like I could eat you alive. Is that normal?"

"Oh, yeah, sure. The only thing is, there's quite a bit of me to deal with. You should have a little of that fish to keep up your strength."

She shrugged in resignation and took a huge bite. "Happy now?"

"Yes. I mean, you ate tons of salmon when we went on that fishing trip to Canada."

"What are you talking about?"

"Pretend we've known each other for a long time. Like we've done a ton of normal things together. Try it sometime."

---

"It's like you're somebody else in bed. Not the old Buttoned-Up Sarah. You break free. You're Wild Sarah, Unbound Sarah . . ."

She stretched luxuriously. "Happy, Exquisitely Fucked Sarah," she supplied. "And Thirsty Sarah. Would you open the other bottle?"

Jeff sampled the buttercream frosting on the piece of cake he had asked the room service waiter to leave when the dinner dishes were collected. "Oh, shit! Ouch!"

"What is it?"

"I just cut myself on this opener thing."

She bounded from the sheets. "Let me see."

"It's okay. I'll look for a Band-Aid."

"No. Give it here." She slid her mouth around the finger and sucked at it until the bleeding abated. "Better?" she said. "Now, shall I cut mine too? And mingle my blood with yours? Like an oath?"

"You shouldn't, no."

"Am I making you nervous, Jeffrey? Nervous in a good way, though. Right? Like that night in Seattle when we had too much to drink."

"The what? Oh, I see. You're doing a bit. Like we're normal, right?"

She sank in front of him.

"At last. Hungry, hungry Sarah," he said.

---

*He was a rather bearish white man, not willowy and fine-featured like his late father and brother.*

*When it began, when he first started coming to her, her fear was so intense, it was almost a living thing, there on the mat with the two of them. Eventually he realized she was afraid he would crush her. It was better when he put her on top of him, he learned.*

*He was never certain which of the slaves had been her mother. He only knew there was no one in particular to look out for her. Someone, somehow, must've taken pity on the girl, saw to it she was fed, didn't allow her to be trampled, plowed under, although there would be nothing they could do to keep her from being misused, by anyone, yes, including himself. If his father were still alive, he'd probably sell her to any buyer at whatever price they were willing to pay. And then God knows what would befall her. There were physicians, doctors at the white hospitals, scientists who took on certain impaired ones for use in their medical experiments. The sick and wounded soldiers were coming home by the hundreds. Maybe there'd be a medical breakthrough owing to experimentation on a mentally shattered outcast, a blind or hobbled black.*

*God knows what had befallen her already.*

*He used to pantomime the instruction: "Don't close your eyes." He could not stop looking into the depthless lake in the eyes shining out of the face of this sand-colored girl who belonged to him. She and more than twenty others "belonged" to him upon his father's death.*

*They had been his inheritance. But they were dead now, nearly all of them. His mother was dead as well, and his uncles, and his imperious, conscienceless brother. More than enough death to go around. Death was busy, if no one else was. All his people were gone, and now every soul remaining, white and black, close to starving. He took the girl and their baby from the cabin and brought them into the house.*

*That first year, the beautiful girl, obeying him, kept her eyes open, maintaining that eerie white stillness no matter how he went about it or how long it took. As time went on, though, she would often begin to cry, then the tears would trigger, from somewhere deep in her being, an unreal bleating. He took it as a kind of signal, and he would ease himself farther into her. Or he would kiss her, deep and long enough to tax her breath. And then his mouth, hungry but gentle, would roam everywhere on her. He would call out her name as he finished, his heart twisting and booming in his chest, hating that she would never hear him say it. Arm across her breasts. Acting out the words:* Stay. Closer. Sleep.

*By now, though, everyone knew how openly he lived with the girl and their child. Some of the widow ladies turned their heads when they caught sight of him. Others pretended they knew nothing at all about the goings-on at his house. The black survivors knew, had always known.*

*Knew that he had moved the beautiful young girl from her quarters and installed her in the big room that had been his and his older brother's when they were children. During the day, he went about the property, where a dwindling number of bony black beings tended the imaginary crops. For a time, he went in the buggy to neighboring spreads, uttered empty words of consolation to the bereaved mothers and wives in a kind of grotesque facsimile of noble manners. Feeling nothing like the fortunate son, the country squire, he* would scrounge in the woods on the way back, and if he came upon the odd critter, he'd kill it and deliver it to the old black woman who'd been cooking for his family since she was twenty. When he was home from his preposterous errands, he took his plate into the room and shared his meal with the beautiful young girl; sometimes it was hominy and sometimes nothing more than fried bread. Butter, milk, chicken, eggs, all recollected as if from the distant past. Like reading about what tools ancestors used, how they dressed and what they ate in another age.

Night came. He suckled at her breasts as though his last hope, as though life itself, flowed through them. He undressed her and himself, then lay upon her for long moments, listening to her heart beat, before lifting her body up to receive him. He had grown so much thinner, she noticed as she bathed him and combed the hair that now crept halfway down his back.

Sometimes, when he was away from the room, the beautiful girl would go to the door and stand with her ear pressed against it, trying, despite her disability, to hear what she thought must be the comings and goings, the talk, the noise in the big house. But in fact, activity in the house had dwindled to nothing.

The second baby came. The same fragile loveliness and the same wondrous eyes as her sister. So unlike ordinary babies. They waited quietly to be nursed. It was as though they knew she could not hear them cry. The big room had become the couple's entire world. In fact, the man wanted only to close the door to the room and remain in that world forever, with his two serene daughters and their mother.

That last day, even the trees were on fire. All the troops must have gone mad. Desecration was the only outlet left to the crazed, ragged soldiers. When he returned from a day's pointless activity, the white man's house was smoldering, and the deeply black woman had both little girls with her. Their father saw them, picked them *both up in his arms, and began to run toward the blackened hulk.*

*The old woman headed slowly for the path. No backward look. She kept walking until she could no longer hear the white man, the young master, screaming.*

CHAPTER 24

*The Bowery, 2000*

Yvonne stood near the meat locker in the kitchen of Sea Grass. "I got your message," she said into the phone. "What's going on?"

Detective Kyle Sansom was on the other end of the line. "We need to meet," he said.

"What are you talking about? We *are* going to meet. In a few hours, remember? You said you'd come up to my friend's loft at six."

"No. I mean before that. I need to talk to you first. Alone."

"Why?"

"Look, Yvonne. I doubt you want your friend and his nephew in on this. Just meet me somewhere first."

"I get off work in an hour," she said.

Yvonne was suspicious. Why did he need her to be alone? It was all out in the open now, right? She had convinced him that the stories about Sarah Toomey's mother—right there in black and white—had to mean something, and that the pileup of coincidences was way too improbable. Maybe he wasn't as ready as she and Kofi were to hang murder charges on Sarah Toomey, but at least he had agreed to join them at the loft and try to figure out their next move.

She told Sansom to meet her at the only place on the Bowery she could think of that would be open this time of day. The trendy new watering holes, constructed on the sites of the old flophouses and stale beer joints, didn't open their doors until six o'clock. That's when the well-heeled youngsters tumbled in from their good jobs, ready to impress one another over single malts and vodka that tasted like penny candy.

"The Poetry Café?" Sansom said. "What the hell does that mean?"

"I guess we'll find out together. I never been in there before either. It's down the block from the address I gave you."

———

The explanation was not very complicated. By day, the Poetry Café offered espressos, prepackaged sandwiches, and a quiet place to sit and read a selection from the bookstore that operated downstairs. By night the fare was *vin ordinaire* to the third power, bottled beer, and poetry readings. With window shades drawn against the afternoon sun, the café was a comfortable space filled with flea market Formica tables, simple wooden chairs, and sundry overstuffed furniture that had likely graced the living room of a semidetached house in Flushing some forty years ago.

They ordered coffee from the slick-haired young man behind the counter and found seats at the back of the room, near the bare stage where, undoubtedly, the performances took place.

Kyle Sansom took out his cigarettes and green Bic lighter, but then he noticed the No Smoking sign near the door. The talk was that there would soon be a citywide proscription against indoor smoking. He let the pack lay where it was, mentally sending the mayor and his clean-air rules to hell. Then he turned his eyes to Yvonne, but he didn't speak.

She sat in silent anticipation for a few minutes, then could wait no longer. "*What?* What are we doing here?"

"I'm gonna ask you something, Yvonne. I want a straight answer. First sign of bullshit and I'm gone."

"What the hell are you talking about?"

"Did you have anything to do with those killings? Either Crawford or Bitty Willetts? If you did, you better tell me about it now."

"Man, are you out of your mind? Why would you even ask me some crazy shit like that?"

Sansom fixed her with another long look. "You remember a girl called Katrina Bell?"

Yvonne's face began to move involuntarily.

"Name familiar?"

She didn't answer.

"I asked you a question, Yvonne."

Her mouth seemed to be full of wood. "The name is familiar, yes."

"And a man named Curtis Baron. You remember him too?"

She looked around then, suddenly feeling like his prey. "What have you done, Sansom?"

"I'm trying to protect myself. I need to hear your end of it. I'm not throwing in with you on these Willetts murders—in fact I'm not getting involved with nothing to do with you—until you level with me."

"And you think I'm just another—"

"Tell me. Now."

———

Yvonne Howard was an only child. And since her melancholy father had died of drink before the age of forty, she and her mother, Willa, had only each other to depend on.

Curtis Baron was some twenty years older than Willa, but he was still vigorous, and as the owner of three profitable corner store properties in the borough of Brooklyn, all in shredded black neighborhoods, he had a talent for making money. A prodigious gambler, he also had the touch for that occupation. Then, too, he was reaping tidy profits from his moneylending activity, which was, if anything, his surest source of income, as strapped Negroes with no legitimate sources for quick cash were in endless supply.

Willa was a nice-looking woman with big legs and a small waist, luscious red lips, and a head of good brown hair. There were plenty of men who wanted her, but Curtis Baron was the one with the dark blue Cadillac and the show tickets and the ready coin. After the years of struggling alone to support herself and her young daughter, she welcomed the attentions of a man who could take her to dinner wherever she liked, keep nice groceries and liquor in her house, and occasionally advance the rent when she found herself short at the end of the month.

Willa, even as she washed and dusted and mopped at the various cleaning jobs she picked up, maintained a dream for her daughter: she wanted Yvonne to go to college. In the early stages of the affair with Baron, she was calculating that he might be the means to that end. Maybe he'd ask Willa to marry him; maybe the alliance with him, wedded or not, would finally bring her the good things that had eluded her all her life. Where once there seemed to be no future, she was now imagining one full of possibilities for her and young Yvonne.

Curtis Baron was not young and handsome, nor was he a kind or even an especially proficient lover. But Willa had struck the kind of deal with him that good-looking women had been brokering since time began.

Predictably, she lived to regret the choice she had made. Once she took up with Baron, she had never looked on another man with anything but pleasant neighborliness. But Baron, being pathologically suspicious, had convinced himself it was only a matter of time before the cheating began. His jealousy had surfaced a few months into their courtship, and indeed after a year of his tyranny Willa planned to quit him. But then she discovered that she was pregnant. His accusations and rages were making even the earliest stage of the pregnancy a living nightmare.

It did not help matters that Yvonne, then twelve years old, despised her mother's wealthy gentleman friend. Baron had arranged an after-school job for Yvonne at one of the convenience stores; she swept out the back room and helped restock the shelves four days a week. It sickened her to hear the store employees bad-mouth Baron all afternoon, and then watch them kowtow to him when he made his daily drop-in. And she was humiliated on her mother's behalf to hear the gossip about his exploits with other women.

The store workers, well aware that he kept company with her mother, seemed to revel in Yvonne's embarrassment. *"He sniffing around that heifer from Macon Street now. Won't be long before she getting some of his money too."* *"Yeah, he like 'em young, don't he?"* one of them would add with a chuckle.

Not a few times, Baron had teased Yvonne long past the point of good fun—mostly about her bad luck in not inheriting her mother's looks. On several occasions he had roughhoused with her as if she were a boy, not even trying to be careful about where his hands landed. Yvonne was growing up to be a tall, strong young woman. Whenever Baron became physical with her, she pushed back. He had enough restraint to stop short of striking her, but Yvonne could feel the threat in his laugh when he grabbed her wrists and held her at bay.

Willa had fought with herself about informing Baron of her pregnancy. On the one hand, she realized that if he gave the baby his name and provided for it, she, Willa, would be yoked to the unpredictable old man for as long as he lived. The prospect of that dismayed her, and she began to plot her escape from him before the pregnancy became apparent. Realistically, though, she knew she had no hope of supporting a second child on her own. And, she rationalized, it was quite possible that the appearance of the baby would soften Baron's ways. He might very well be so pleased to have his own child that he'd put all the jealous nonsense aside and become a doting father. Clearly, he was in a position to make life comfortable for all of them, Yvonne included. That kind of happiness might still be in reach. Willa decided to hang on. She would tell Curtis about the baby in another week or so, as soon as the doctor said everything was proceeding well enough.

Katrina Bell, known by all in the neighborhood as Twister, was a wild little thing, and had been for as long as anyone could remember. It was nothing out of the ordinary for a man to begin assaulting a community as a child and continue to do so into adulthood—school bully to gang member, hold-up man, pusher. Few expected the same from a little girl. Katrina Bell had been a terror in the preschool sandbox, an ongoing disruptive element in the schoolroom, an incorrigible adolescent with more experience in the juvenile justice system than the court-appointed lawyers and counselors fighting to keep her out of Spofford. To no one's surprise, fast Katrina grew into a promiscuous young woman—at a time when the standards for acceptable sexual behavior had been all but discarded. When the newest crop of ugly drugs tore through the dark neighborhood, Katrina Bell had snapped to their call like a hound dog heeding a high-pitched whistle. By the time she was twenty-one, Twister, the wiry little predator, was a low-end hooker who slept wherever she fell at night. And, oddly enough, those older folks who had feared or reviled her when she was sassy and dangerous now took a kind of pity on her, and possibly a kind of satisfaction in her plight. Twister had at last been neutralized.

Just as Willa Howard was gaining hope that fatherhood might turn Curtis Baron away from his nasty behavior, Yvonne, too, was beginning to think that he might be redeemable. She had noticed him passing dollar bills to Twister whenever she came into the store to panhandle. The store manager's first impulse was always to shoo her away with the vilest language he could summon, but Curtis Baron had taken to silently donating a buck or two and then ushering Twister out firmly but not unkindly.

One evening, a Thursday, Yvonne was nearly done with her duties at the store. Her last task for the day was to break down the empty cardboard boxes and take them out to the alley behind the store. She had once or twice been frightened by rats out back, so she stepped carefully. She came out quietly enough that Curtis did not hear her. He was standing near the chain-link fence, his back to her. It wasn't until she was a few inches away from him that she noticed Katrina Bell kneeling before him on the filthy ground as she fellated him.

Yvonne wanted only to disappear; she had not meant to make a sound. But a wheeze slipped out of her throat. He whirled to face her.

It was too late to pull away when he lunged for her. He snagged the front of her dress and pulled her to him, the zipper to his trousers still undone.

"You want some of this good thing? Yeah. You a pitiful ugly bitch, ain't you? Ima give you some right now," he said.

He pinched her nipples cruelly, dug one of his fingers into her crotch, pushing inside her panties. He pulled her into the storage shack, and sodomized her. It was over in a few minutes. She fell away from his grip, wiping furiously at her clothing.

"You say anything to your mama, Ima kill you and her both. And I got plenty more for you tomorrow night, after your mama goes to sleep."

Yvonne ran. Back through the store and all the way home.

Yvonne did not speak a word as she ate dinner with her mother that evening. After, while Willa watched TV, Yvonne went to her room, and remained there for the rest of the night. When it was time for bed, Willa knocked at Yvonne's door, but Yvonne pretended to be asleep.

The house quieted after a while. Yvonne lay awake for hours. When her little travel alarm clock read 2:00 a.m., she picked up the bag containing the things she had gathered up earlier in the evening and slipped out of the front door.

On the moonlit street, Yvonne felt little fear. Spurred on by hatred, she had a mission. Her mind was focused, her footfalls were sure and purposeful. If ever there was a night when her personal safety seemed irrelevant, this was that night. She felt prepared to eat the heart of anyone daring to interfere with her plan.

Half a block away from the corner store, she picked up several abandoned construction bricks and added them to her tote bag. Then she walked directly to the area behind the store and shook out the contents of the bag.

The first brick shattered the glass in the storeroom window. Yvonne wrapped several of the oil-soaked rags around a second brick, retrieved the box of kitchen matches, set the cloth alight, and hurled the bundle in through the hole in the window. She waited until she saw a plume of fire glowing against the glass before moving around to the front of the store, where she repeated the process, throwing the missiles through the spikes of the iron burglary gates.

As the sounds of popping glass and the clouds of muddy smoke accelerated, Yvonne turned back toward home.

While she waited in the shadows for a sudden burst of traffic to pass, she heard the first scream. There was no mistaking it. The horrific shouts were coming from inside the burning store.

Curtis Baron heard the agonized screams too. He'd arrived on the scene before the firemen.

The shrieks from inside still shattering the air, Yvonne watched from a darkened stoop across the street as he fiddled wildly with the gates at the front of the store. He threw them open at last and stepped into the entrance just as a fireball raced at him belching red death.

Curtis Baron jumped and rolled and hollered. Nothing helped. As the neighborhood looked on, he was incinerated in the doorway of his place. The screams inside had stopped by then.

The fire engines and ambulances were now barreling up the street, dozens of onlookers gawking and running about, hysterical tenants from the adjoining building tumbling from their apartments. Yvonne slipped into the crowd, then ran all the way home, the wind beating in her lungs.

It was all they talked about that next day. Mr. Baron's store going up in flames, him dying in the fire along with no-count Twister. Word was, somebody set the fire deliberately. And small wonder. Nobody could stand Curtis Baron except that stupid woman he was keeping. *Didn't I say one day God was gonna get that rich niggah for all the shit he done to people?*

Willa Howard, having never had the chance to inform Curtis Baron of his impending fatherhood, moved into the housing project on Ocean Avenue, not long after his death. Some people in the new neighborhood said Willa was simpleminded. That wasn't so. Before she and Yvonne left the old neighborhood, Willa had been assaulted, struck on the head with a pipe, so that, in addition to losing her baby, she sustained mild brain damage.

She made friends among the other welfare women and they kept one another company, watched the soap operas together, played cards, went shopping. Yvonne, who had become a guarded, silent teenager, made few friends. She graduated high school and took a series of poor-paying jobs—supermarket cashier, nighttime waitress—looking after her mother until Willa's death from a stroke.

"They questioned you," Kyle Sansom said. "You must've been seen that night."

Yvonne nodded.

"Your juvenile records were sealed—"

"And you went messing around until you got 'em unsealed," she said. "Didn't you?"

"Hey, look. I had to find out a few things for myself. I never did understand why you were so interested in getting justice for a hooker you used to see behind bars. I had to know."

Yvonne was fighting tears. He took a paper napkin from the dispenser on the table and handed it to her.

"They couldn't nail you for it though."

"No. Thank God he was a black man, right? It never went any further than a couple of detectives questioning me and my mother. And the one man who claimed he might've seen something—last anybody saw of him, he was driving away in Mr. Baron's Cadillac. So I got away with it. But that didn't make it any easier to live with."

He didn't speak for a while.

"Richard used to say something when we were still partners. He said the thing he always hated the most was what happens to the girls. So many bad things can happen to them, it must come to a point where they accept the awful stuff, figure that's just the way things are, don't expect any better. We should look out for them, he said, and treat them like they matter."

"The fuck are you saying to her?" Bean was standing over them, a take-out container of coffee in hand. "Yvonne, what's wrong?"

She wiped her eyes. "Nothing, baby. This is the detective

I mentioned. He's coming up to your place. To help us." She looked at Sansom. "Right?"

Sansom picked up his cigarettes along with Yvonne's discarded napkin, which he crushed and then threw back onto the tabletop. "Yeah," he said. "Let's go."

CHAPTER 25

## *SoHo, 2000*

The hotel lounge was on the mezzanine. Settees and armchairs in red leather, bold industrialist Russian art on the walls, a Brancusi on a marble pedestal casually pushed into one corner. Sarah and Jeffrey drank their cappuccinos standing at one of the magnificent arched windows.

"SoHo's passé, I guess, but I still like it," he said. "Let's get a place somewhere down here. A pretentious loft."

"Get a place. A place to live? Together."

"Yes."

"You mean, someday, don't you? You mean, let's pretend that we will."

He didn't answer.

And he didn't say the other thing that was on his mind: Mariette knows. Everything.

She had waited until the girls kissed him good night and went off to their room. Then Mariette had announced in a tone that left no room for argument or denial, "You're fucking someone. Quite a lot, apparently."

Daniel Bender, Jeffrey's father, had said it many times during Jeffrey's young life: Take responsibility for your actions. That's what a man does.

They could see the lit display window of the Yves Saint Laurent boutique from Jeff and Mariette's living room. He looked down at it. The mannequin had been switched since he'd last noticed. This one was all in pink, with a winsome newsboy-type cap on its hairless head.

"So," Mariette said, "what's the story, Jeffrey?"

He emitted a loud *oouf.*

"Sounds complicated. You'll have to do better than that though."

"I know." He picked up the Raggedy Ann that their youngest had left on the floor, placed it gently on the sofa, and then took a seat next to it. "Let's have a scotch first, okay?"

Mariette smiled. But not at him. Then she placed the bottle before him.

"I don't know exactly what I'm doing," he said. "Not exactly. But I may have to move out for a bit. I think you're gonna want me to."

"Stop crying, Jeffrey."

"Right."

"I'm serious. I'll brain you if you don't. You silly fuck."

What was the expression Dad used? The fat is in the fire.

No excuses, he resolved. Don't say you couldn't help it. And don't say you love her—that'll just make it worse. Best to give Mariette as few details as possible for now.

They talked a while longer, Mariette's posture knotted, her questions clipped. She made a veiled threat concerning his future access to the girls. He let that one pass. No use starting the custody and visitation shit at this stage, he told himself; just let it roll off you. Not easy to do. No more little arms around his neck. No *Guess what, Poppy? There's a surprise!* No more searching under the furniture for the Barney doll and the make-believe lipstick. Losing his daughters would be like lopping off an arm.

And still his being silently called out for Sarah. Where was she now? Bathing? Reading? Love her. Did he love her? Some black guy from the mailroom at work had once asked him about Sarah—was she single? He was twice Jeffrey's size, but Jeffrey wanted to rip his lungs out. Keep the fuck away from her, he nearly said. Instead he merely shrugged in the guy's direction. Where was she now? Standing at the window in her short green dress, waiting for him?

At the end of the confrontation with Mariette, tired, he told her he'd sleep in the sewing room.

"You will if you value your life, you prick." Bedroom door slammed shut.

Jeffrey took a long walk after she left him in the living room. He headed down Madison, the nighttime streets deserted and cold. Past the Whitney, past the Carlyle, where he and Mariette used to drop in for drinks in the days before the children came along.

So, ready or not, a new chapter. A new life, with the mystery that was Sarah Toomey. So, the fat is in the fire, Poppy.

Outside in the late winter sun, Jeff and Sarah held on to each other. He bought a scarf for her at a little shop on Prince Street filled with exquisite Thai silks and silver, Javanese carvings and vintage kimonos. They bought pastries at Dean & DeLuca and continued to walk while Jeff devoured them. Then Sarah noticed an antique store on Mercer Street. It looked familiar somehow, she said. But she couldn't quite recall why.

"Let's go in," he said.

The middle-aged Chinese saleswoman was especially welcoming as she showed off her impressive collection of brass gongs and eighteenth-century tea services.

"I'm wondering," Sarah said as the woman invited her to examine a high-polished footstool, "have we met?"

"You bought a lamp," the woman said.

"Oh, yes. The lamp." She turned to Jeff then. "Maybe two years ago. I bought a lamp for my study at home. I *have* been here before."

"Very good, Miss Amnesia. Anything else coming back to you?"

"Well, I think I remember seeing some charming puppets at the back of the store. They were on little wooden stilts."

"Yes," the saleswoman said. "From Bali."

Jeffrey looked at Sarah in amazement. "Girl, you are an Alfred Hitchcock movie."

They fell into near silence after the encounter at the antique store, walking for blocks, hands entwined. He squared his shoulders, beaming, as if he were drinking the air. My God, I think I'm good for him, she thought. I've been good for someone. She looked at Jeffrey's profile as they stood gazing in a boutique window and was moved nearly to tears by his bumpy nose. She let herself relive every minute of the dizzying pleasure she'd known. But then there was a sudden rush of the scraped-out feeling that came when he left her—hurting, all at sea. She pressed closer to his banker's blue woolen coat.

The stuff of everyday living and loving, all of it new to her, foreign. It had come to her late in life. Too late. And when all this was gone—and somehow she knew it soon would be—there would be no returning to the old way of living. She was grateful that he couldn't see her thoughts; didn't know how she was ratcheting between the only real happiness she had ever known and utter, screaming despair.

At his unspoken signal, they turned back toward the Europa.

"Did you have a grand wedding, Jeffrey? The bride all in white. Lavish flowers and hundreds of guests?"

"I don't know about the hundreds. But yeah, it was a pretty big-time wedding."

"And did you take a trip after? A honeymoon?"

"We went to Italy. Some friends of my dad got this apartment for us in Rome and then we drove all around the country for a month. It was great."

"You were deeply in love with Mariette?"

"I guess." He moved her onto his lap. "But it was way different than me and you. Well, everything is different than me and you. Yes, we were in love, sure. You—you're like totally new territory. Smart and competent and everything. But—"

"Naïve. The country mouse."

"Don't be insulted. It's nice. It makes me feel . . . What? I'm really telling on myself, right? I'm just trying to say you make me feel strong, strong enough to protect you. And protect you I will, Sarah. I'd do anything for you. I just wish I could get at whatever it is that's clawing at you. Look at it, name it. Find a way to kill it."

*And what if it's stronger than you? What then?*

He was rocking her gently in his lap.

"What do your little girls look like?"

"They're knockouts. Luckily they take after Mariette. There was a boy too. Going to be a boy, I mean. But we lost him." As he talked, he absentmindedly ran his hand along her stomach.

"Can I tell you something kind of secret about me?" she said.

"Tell."

"It's about having children. I'm terrified of it. I always have been. I used to tell myself I just didn't like them. That isn't it, though. I'm scared to death of the whole thing."

"Why?"

"I don't know. I suppose it's something—something else—from what you call my dark past. More proof I'm not a normal woman."

"What if things turn out with us and we're together for keeps. You wouldn't want to make a baby with me?"

Helpless sorrow in her face.

"Why don't we just wait and see if you change your mind about that. Maybe I'll knock a baby in you one summer, while we're on vacation."

"We'll be vacationing in Provence, perhaps."

"No problem. And by the way, you're no mouse, baby. Not anymore."

———

Jeff pulled a sheaf of papers from his briefcase and scanned them while Sarah bathed.

"Hey, you know what?" he said when she emerged from the

bathroom. "Keep going about that dream. The one you started talking about before dinner came."

"It was really horrible." Sarah got up to refill her wineglass. "And the weird thing is that it took place in the bright sunlight. Burning hot. I was a bad person, I remember that."

"How do you know you were a bad person?"

"Not just bad. I must have murdered someone. There was blood everywhere, almost as if I was swimming in it. And I knew I'd done wrong. I knew the sun was going to catch up with me and I'd burn to death."

"Boy, what a guilt trip."

"You're right. When I woke up, I had an overwhelming sense of guilt."

"Jesus, Sarah. You punish yourself even in your sleep. Look, you sucked it up big-time. Ace law school. Support your mother—and let's face it, she must have been some kind of distant, withholding number, because you can barely remember her. What do you have to be so guilty about?"

"I told you all along, I'm a mess."

"Which is why I keep talking about you seeing a shrink. You know, a good therapist could probably help you to remember a lot of things."

"I know. And I am. Thinking, I mean."

---

She was sleeping peacefully enough, but then Sarah woke suddenly. She had had a vision that came and went in a couple of seconds: She saw Lila, the cold—or was it *distant? The distant, withholding number*, as Jeff had characterized her, sitting in the

Wilmington apartment, on a tufted green chair, silent, staring at nothing in particular, her eyes all milky and dozy. And in her fingers—well, it was ridiculous, but Lila, *her mother*, was holding a reefer.

Marijuana.

Really?

## CHAPTER 26

# Berkeley, California, 1987

The party was in a rambling house high in the Berkeley hills.

Leading her by the hand, Marty Haysbert took his prize student, Sarah Toomey, on a grand tour around the great room that was pulsating with people and chatter, laughter and music. He hugged friends collegially, exchanged peace signs or air-kisses with those too far away for touching.

A young man in a tattered tee shirt was expertly rolling a spliff with one hand. Another giant-size joint was making the rounds and Marty helped himself to a deep draw from it, then held it up to Sarah's lips so she could do the same. He raised his eyebrows. "They've got a pool, you know. Drop a tab of something, we could do some serious relaxing."

He continued his promenade around the room, Sarah in

tow. "As ever," he said, "a staggering panoply of intoxicants. All's right with the world. Should we hunt up the coke?"

"You go ahead," she said.

"Okay. Sit tight. I'll be right back."

A knot of guests standing by the television greeted him warmly and pulled him into their circle. It was too noisy to actually hear them all inhaling, but from her perch on the sofa arm Sarah watched their eager snuffling, taking careful note of how they used a finger to close off one nostril while vacuuming up the powder through the other. Who knew when she might have a role as a coke-loving party animal, a term Mr. Haysbert had taught her. She'd have to know procedure.

In an adjoining room the host was explaining to a well-dressed couple that both James Brown and Aretha Franklin had recorded songs entitled "Think." It was the Aretha version that the rainbow coalition on the dance floor were enjoying, heads bobbing, fingers popping, hips engaged.

Marty caught Sarah by her waist and they continued their survey of the house. He took her hand and kissed it playfully. "Having an okay time?"

"Of course," she said.

"It's every kind of party, see? A raucous political debating party, a stoned-out party, a drunken one, a dancing one—all at the same time. I wonder if that's what Dick Diver in *Tender Is the Night* meant when he said he was going to give a terrible party."

"Or perhaps this one is just a terrible party."

"Good line, Sarah . . . Shut up, as Little Richard would say." He kissed her a little while they laughed.

And the guests kept arriving.

A while later he went to fetch a drink for her. When he returned there was an excitement in his voice. He plopped down next to her. "I just heard," he said. "Bella is going to be here, they said."

"Bella," she repeated, clearly not following.

"She's a brilliantly strange stand-up. Except, no, you can't really call it stand-up, not exactly. It's just—you have to see her to understand."

"She's a performance artist, is that what you mean?"

"Yeah, I guess, but—you know how I'm always telling you guys to be courageous, be available, dig deep? Bella doesn't just dig, she excavates, eviscerates herself. It can get scary. She like sets herself on fire. Like whatchamacallit . . ."

"Auto-da-fé. Self-immolation. Certain monks do it, I believe. In order to protest."

"Um. And you never quite know who she's going to be. Amos and Andy or James Mason or Eleanor Roosevelt. I guess she's kind of everybody and nobody," he said. "She never tells who's inside there."

Minutes later, a craggy, full-throated cry went up over the noise and the music: *"Goddamn, y'all!"*

The response from the crowd was thunderous.

"Need I say?" Marty left it there.

The boomy voice went on: "What drug are y'all on? I just left a party full of niggahs and even they wasn't dancing like y'all are."

The short, stout woman in a red beret was full breasted, with a puffy torso and legs like twigs, making her look like an over-fed blackbird. It was a good twenty minutes before the crowd surrounding her thinned out sufficiently for Marty to get close. When he did, he hugged her, and then turned around. "Bella, let me introduce—"

She interrupted, "Miss Hemings, I presume."

"Stop that. This is Sarah Toomey. She's going to be a great actor."

She trained her glance on Sarah, didn't speak for a minute, then said, "Right on, Marty. I gotta say, for your age you doing pretty good. But why wouldn't you, your nose full of snow and something this pretty sucking your dick. Like the song say, Who could ask for anything more?"

"Jesus Christ, Bell. Even for you . . ." He turned to a stricken Sarah. "I'm so sorry, honey. Bella's cranky, she hasn't killed and eaten her first antelope today. And Bella, you should fucking apologize to Sarah for that filthy thing you said."

"All right, all right, Sir Glad You Had." She bent at the waist. "Fair lady Sally, I mean Sarah, I'm sorry."

Sarah nodded acceptance of the apology, but took a few steps backward.

One after another, partiers stepped up to pay obeisance to Bella. She drifted off with a group of them, dourly insulting them between swigs from the champagne bottle she was carrying.

Half an hour later, an eager, milling knot of people began streaming into the children's playroom. Toys were here and there on the floor and atop the bookshelves. Teddy bears and beach balls and yellow cabs and red fire engines spilled out of the huge wicker trunk in one corner. The partygoers settled themselves on the floor, on the ledges of the big curtainless windows, atop the sturdy wooden table that held a Parcheesi board and a lone sneaker.

Sarah looked at the procession in puzzlement.

"Bella's on, looks like," Marty explained. "About to do—I don't know—whatever the fuck she wants to."

Sarah hesitated to follow when Marty started walking toward the playroom. "Don't worry, honey," he said. "She's moved on to mortifying somebody else. You really should hear her."

The two of them followed the others.

From the makeshift stage, made up of two low wrought iron tables pulled in from the patio, Bella looked out over the crowd. "I got a story for y'all. I call it a story but, believe me, it's all true. Swear on my mama's grave. And I just went and put flowers on it this morning. Bitch gonna be mad as fuck when she wake up. Yeah, who's laughin' now, Mama?

"Oh, look! It's black Hansel and Gretel." She was talking to a couple up close who sported matching cornrows. "How y'all doing? Y'all better sweep up all those cornbread crumbs before you leave out of this house.

"Okay. Listen. This tale comes straight from the mouth of a confidential source, my very own Deep Throat, you dig? And just to show you I'm serious, I'm not even gonna make a joke about that. My source is a cat goes by the name of See-ya. He's lived many lives, that motherfucker, and he don't love nobody.

"He was the nigger at the door of no return, who got a nickel for every nappy head he delivered. He used to call out to the luckless son of a bitches about to take that long journey to America: *Bye, y'all. See ya.* He was the nigger roping in the suckers on 125th Street with three-card monte. He a bank officer. He a jackleg deacon at yo mama's church, who rapes you. He a used-car salesman. The life insurance man. He the real raisin in *le soleil.*"

After another ten minutes of profane minstrelsy, "I'm gonna wrap this up soon, y'all. Like they say, Always leave 'em laughing."

Bella nodded a grudging kind of thanks to the crowd. "Okay, okay, y'all, I know you love me. Or maybe you hate me? Or maybe you just sick of me. Those things can all happen at the same time, yeah? Sure, they can, just ask my wet-brained mother. Y'all were left with a grandma who tried to wash you with bleach, right? No? Well, never mind."

Bella looked out over the crowd. She was breathing heavily, taking her time. Finally she announced, voice like the tolling of a weighty bell, "Tonight's merriment is not finished. Now I'm going to present a young lady with a hell of a tale to tell. I know she must be weary as hell of talking about the Thomas Jefferson shit. So we're granting her a break from that tonight. Sally, come on up here and let me pass the talkin' stick to you, girl . . . Come on, Sal. Where you at?" Her eyes roamed over the audience "Ah, there you is. I see you. Get up here, Sally! Show 'em what you got, child."

A collective murmur went up as the people in the crowd looked around, trying to determine who she was speaking to. With horror, Sarah realized that Bella was looking at her, pointing the microphone at her. She shook her head no, no no please no. She tried to flee, but somehow she could not move, her feet would not obey.

Marty's face read confusion as he looked from Bella to Sarah. "This isn't something the two of you planned?"

Sarah bristled. "Of course not! She means to humiliate me, obviously. I don't understand why."

Bella went on milking her audience. "Give the little lady a warm welcome, folks. Like on the old Ed Sullivan show. Let's hear it for the girl. *Sa-rah, Sa-rah, Sa-rah.*"

The crowd picked up the chant.

Marty made a useless stab at shushing them. They couldn't even hear him.

*Sa-rah! Sa-rah! Sa-rah!*

He reached for her hand, ready to aid her escape from the room. To his astonishment, she was walking toward the stage.

"Here you go, baby," Bella said. "Kill these motherfuckers."

Sarah took the microphone and looked out at the crowd.

Marty had moved up to the very front by then. When she

caught his eye, she pinned him with her stare. After a minute, he shrugged, then called out: "Go for it, Sarah. Anything."

"*I tell you,*" she began, and paused there, and already the slightest accent, barely there, something with a certain lilt, could be discerned—from just those three words.

"I tell you, that Monsieur René, he cry like no man never cry before. You can't know no man grieve hard as he did when we lose Miss Arlette and her babies.

"All the boys want Arlette when she's a girl in school. And when she is grown, all the men do. Since she so beautiful, Arlette used to that kind of attention. But once she meet Monsieur René, she don't study no one else. He buy her this house, one of the finest ones on Dumaine, come to be with her every day he don't have to go 'way for his work or be with his *père*, and she happy like I never see her since she was a child with her birthday cake. Her mam Miss Emma tell me: Josie, we manage just fine without you now. You go to Arlette and do for her in her house same way you always work for us. Watch over her like when she was a baby.

"And so I do. 'Cause she my heart, that girl. That Arlette.

"Since the day he set eyes on her, that devil Pernell Willetts never give her a minute's rest, and she never give him a minute's notice. He had nerve to try to call at her papa's house, he want to court Arlette, ask her to marry with him. It was almost funny. No accident how he wait till Arlette's papa pass away. He had to know Mister Joseph take a cane to him, he see him at his front door. Pernell run a fancy house, using those ignorant girls, selling them like he sell them cigars and that whiskey. Like he sell any kinda evil you can name, and so much you never even heard of. All he do is sow unhappiness and ruin.

"Arlette start to lose herself. We don't like how she spend her evenings with people nobody in this part of town know. I see she had started messing with that bad medicine. Pernell Willetts and half a dozen others selling it, getting richer, offerin' it round at his parties like it was lemonade. *Everybody takes laudanum, Josie,* she saying to me. *Doctors give it to people all the time. It can . . . cure what ails you, and it helps you unwind.*

"Unwind! It make a ghost of you, I say.

"But then she meet Monsieur René. Never see anything like them two, loving each other like that. Arlette like the weight of the world been lifted off her shoulders, like they say, she don't walk on the ground no longer, she walk on air. Monsieur René like a man found his reason for living.

"Sometime I come upstairs to soap her back, and I find the two of them in the *bain*, she rared back in his arms and both of them near sleeping in that water, looking like—I don't know— like two beautiful pebbles in a teacup.

"That devil Pernell still don't leave her alone. He have nerve to leave flowers outside this house. Nerve to send letters saying he gone get her back, like as if he ever did have her. Follow her when she go to visit her mam. Wicked he is, but he ain't a fool, Pernell. He got sense to know René kill him if he keep troubling us.

"We had us joy in this house when Arlette say she was expecting. Double joy when we find out there's a second one in there. Arlette's *maman* pray with me the whole time of the birthing. Hour after hour. And when it's over we got us the two best baby girls ever in this world. How they mam and daddy love them twin babies, 'specially Monsieur René. His papa never gonna claim them as his blood grandbabies, but I think he sweet on 'em too.

"Miss Emma say she can die happy. Arlette safe and René treat her like a queen, and most of all, the gorgeous twin babies be provided for.

"All us being happy—that don't last much more than a year.

"I don't look at it as no kind of excuse, but Pernell had to be crazy. Bad living and jealousy eatin' him alive must've rotted his soul till it was like a sore tooth, and it musta made him crazy. Nobody in they right mind could do what he did. Take them children away from they home and smother them. It do no good to take something beautiful and try to stomp it out like a campfire. No matter what you do, they still be beauty in this world and you still be ugly, and damned.

"That Pernell Willetts better be glad my Arlette kill him. That devil *rather* be dead than see what Monsieur René father have in store for him. Old Monsieur is part colored, but he got power in this New Orleans city. He have Pernell Willetts boiled in oil in the middle of Jackson Square. He have him skinned and boiled. And besides that, my *grandmère* just gettin' started to work roots on him, after I tell her what Pernell did.

"Arlette lit out of here in my cloak that night. I didn't see her do it, but she musta took my long knife from out the kitchen drawer.

"She storm into Pernell's saloon, see him drinking at the bar. I guess she run up behind him fore he could turn around. She put that blade in his back deep. Took it out and do it again. Yessir. And when he fall to the floor, she drive that knife straight in his black heart.

"Nobody know where that poor girl spent that night. But early next morning, city police find her in the lagoon. Floating.

"For a whole day Miss Emma can't even stand up on her feet. But then she get out of bed and come to the house. We both washing Arlette and putting her in her gray dress, while René in the girls' room, sobbing, howling like somebody's old dog, him, sitting on the floor near the empty cradles.

"Me, I stop my crying and wiping at my eyes, I have work to

do. But tears in my throat all the time. Maybe long as I live. But today, we busy, we gone bury Arlette with her babies."

———————

The room was silent for a long moment before the applause exploded.

Marty Haysbert stood speechless. He waited until the noise died down and people began leaving the room in search of food and drink. Then he stepped up on the stage where Bella and Sarah stood. Bella was shaking her head. "How did I know?" she said, grinning.

"Don't ask me," Marty said. "How *did* you know? For that matter, *what* did you know?"

Bella didn't answer him. She turned to Sarah, held her palm out. "You gotta give me five, Lady Hemings."

Sarah looked down at the extended hand. "Sorry, what?"

"Let me give it to you," Marty said, and slapped Bella's hand with his own palm. "We've seen some kind of channeling, or something, here. Right? People are going to be talking about this for years to come. Right? Or did that not really— Are we all tripping?"

"I don't know," Bella said. "I run on hate, buster. That's what gets me out of bed every day. I don't know what animates people like the woman we just heard from."

"God, Sarah, where the hell did that come from?" he said. "How did you do that? I mean, *say something*."

She didn't.

"Sarah?"

Still no answer.

"I think the party's officially over for us," Marty said. "Ready to go, Sarah?"

"Yes. Good night, Bella."

As he helped her down from the table, he looked back over his shoulder while pointing to Sarah, then he pointed to his own chest and mouthed the word: *mine.*

Bella chortled. "You wish."

A second later, Sarah folded at the waist. He caught her before she collapsed.

## CHAPTER 27

## *The Bowery, 2000*

"So, what did this preacher say?" Sansom asked.

Kofi made a face. "There's no quick answer to that."

"What is he, senile or something?"

"Uhn uhn. He's old but still sharp. I meant, he was helpful up to a point. But he was being careful in what he said about Lila Toomey. I think he knows more than he wanted to say on the phone. Maybe a lot more."

Yvonne handed Sansom a pumpkin muffin. "Try one of these," she said. "I think I oughta go down there and try to get something more out of him."

"How are you going to make him say anything he doesn't want to?" Kofi said.

"I don't know." She turned back to Sansom. "What you think? Here . . . this cream cheese'll go good with that."

"Talking to him in person is the way to go," Sansom answered between bites. "He's much more likely to spill something face-to-face. He's a minister, right? So maybe she confided in him. Maybe he wants to keep her confidences, but on the other hand he's guilty about withholding information about a murder. You gotta play on his conscience."

"One of us should get on it right away," she said. "I was sort of hoping you'd do it."

He snorted. "Yeah. I figured that's where this was going." He mulled it over for a minute. "You gotta remember, this would all be unofficial. I'll tell him I'm a cop, but I'll have to explain he's not obligated to answer a damn thing. Everything I'm doing's unofficial, for now. The attorney who repped Lila is long dead. But if I could get something solid out of this preacher . . . if he, or anybody else, could provide us with some kind of motive for these killings . . ." He took his cigarettes out. "You mind?"

Bean spoke up then: "Normally I'd say yes. But in this case I'll make an exception—and actually there's something you could do for me."

"Like what?"

"I want to go with you. To Wilmington."

Kofi was astonished. "What are you talking about, Bean?"

"Cool it, K. Just hear me out. I want to help Yvonne."

"You helped me enough already, sweetheart," she said.

"Okay. But it's not just about you. I figure I can shoot some great stuff down there. You know, the church this dude used to preach at, the nabe where this Sarah chick grew up, maybe some video at a Negro cemetery where her mother might be buried. It ought to work fantastic alongside the things I shot at her apart—" He halted there, unsure whether Sansom knew about his and Yvonne's break-in. "I'm just saying, I've never been to Wilmington before. And it would be awesome to hang with a for-real detective."

Sansom looked dubious. "Hang?"

"Don't worry about it. I'm not going to be in your way. I'm just putting together a document, get it? This stuff should be documented. And besides all that, this preacher would probably feel better with a regular brother in the room—you know, not a cop, just a regular guy trying to keep somebody else from getting killed; it wouldn't feel so much like you're threatening to bust him or get him to testify about anything. Makes sense, doesn't it?"

"He might have a point at that," Kofi said. "And speaking of cops, Bean, every time you get tempted to act crazy, just remember you're with one. If you come back here in handcuffs, don't call me."

Bean looked at Sansom. "So? You down with this?"

The detective shrugged. "Why not? It's no crazier than anything else about this case. A couple of things though. Do you know what 'shut up' means? And 'get lost'—you know how to do that when I tell you to? No questions asked. 'Cause if you put a foot wrong with any of your *documenting* crap . . ."

"Shut up. Check. Get lost. Check."

"Thank you," Yvonne said. "Trains every couple of hours from Penn Station. Or do you want to fly the commuter plane? I can cover all your expenses."

"Skip it. Cook me dinner after I crack this goddamn case open and they make me chief of detectives. Anyway, I hate airplanes. Amtrak's good enough for me."

"You'll be staying for a little something to eat, won't you, Kyle?"

"Take a rain check," he said. "I've got a couple things to do before taking these vacation days."

Kofi, who was now deep in conversation on the phone, waved his appreciation as Sansom headed for the door.

"He's trying to get an appointment with this museum lady," Yvonne explained.

"Museum?"

"Yes. Uptown. Kofi says this woman up there might know what the story is with that blanket that was in Sarah Toomey's place. You saw the photograph. The one with the snakes and crosses and what-all."

"And Uncle Remus in the middle of it. What does that have to do with anything?"

"I don't know yet. But I think it must mean something. Kofi says my hunch might be right, that the blanket could be 'symbolic' of something. There's this lady who might know more about it."

"Symbolic. You don't mean, like, the *spirits*? Like some kind of woo-woo?"

"A lot of people believe in that stuff. Maybe Sarah Toomey and her mother did. I never met a black person yet didn't have some kind of superstition carried up here from the South."

"Mother of God. You're talking about some southern shit? Yvonne, I hate southern shit."

CHAPTER 28

*The Bowery, 2000*

Everybody knows the Bowery is haunted. How could it not be?

Even so, Burt Winnick—who had grown up in the Belgian Congo as the only child of two white Christian missionaries—was unprepared when he saw his first ghost.

Seated on a high stool in the locked reception booth, Winnick, the daytime manager of the Third Street Christian Refuge for Men, looked in astonishment at Sarah Toomey. He'd seen a bit of just about everything in his thirty years slinging soup and handing out towels and mopping up vomit in the funky old structure. But nothing like the apparition that had emerged out of the shadows and was now staring wordlessly at him. The beautiful young woman was cool as marble and her curly blond hair was damn near transparent.

When it is your time, Burt Winnick recalled his mother saying, be ready to meet your maker. Winnick was ready. And now he was looking at just the kind of angel he'd always hoped would come for him, wrap him in her bosom, and take him to his rest.

One thing, though: there was a big smear of blood on her face.

Finally, Winnick found his voice. "We don't take women here, sister. You want the Sixty-Third Street facility."

Sarah went on staring at him.

"What's the matter with you, sis? You hurt? You want me to call an ambulance?"

He climbed down from his perch and started toward her. But by the time he unlocked the reception-room door and hobbled into the hallway, she had vanished.

At the corner of Second Street and Bowery she came upon a spindly white man steadying himself against the gray stone building that housed a Hare Krishna boutique. The aged hobo, whom the others at the shelter called Minn, had lived far longer than anyone would have predicted. He had been a Bowery denizen since the early 1960s.

Minn was drunk. Undeniably drunk. But not so out of it that he didn't realize what the ethereal-looking woman in the white dress was doing. She was sniffing him. She had walked up very close to him and bent toward his chicken-yellow flesh. Then she commenced to smell him at the armpits.

It so startled the old wino that he dropped the paper bag he had been holding. He heard the muffled tinkle of glass, looked down to see his half pint turn to a dark stain in the bag.

Sarah reached inside the top of her dress and pulled out a crisp twenty-dollar bill, which she pushed into Minn's hands. She mumbled something as she did so.

"What's that you say?"

"I said, tell me where he is."

"Who? Who you looking to find, missy?"

She stepped back and regarded him sharply. "There's another one." She wiped at the blood on her face. "Where is he?" she asked again. "He's very close. Isn't he?"

"Gal, you're drunker than I am."

"I'll give you more when you tell me where to find him."

"More? Okay. Just tell me what he looks like. One of the black fellas? That who you mean? He beat on you or something? You looking to get back your own?"

Sarah shook her head in impatience. She turned away from him, eyes scanning the street.

"Just a minute, just a minute," Minn called. "Lemme help you find him."

But she did not stop. She had spotted another derelict, a black man with one leg, slowly making his way across the avenue on his walker, and she was heading straight for him, extending a twenty-dollar bill. Minn heard her demand, "Where is he?"

CHAPTER 29

# The Georgia Backwoods, 1865

While he preached, Jack kept his voice low. And he kept his hands upon their heads as they knelt before him. There was a perilous journey ahead, he told them in the gravest tones. But also ahead were rewards beyond their imaginings. The enemies were coming, the battle was coming, no stopping any of it now, so they'd best prepare themselves. They'd best be clean of soul and ready to assume the throne awaiting them, as soon as they banished the beast.

"What we gone do to him?" Abner asked.

"Slay him," Jack said. "Kill him dead."

"He gone kill us too?"

"He'll try, child. Like I told you. Think he can blind you with his temptations. Think he can fool you with his lies. But none of that's gonna stop us."

Monroe squirmed, tried to pull away from the pressure of Jack's powerful grip on the top of his skull.

"When we gone kill the beast?" Abner persisted.

"Soon as we get to the sea," said Jack. "That's where the battle will be waged. We gone turn it red with the blood of every devil. Spill they blood. Feast on they flesh. That's what he said. Then we go right on 'cross to glory."

Monroe made a strong twisting movement and at last escaped the preacher's grasp. He scrambled to his feet. " 'Cross to where? How?"

"The heavenly white ships . . . the *ships*, man. Haven't you heard a word I say?"

Monroe stared.

Jack turned mocking eyes on him. "You tired of praying, Brother Monroe? Think you worthy of glory now? Or don't you have to earn that crown?"

Monroe was weighing his words. While he calculated what to say, Abner spoke up: "I want a glory crown. Ima kill a beast."

Jack beamed down at him. "Let me hear amen."

Preacher Jack closed his eyes, bent his head in silence as Abner, now on his feet, slashed at the night with an imaginary sword.

In the fast-descending darkness, Monroe started to kick the fire out. Suddenly, from the high clump of grass behind the banked fire, there was a rustling noise and the sound of voices. Monroe ran to the arsenal of weapons they had stolen from the trapper's place and grabbed up a skinning knife.

A Negro couple stepped out of the high grass, the man's black hands held high, palms outward. Behind him was a woman who kept her hands folded in front of her.

"We mean no harm," said the man, his eyes on the knife. "We just hungry."

Monroe stared at the woman, who was not so young, but

very pretty, with a plump face and light brown eyes. She was in turn fixed on young Abner. When she smiled tenderly at him, he backed away from her.

Both the man and the woman wore jackets with dull metal buttons over their garments. They were not field slaves, Monroe decided.

"Where y'all going?" he asked.

"To that old mill on the turnpike," the man answered.

Preacher Jack had said nothing so far, but at those words his head snapped up. "Mill, you say?" he demanded.

"Yes. 'Bout six miles from here."

"What for?"

The stranger could not comprehend the fire in the older man's questions, yet he answered calmly. "Work. Union soldiers camping there. They paying money to work on the roads."

Jack knit his brow.

"Give you food and tents too," the woman added. "And there's a doctor with medicine."

Jack thundered laughter. "That's where you go? To toil in their fields? With Armageddon at hand?"

"We not going to the tents," Abner said. "We going to kill the beast. He in the sea."

Monroe addressed the woman: "Who told you? How y'all know about the tents—and the pay?"

The man, his face growing tight, placed a silencing hand on the woman's arm and started to respond, but Preacher Jack would not allow either of them to speak. "As clanging brass!" he boomed. "None so blind."

Silence fell over the group like a spell.

It was the woman who broke it. "You ain't but ten or so, are you?" she said softly, and walked toward Abner, her hand extended.

He eluded her touch. Then he used his would-be weapon to stab at her belly.

Monroe grabbed his ragged shirt collar and shook the child so hard, Abner gasped for air.

Jack looked into the face of each stranger. He was breathing heavily. "If they hungry," he said slowly, "give them beans."

The Negro watched warily as his companion followed Monroe over to the sacks of rice and beans. As Monroe made bundles from shredded cloth and poured rice into one, beans into another, he spoke quietly to her: "You done seen those soldiers before?"

"Yes."

"They giving out food? And putting folks to work for money?"

She nodded. "We heard."

"That's your man you with?"

"No. My uncle. He knows the way. Why don't y'all go with us?"

Monroe didn't answer.

"Y'all should come. Least the child would be safe."

His eyes flicked in Jack's direction and he shook his head.

"Your daddy?"

"No. He's a preacher. Jack Willetts, from the Clarkson place, like me and the boy."

When they returned to the others, she made a small bow in Jack's direction. "Thank you, preacher."

Jack did not acknowledge her words.

She went on, speaking shakily. "When we smelled your fire, I said to Uncle, 'Maybe there's folks we might camp with tonight.'" She laughed nervously then. "Being there's no moon and all."

"That's right," her uncle put in. "Selena gets afraid of the darkness—"

Jack cut him off. "She's not fit for war."

"No sir," Selena said. "That's what I know. None of us fit. Least of all, me. We hungry and rest broken. Feel like I'll never be strong again."

Somewhere, an owl hooted. Then Jack heard it cackle and cough.

Jack strode over to the pair. "Here," he said, "here's your strength." In a single movement he unwrapped the bandage from his wounded arm. Selena cried out. There seemed to be points of blue-and-yellow light rising up like fireflies from the infected flesh.

"You will not stay these warriors," Jack pronounced, pointing to Abner and Monroe. "By God, I will tear thy limbs from thy body and thee will sink to the same bloody hell as thy captors." He spat on the ground at her feet.

She turned, tore off through the grass.

Before her uncle could follow her, Jack stepped in front of him and used his long knife to slice at the man's coat front. The little buttons fell to earth in a gentle shower. Jack retrieved them and solemnly distributed them to his soldiers.

## CHAPTER 30

## *SoHo, 2000*

On the other side of the glass wall they could see a few of the guests in their workout gear, astride the exercise bikes or doing sit-ups.

But they had the pool all to themselves. They'd been floating for a long while, holding hands, silent.

Jeff sighed in contentment. "Well, this is obviously something you *do* remember. You can swim."

Sarah grinned at him. "You're right. I can. My Nanny Bea used to take me to the Y. That's where I learned how. And a few times my mother took me to the beach. I was afraid at first, but I came to love being in the water."

"In the summer," he said, "we used to go visit these friends of my dad. They had a big ostentatious place on the island. And a gigantic pool. I'd lay there on one of those cushions, looking up at the sky. Waitin' till some lady in an apron made my lunch. Little entitled bastard. But in my defense, sort of, somewhere inside I knew how lucky I was."

"I guess I was lucky too. I have a feeling there were all kinds of opportunities for something awful to happen. But here I am, here I still am. With you." She turned to look at him. "Lucky."

The leisurely walks through SoHo were the high point of their hotel getaway. They found a fantastic little place for lunch, and went there every day that Jeffrey could get away from work. They "decided" on a loft in a remodeled building on Wooster. Sarah liked the sound of the street name. The fact was, it would be months before they'd actually be signing a lease, phoning the movers, and so on. Jeff was thinking he'd move into Sarah's place in the interim. Did she think that would work?

When Sarah said yes, oh absolutely, she was laughing.

What's so funny? he asked.

She didn't answer because— How could she phrase it? It was funny because it was never going to come true. Being loved by Jeffrey, living with him, waking up mornings in his arms, the two of them going to work together. So normal that it seemed totally out of reach.

They'd walked for hours, and when they got back to the Europa, Jeff suggested an afternoon nap. Like we're in kindergarten, he said.

She nodded off soon after they tumbled into the downy fluff of the king-size bed, but, drowsy as he was, Jeffrey didn't sleep.

Sarah lay on her stomach, sprawled across his chest. He

looked down at her as she tightened her arms around his torso. *A glorious prisoner, that's me.*

He closed his eyes, but even with them shut, he still saw the slope of her back, saw himself nuzzling into it, his hands encircling her from behind, finding her breasts. One hand traveling slowly downward and then over the rise of her hip, and then feeling her moisten. He opened his eyes. Wow, the sun had brought a miraculous blush to her face. Yeah, that's the ticket, Sarah: get *more* beautiful. She began to fidget, mumbled for a minute, and then snored contentedly. He smoothed out a tangle in her hair.

His thoughts ranged all over.

*Ahead to the future*— Was the life with Sarah he'd been imagining going to happen for real? Was he blowing up his marriage, his life, for an affair that was going to flame out in a few months? What was Mariette going to tell the girls when they asked why Poppy wasn't there anymore? What would he say to them?

*Back to the past*— To Toby, his best friend, his roommate in the Penn days. Whenever Jeff left their shared apartment to go on a date, Toby would announce in a stentorian voice, "On tonight's episode of *How Much Pussy Can One Man Handle* . . ." He was a successful sitcom writer now.

When the separation from Mariette was formalized, he'd call Toby and tell him the news. Mostly, he needed to tell him about Sarah, if he could find the words.

Sarah slept on.

Christ, that thing, or things, whatever—the trauma—that made her this way, it must've been a motherfucker. Something unimaginable. He wanted so bad to help her exorcise it, but he had to be careful not to push too hard. They'd talked about her going to a shrink. He almost had her convinced.

Flawless beauty aside, she was a black woman born in America, with a black mother and black ancestors, which meant loss, murder, grief. He couldn't begin to know how centuries of racism land on the back of any one person. He wished he did know. But Sarah sure as hell couldn't school him, because she couldn't remember most of the things she'd been through. When he asked about the segregation in Wilmington, she could only repeat a few things she recalled her Nanny Bea saying about "the old days."

We made the rules, wrote the histories, *We* scorched the earth, killed the buffalo, befouled the air and poisoned the streams, and finally, finally cut the dark millions loose, sending them off on another endless fucking odyssey. I'm not black. I'm a "We." And there's nothing I can do about it. I'm a man, a white man, I'm rich, I'm still young, and the only woman I want, wants me. And our wanting ain't cute. Not anymore. Our thing has jaws and teeth and it's greedy and unpredictable. And we go so deep inside each other, I take her so completely—it almost makes me feel like a cannibal. So yeah, basically, except for the murder I'm gonna commit if Mariette tries to take my kids away, basically no complaints.

*The recent past*— Yesterday's little adventure. He had an appointment with a client uptown. He and Sarah made a plan to meet up afterward at a tony black-owned place that was currently setting the standard for New York hip.

He ordered his Absolut on the rocks from a bartender in a Hermès tie, a guy the other side of fifty, very tall, colored like a sun-burnished cowboy, profile chiseled out of granite, contemplative, with slicked-back hair. Jeffrey settled into the comfortable seat at the bar and they exchanged a few meaningless, cordial words, what you do when you're the only person sitting there. Ten minutes later, Sarah walked in. He turned on the stool to watch her as she approached. She was in black, her dress long, dead plain, and like a second skin. Impeccable pointy-toe boots with hardware—tiny silver skulls—running up the sides. Biker chic. New York costly, and worth whatever the cost. All that was missing: tattoos. No doubt, she'd bought the outfit at one of the Nolita boutiques that had popped up in the last year, at the same time that cluster of streets in vanishing Little Italy had come to be called Nolita. She headed for Jeffrey. The bartender, expressionless, only the eyeballs working, switching several times from Jeffrey to her and then back to Jeffrey. She said nothing, just stood there looking into Jeff's eyes.

Oh, Sarah. That slow smile of yours. What is it saying today, baby? *I'm just a little puppy?*

*Try to keep up, fool?*

*Be very afraid?*

Fuck. So she's crazy. So what?

He stood, took Sarah and lifted her onto his vacated seat, and they began to kiss. Seriously.

What was the bar guy thinking? Does he hate me now? Fuck him too. *She Is Mine.*

The guy turned away and walked the length of the bar to busy himself at some task.

He returned in a while, and directed his words to Sarah. "To drink?"

"I'd like a red wine, please." She paused there, listening intently to the music wafting over the bar.

"Something the matter?" Jeffrey said.

"I think— That song. That voice. I think maybe I heard it once, somewhere."

The bartender was refilling Jeffrey's water glass, but he was looking at Sarah.

"It's Ella Fitzgerald," Jeffrey said. "You probably have heard her, love—somewhere before." He thought he could see the tiniest shift in the bartender's posture. *Who did you think I was going to say—Moby?*

The bartender then placed before them a stiff piece of stationery only slightly larger than a playing card. It was the menu.

―――――――

Sarah stirred, sat up and yawned. "I thought you were sleepy," she said.

"Nope. I just watched you."

Pulling the tee shirt off over her head. "Keep watching."

"Whatever you say. Aha. Good girl."

CHAPTER 31

*Harlem, 2000*

"I really appreciate your taking the time to see us," Kofi said.

The woman he was speaking to was about forty, hair cropped nearly down to the scalp, petite, trim, and beautifully dressed in a clay-colored knit; an impressive chunk of lapis lazuli hung from a silver chain around her neck. She greeted Kofi warmly. Vy McKim, one of the founders of the Contemporary Museum for African-American Art, was married to Porter McKim, a renowned sculptor and a friendly acquaintance of Kofi's.

"Please excuse me. I'll be with you in a moment," she told him and Yvonne, and then hurried away.

Yvonne turned to Kofi. "What is it she does?"

"Shows people, mostly VIPs, around the place. Tells them the story behind the paintings or whatever they're looking at. She explains stuff, talks up the artists. But mostly she tries to get them to open up their wallets. I hear she hit up the mayor for some big bucks out of his own pocket."

Yvonne nodded. She shivered a bit. Figuring she ought to be wearing something nice when she met this cultural heavyweight McKim, she had chosen her blue silk dress. But the museum was too chilly for her outfit. She pulled the collar of her lightweight jacket close around her neck.

"This way," Vy said as she beckoned to the two. "Why don't we go up to my office."

They were shown into a spacious glass-walled room with a jaw-dropping array of African metalwork on a series of bleached wood shelves. On Vy's desk was the predictable volcano of paperwork. She gestured them to two of the three Breuer chairs in the room. Genuine vintage Breuers, Kofi noted, running his hand over the worn leather. Envy wasn't a major sin, was it?

There was a bit of obligatory small talk: the stunning gentrification going on in Harlem; what good publicity the recent *Artforum* piece on Porter's work was; and wasn't it a strange coincidence how Kofi's mother too ran an art gallery.

Kofi was circumspect in his narration of the events that had brought them to the museum. He never mentioned Yvonne's former occupation or her relationship to Bitty Willetts; and especially there was no talk of people meeting their deaths covered in slime.

No, what he wanted to talk to Vy McKim about was the arresting quilt that Yvonne and Bean had found in Sarah Toomey's apartment.

Vy took the enlarged photograph he handed her, studied it for a moment. "Oh, it's a story quilt. Just looking at this photograph, I can't tell much about the workmanship, but it's very interesting. There's a pronounced quality of fear in it, so much menace. Like a representation of evil."

"I'm with you on that," Yvonne said. "I can hardly bear to look at it."

"A story quilt," Kofi said. "Three or four years ago, wasn't there a gallery or a museum somewhere with a show about quilts?"

"That's right," Vy confirmed. "The Whitney did a wonderful job with them." She walked over to a metal cabinet and pulled open one of its shallow, elongated drawers. "Here's the poster from the show. The one shown here was one of the nicest things in the exhibit. Lovely, don't you think?"

It was. Sewn using a variety of pastel colors, the quilt featured at its center an indomitable-looking old black woman in a narrow-brimmed straw hat. Along the borders of the quilt were some of the same objects featured in the one found at Sarah Toomey's apartment: stars, milk buckets, and so on. Only this piece held none of the darkness that characterized the one at Sarah's. The central figure in it was strong but in no way demonic. In fact, the whole character of the piece was charming rather than chilling.

Vy removed the catalogue for the Whitney exhibit from a bookshelf overhead and handed it to Yvonne.

"It's not my area of expertise," she said as Yvonne thumbed through the book, "but I did see the short instructional film that accompanied the show. Apparently, a number of quilts more or less like this one were made to give directions to escaping slaves about which routes to follow or what areas to avoid. Each of the objects at the borders of the quilts had a specific meaning. It was a kind of code. An anchor might mean that a boat was ready to carry them someplace; a milk pail perhaps told a slave on the run to look in the sky and follow the Big Dipper. It was all very complicated. Of course, most of those quilts didn't feature a person's face; they were a lot more abstract. Maybe the one in your photograph was done after Emancipation. Rural black women are known for their quilting abilities, you know. Even to this day."

Kofi regarded her with a twist of the lips. "Some of this is coming back to me now," he said. "I have heard stories about things like that. But I never paid too much attention to them."

"What's the matter? Don't you believe they're true?" Vy said with a little smirk of her own.

"I think it's gotta be at least fifty percent wishful thinking on the part of the scholars who tell us about these things. I guess I'm just not as credulous as a lot of us are."

Vy laughed out loud then.

"Sorry," Kofi said. "Am I being pompous—a bad race man?"

"That's between you and your little black consciousness. But it's okay. Porter's not very 'credulous' either. But that hasn't stopped him from using quite a bit of it in his work. The images, the symbols, the traditions—all of it has tremendous power in any case." Then she added, "*N'est-ce pas?*"

"To be sure," he said.

"Getting back to your photo."

"Right. What do you think of it? You think it's just decorative— grotesque as it is?"

"Don't get me spouting off about something I know so little about," Vy said. "It could mean anything or nothing."

Yvonne put the catalogue aside and asked, "So what do the snakes and skeletons tell you?"

"I'm sure I don't know. But I can tell you who might. When they put that catalogue together, they consulted someone who knows a great deal about the subject."

"Who?"

"An incredible woman who lives in the South, a homegrown scholar. Quite elderly now, and she was too ill to travel up here for the Whitney thing. I understand she's spent her life gathering oral histories, transcribing slave narratives, tracing family trees, and so on. She has extensive knowledge about quilts, and apparently she owns some exquisite examples. Several southern universities have had her lecture in their ethnic studies programs. I don't think anybody would dare write anything on the subject without consulting her. Her name is—"

"Carrie Joshua," Kofi said. "Her name came up in some research I was doing. I can't believe I forgot about that."

"Well, there you have it," Vy said.

"Do you think," Yvonne asked tentatively, "she'd talk to me? Have you got her phone number?"

"Me? Oh no. But I believe she lives in a town not far from Macon. I'll make a phone call to a friend at the Crafts Museum and see what we come up with."

Twenty minutes later Kofi and Yvonne were thanking Vy for all her efforts.

"We'll let you get on with your work now," Kofi said. "You must have a lot to do."

"Sorry I can't ask you to lunch," she said. "My day is more overbooked than usual. But I can recommend some wonderful places to eat in the neighborhood."

"That's all right. We're pressed for time too. I have to get you and Porter downtown sometime. Take you to dinner. I owe you."

"No, you don't. But I would call your attention to our donation box downstairs. We take checks."

Once they were outside again, Kofi thought better of his decision not to stop for lunch. "You know what I'm thinking?"

"No," Yvonne said.

"Two things. Chicken. And waffles. Come on. I know a place on 138th. I can call Amy Rice from there."

"Who is— Oh, right—your sister's old girlfriend."

---

"I didn't know you had a car," Yvonne said. "My old piece of crap died long ago."

"It was my mother's. I keep it at a garage on Varick. Don't use it much. But it comes in handy once in a while. Like for taking you to the airport tomorrow."

"The airport." Yvonne sounded giddy. "I'm going to go flying down South, to Macon, Georgia. Probably lose my job. And what do I know about the goddamn South? Nothing. But I got this far, Kofi, and I can't let it go. I can't. I don't know anyplace but New York. I don't want to have to kill some cracker says the wrong thing to me."

"You can handle it. Actually, Macon's kind of nice as I remember it. And like I told you, you're not going to be all alone. You're going to have Amy."

"I guess you think this must be the final proof I'm out of my tree," she said, trying to laugh.

"No. It's proof of how fierce you are. You might have made a brilliant medical researcher, Yvonne. Or maybe a homicide detective. I don't think you're crazy. I think you're magnificent."

CHAPTER 32

*Wilmington, Delaware, 2000*

The church was still standing, weathered, to be sure, patched here and there, but with a kind of graceful modesty.

Reverend Joseph Thayer was no longer the resident minister. He'd retired some years ago. But he remained a fixture on the premises, coming and going altogether freely. And he maintained the keys to everything, to the massive, timeworn front door, to the sacristy, to the small dining room below the stairs.

It was only now, as he watched the two tall men walk up the path to the church door, that he made the decision. The dead are dead, let them be, he'd said to himself in the past. But the New York police were looking into a series of hideous murders, of innocent people, and they needed his cooperation. The dead are buried, yes, but sometimes their secrets can't stay buried with them. In fact, sometimes they mustn't stay that way. He made the decision to tell the New York visitors everything they wanted to know. The question was, would they believe him?

Yes, he told Kyle Sansom and Bean, like her mother before her, Lila Toomey had been in his congregation. From the very first, he knew she was a troubled young woman.

"You helped her out when she was arrested," Sansom said when they were all settled with their coffees in the kitchen. "Sheltered her, found a lawyer for her. I understand he's passed away. But he wound up getting her off."

"She was in need of so much help. So much."

"I think now you're maybe talking about psychological help," Bean said.

"I am, yes. She came to me when her soul was in crisis, which is what she should have done. Bringing peace to her soul was my business, my duty. And my failure. It turned out the best advice I could give her was to seek a different kind of help."

"But she didn't seek it?"

"Lila was a good person, a very intelligent woman, but she was . . . I don't want to say she was haunted, because that would mean— Well, all the things that made her so fearful, I'd be admitting they were real."

"What things?" Sansom asked.

Reverend Thayer sighed, turned his eyes away. "Not just ungodly . . . horrible things."

"She thought she was under some kind of crazy spell or curse or something," Bean said. "That's what you mean, isn't it?"

He nodded. "The truth is, those things did *haunt* her. And they ruined her life, really. She told me there was a young man who loved her very much, and she loved him as well. There seemed to be great happiness at hand for her, and she should have just grasped it and thanked God for it."

Sansom nodded his head ever so subtly toward Bean, indicating that he should continue the questioning.

Bean said, "But—?"

"But she was convinced she was going to be the cause of his death. He was bound to die, and die horribly, she'd say. How can you know that, I'd ask. I just know it, she'd say. I don't know when and I don't know why, but it's coming.

"I'd watch as she pounded her own forehead with her fists, trying to drive the thoughts out of her head. But then she would recover, resign herself to it, and say she was helpless to stop what was going to happen, but the one thing she could do was make him happy for as long as they had together.

"Do you understand what I'm telling you? After all that self-blaming and suffering, she would return to being a lovely, rational girl, and she would dry her eyes and thank me and leave. Until the next time. It was torture for her, understand, to always be on alert for the worst thing in the world to descend on him— and on her."

"And you knew him?"

"No. Only his name. He was called Eugene. Eugene Willetts."

"Willetts. You said Willetts?" Bean and Sansom exchanged quick bug-eyed glances. "And he was the father of Lila's child? Sarah."

"Surely he must have been. And as you know, he was indeed killed. Before Sarah was born. Lila was devastated, of course, but she claimed to also feel a sense of relief. In her mind, some unknown force had decreed things had to happen as they did. Now it was over, the torture was over. And she went on taking the blame for his death."

"She said that? She admitted she murdered him?"

"I didn't say that, and I didn't believe that."

"But she confessed it to you."

"Confessed that she summoned a horrible entity from some other world. Summoned it or . . . or became it, perhaps—she didn't know which—and this was the thing responsible for the unspeakable death of the man she loved. Is that what you mean by 'confessed'?"

"Did Lila ever get with anybody else. After?"

"No, I think not. Another parishioner, an older, more settled man, had always been interested in her, followed her about, pressing his suit, but she never responded to him. Finally he gave up. 'God must've made her so pretty to make up for her not having any feelings,' he said. I suppose it was the rejection that made him a bit ugly."

"Did you ever think maybe Lila just straight-up killed the Willetts kid? Either because she was mentally ill or just really pissed off at him. And she was conning you all along, like setting up an alibi."

"No. Never that. How could I know what really happened to that poor boy? Lila was clearly delusional, disturbed. Should I have allowed her to go to prison for the rest of her life if she'd done nothing wrong?"

Sansom spoke again. "And never tell the police, right? Because when somebody *confesses* things, it's sacred. Even if you confess to killing JFK. It's sacred. Right?"

"You are a Catholic, sir?" the reverend said.

"Was, Dr. Thayer. Was."

"Detective, I think you may look at Lila Toomey as simply someone who got away with murder. That isn't true. She escaped nothing. What she was, was a soul that had visited hell, or had it visited upon her.

"She was other things too. A daughter whose own troubled

mother died young. A woman alone with a child to raise. She never recovered from Eugene Willetts's death, but she was able to go on and provide an education for her child, Sarah, and bring her up to be a splendid woman who is now off on her own. Is that scenario so different from millions of single women, especially black women, who face hardship but somehow find the strength and resolve that are called for?

"Lila was able somehow to keep the demons in her mind at bay, year after year. She was no one's idea of a fulfilled person, but never again did anything happen— I might as well stop there: nothing more ever happened. Except, there is one other aspect of the story. I don't believe you know about it. And now I think you must."

Sansom and Bean waited.

---

Yvonne raced into the room, held her head close to Kofi's so that she could hear the report Bean was phoning in.

At the end of his recitation of all he and Sansom learned, he added, "Wilmington is a trip. The food's good though. Is Yvonne okay? Ask if she knows how to make fish stew."

"She's okay. Considering. It sounds like you did solid work there, my dude. I'm proud of you."

"I saved the best for last, Kofi."

"What best?"

"Is Yvonne still listening too?"

"Yeah."

"There were some killings down South. Before Lila and *her*

mother came north. Police down there questioned someone with the last name Toomey."

"I don't believe it."

"Believe it. Straight from the mouth of Rev Thayer. He had a lot of years to poke around in this thing. I think in the end he decided he didn't want to know any more."

"Last name of the victims of these killings?"

Bean laughed. "Come on, K. You know it's Willetts."

"Oh my God." That was Yvonne.

"Both of you—you may want to sit down for this," Bean said. "It's about Lila's baby daddy."

"I hate that expression, and you know it."

"Okay. I'll say it straight. Sarah Toomey's father was a Willetts. His name was Eugene. So, Sarah's got a double mojo on her—she was born to kill Willettses, but she's one herself. You fainted yet?"

"I'm just trying to take it all in. Where in the South?"

"Hang on, I'm looking at my notes. Okay, Galilee. Like in the Bible? Galilee, Georgia."

"Where's Sansom? With you?"

"No. He went to talk to this retired cop who caught the case. I've been trying to talk to the old lady who lived downstairs from Lila. But she's not well, and she doesn't want to talk to us anyway."

"You're doing that on your own? Without Sansom? You better stop that, Bean. And where are you now?"

"Shooting. I'm getting some unbelievable stuff. Plus, I met this girl in the place where we ate last night."

"You be careful, you hear me? Just get back safe."

"Yessum."

"When do you get in tomorrow?"

"Late afternoon. I think. Depends what Sansom says."

"All good. Solid, solid work, man."

"See ya."

"Wait. Just—love you, that's all."

Yvonne added quickly: "So do I, honey."

## CHAPTER 33

# *NoHo, 2000*

The hotel room was warm. Jeff threw off his coat and went into the bathroom. When he returned, he motioned her over to him with a small movement of his head. She obeyed, wordless, abandoning the scrunchie she'd been using to keep her hair off her neck and shedding her underthings as she stepped toward him.

He began to work her where she stood, kept it up until she collapsed into him. He picked her up and put her on the bed. "I'm gonna taste you right now," he said. "All day I've been thinking about it." She babbled something. He laughed. "You're talking out of your head, baby."

A while later she was sitting astride him, moving with excruciating slowness, making him mewl, beg.

"Tell me," he said. "Tell me how much you love me."

The scarf he'd bought her traced a silver blue parabola in the air as she brandished it, slipped it around his neck. "This much," she said, tightening her grip until her knuckles whitened.

"*Tell me!*" Jeffrey choked out. But she shook her head no. She bit savagely at him, drawing blood. "And the next time," she said, "when I tell *you* to stop . . . don't. Or you'll be sorry."

They'd found a way to suspend time. When at last they were spent and weeping, he lay back on the pillow with a fake plea for mercy. "Okay, sugar," he said. "Go ahead and kill me."

Sarah rose from the bed and stumbled over to the distressed wood desk, where she began writing with great concentration on a sheet of hotel stationery.

"What's that you're doing?"

"Writing you a letter."

"A letter. What does it say?"

"Everything I feel."

"What a goofball you are. Why don't you just say it? I mean, you're utterly fetching sitting there naked like that, but I'd like to hear you say it before we're back in what passes for the real world, like, tomorrow. This little idyll is just about over."

"I know."

But she continued writing furiously. He could see that she was crying.

"It's everything I feel, Jeff," she said through the tears. "Keep it with you forever."

He leaned over her. "I will, I will, my beautiful fucked-up Sarah. But why are you so sad?"

*Because you weren't strong enough. No one is.*

## CHAPTER 34

# Coastal Maryland, 1969

"Used to be they didn't let nobody colored come on this beach, till a few years ago," Eugene said. "Gem was telling me about it."

Lila shook out the faded green blanket and dropped it on the sand. "Stop looking over your shoulder," she said. "Or maybe you think they still don't want us on this beach."

He laughed nervously. But after a few moments he was peacefully silent, holding her against his chest while they listened to the water's low music.

It was a bit cool for the beach, but Lila had convinced him he'd like it on a morning like this; it would be beautifully gray and quiet, she said, calming. They got up early and made sandwiches, caught the bus at the downtown depot, napped on the short journey.

Lila wanted to be in a calm place too. She was debating with herself. Should she tell him now that she had missed her period, and not by just a week, or even two? More than five weeks, and counting. The chances were huge that she was pregnant. She thought perhaps the outing at the beach might be a good time and place to break the news. But somehow, she couldn't say the words. Indecision and fear had paralyzed her.

Chances were, he'd be fine with her having a baby. In fact, he might be overjoyed. Eugene would figure it was nothing more than the natural order of things—man, woman, love, babies—didn't everyone?

And she could predict his stance if she tried to mount an argument against it. Not enough money, she'd point out. Other people manage, he'd say. No steady job for you, she'd point out. So what? Grandma Gem will help us out.

One thing was sure: the possibility of an abortion would never even occur to him.

As for her, it was complicated. She knew instinctively that she'd spend the rest of her life in fear for any child of hers. Fear for its safety, fear for its sanity, fear for its life.

She could have an abortion all on her own, say nothing until after the deed was done, and probably break his heart when he found out.

Well, she'd probably start showing in another couple of weeks. Would it be so inappropriate to just let him discover it for himself? Inappropriate, or just stupid. And maybe, no matter how lost and burdened she herself was, any child of Eugene's was bound to go through the world with God's light on her, or him, protected, and incapable of doing ill.

Some warming sun was breaking through the gray. Eugene said something about coming back here, to this very spot, in the summer. They could swim way out and then, when they were sitting here, they'd eat Lila's cornbread and . . . She wasn't paying attention. Lila let him feed her one of the cookies she had baked, and in a few minutes she was asleep.

---

Running. In a neighborhood she didn't know. *Where am I going?* There was a long smear of blood down the front of her sweater. Her sneakers were wet with it. There was even blood in her teeth. Something flashed in and out of her mind—*they* didn't let nobody colored come to this beach. Meaning white people. Had she and Eugene been attacked by racists?

No. It wasn't that.

All at once, her knees buckled. She was lying face down on the sidewalk, screaming inside her own skull, but making no sound. It was the first of many times over the course of her life: screaming inside her head, no one to hear it, nor to hear her wretched begging God to make it not true, asking what had she done to deserve it. What had Eugene done.

Lila had not expected to love or be loved. Certainly she did not expect to find love in the person of a rangy, self-effacing boy who lived with his grandmother. But he was dead now, and she was complicit. If that could happen alongside love, in spite of it, then there was no such thing as love.

A white man in uniform was standing over her. He was saying something. She saw his lips move but she couldn't hear anything. The policeman lifted her off the ground. She couldn't hear, but she looked at his lips as he formed the words, and she understood. *Are you hurt?* he was asking. *Are you hurt? You need help?*

Lila nodded, yes.

And then she found her voice: *"We needed help. Oh, Jesus, why didn't you help us?"*

CHAPTER 35

## *Wilmington, Delaware, 2000*

*This is so fucking crazy,* Sansom thought.

He sat on the hotel bed and slid one shoe off. It seemed to take forever. He'd drunk more at dinner than he meant to.

I bet that kid's going to come stumbling in at three and wake me up. Or maybe he won't show until the morning. You can screw all night when you're that young.

The waitress was good-looking, what you'd call sassy. Bean had hit on her, and they kept up the flirtation through the whole meal. "So you're going to party with your new girlfriend," Sansom said as he left Bean at the table.

"Yup."

"Just don't bring her in the room, okay? And don't bring any drugs either, even if it's only weed. I mean, think about who you're traveling with."

"The law?" Bean said.

"That's right, I am the law. Far as you're concerned, anyway."

He let the other shoe fall softly to the carpet. He wanted to dislike Bean, but he couldn't. Maybe nobody could, he thought, and that's why he's such a brat. And that stupid camera of his. Jeez, it was like it was sewn onto the front of his tee shirt. But damn, the effortless way he had of talking to people, to anybody, getting them to talk to him. That was some kind of gift. Plus, he was a real smart kid. Plus plus, women seem to be drawn to him like flies to a peach left out in the sun. Little bastard.

At Sansom's signal, Bean had taken the lead in interviewing the old minister. He'd done a beautiful job. The reverend was certainly a surprise. Sansom didn't know what exactly he'd expected, but the slight old man had been a study in self-possession and dignity, speaking quietly and talking with such clarity of mind.

Well, what *had* he expected the old black man to be like? A bombastic fool? Some stock character black preacher rolling his eyes, sweating and quoting the good book?

Sansom thought of something his friend Richard's wife said once: *I love it when they say one of us is "so articulate."*

It struck him suddenly that everyone he'd dealt with lately was black. Everybody living and dead—the schmuck who'd tumbled out of that umpteenth-floor window, his ex-con sister, Yvonne and Kofi and Bean—even the woman they all believed was the killer, this Sarah Toomey.

He reached toward his jacket in search of his cigarettes, then remembered the smoking ban. He cursed under his breath, then lit one anyway.

He was like a lot of the white cops he'd come up with on the force, knowing little to nothing about the black people in whose lives they would soon become a fixture, a fact of life— and as often as not, an enemy. Many of those cops were right up front about having no great love for African Americans, to put it mildly. There was in fact a cadre of dyed-in-the-wool, all-out poisonous racists at the precinct. *Niggers.* Sansom heard his fellow officers use that word dozens of times a day. It was like they were inventing reasons to use the word, they just loved the sound of it. He'd heard the stories about some of them recruiting for the Klan too. It was a rumor he didn't dismiss out of hand.

Every one of those idiots thought of himself as "real police," a hard-ass who intended to take no shit from *them.* He could have, he should have called them out, told them to shut the fuck up and just do the job. And it wasn't only the ugly race stuff. It was all the macho nonsense, the dumb swaggering, the locker-room humor. Not to mention the freebies at the massage parlors. Occasionally the loathing for them would rise in him like heartburn. But he did not take a stand. He did nothing. He was like most of the men—and women—who'd joined the force to feed their kids, help to beat back the tidal wave of dumbass shit in this city. No, he didn't take a stand. Instead, he learned to put his head down, studiously avoid the bars where they hung out and the backyard barbecues in their shitty single-family homes, and he went on outperforming them at everything from lifting weights, to filling out a report in lucid standard English, to the shooting range exams. He aced his night classes at John Jay as well. He was on the path to a spot in Serious Crimes, or he would die trying to get there. He told himself that once he had rank over the idiots, he'd kick butt. But he knew that wasn't true either. Go along to get along.

Sansom initially sized up what was then his new partner, Richard Harmon, as "soft." He'd have bet the polite, quiet transfer from a posh precinct in Riverdale was going to wash out before his first year "in real life" was up. It didn't happen.

Richard was the nicest person in the world, and for that reason Sansom worried about him every day, was actually happy when Dick quit the job. He was the sort of straight arrow that pissed slackers off, brought out the sadism in them. But he was the real deal, and while Sansom kind of thought of himself as the teacher, it was Richard who ended up showing him a thing or two. Patience, for one thing, intelligent listening. Dick had taught him that by example—and got him eating less fried food.

End of shift one night, Richard stopped being a cop. He left the combination lock open on the door of his locker and handed his badge and weapon to the desk sergeant, went home, and didn't come back. That happened after Kyle had passed the sergeant's exam, so they were no longer partners. When questioned, the desk sergeant could only report that Richard looked terrible, spooked. Clearly he had been crying. Richard said he'd never discuss it, and to this day he never had.

No proof, of course, but he must have seen something, heard something he wasn't meant to, and sure as shit, another cop had to have been involved. One thing Sansom knew without being told, it was something bad, it was *way bad*. Dick went to work in the private sector. Nobody could blame him for not starring in *Serpico 2*.

Sansom and Richard remained friends even after Richard's out-of-the-blue exit from the force. In time, he fell in love with a divorcée named Sheila and announced that she'd agreed to marry him. He didn't mention that his fiancée was black until the night Sansom was going to meet her. Sheila was her own kind of surprise; handsome, funny, great body, and tough as leather. She'd worked in the prison system for years along with her good friend Yvonne. Sansom eventually started calling her Clint Eastwood. She liked that.

Sansom went into the blinding-white hotel bathroom, considered changing into one of the plush bathrobes on the hook behind the door, but in the end did not touch it. He reached into his travel case and retrieved his bottle of aspirin, along with his bottle. Took a very long pull. Yvonne's life story was still with him, at the back of his mind. Her luckless mother was there. The teenage hooker roasting in that shed, screaming, she was there. Curtis Baron too. That was something else about policing and race—the number of dead blacks he'd seen over the course of his career. Yes, white people did their share of shit, and their rightful portion of dying. But the black bodies—so many. Jesus, so many. Gang wars; murders over utterly stupid shit; death by cop; ugly ends in ugly one-room apartments; bullets gone cruelly astray into little backs, necks, chests; the kid whose mother had found him in the trash can at the rear of the building.

He had a final swig and then recapped the Scotch.

His climb out of the ranks of the uniformed continued. Johnnie Walker became an even better companion than Richard. Or anyone else, including his wife, Nora. Nora no longer even trying to be careful of his feelings. She would talk on the phone to . . . whoever he was . . . whoever they were . . . talk right in front of him, stay out all night when she felt like it. Apparently, the last one was not just sex, it was love, that last one. She lived with him in Hoboken now.

Yvonne was all out of words now that she'd told Kofi about Curtis Baron and Twister and the fire that had taken their lives. She'd also talked about the impoverished years leading up to that event, and the lonely ones that followed it; her sweet and hapless mother; the baby brother never born. At the end of the tale, in his arms, she wept for the whole of the past.

"I'm glad you told me. You must have been waiting to be punished all this time. No wonder you went to work in a prison."

"I'm so tired of it, Kofi. I'm tired of carrying it."

"I know. But you were a child. You didn't mean for those people to die. And there was nobody you could trust with that secret. Nobody you could trust, period. Don't worry, Yvonne. You're going to put Bitty and her brother to rest. You're going to get this pain out of your heart, and you're going to get your redemption."

She dried her eyes. "Maybe. Maybe, if you don't mind hanging on to me for a while longer."

"We're going to hang on to each other. Now, are you sure about tomorrow?" he asked. "You don't have to go through with it, you know. It's anything but guaranteed you'll come back with the answer."

"I know I don't have to go. But it's the best way I can think of to finish things. If it turns out the quilt means nothing—if I can't get to the bottom of all the killings—then I can't. But at least it'll be over, because I tried my best. And maybe then I'll have my . . . my what was it?"

"Redemption." He chuckled then. "Something holy must be waiting for you in Georgia, baby. First you're going to find out what's shaking in Galilee, and then you're going to Mount Whatsit to see Carrie Joshua. Sounds like Macon County is gonna be full of redemption."

Kofi helped her undress and put her into her own bed and then cleared away the things from the Chinese takeout. They made love quietly, as though they'd done it a thousand times before, and after they kissed good night, Yvonne slept the night through.

CHAPTER 36

## Georgia Swampland, 1865

The narrow creek traveled east and then became lost in the salt marshes leading out to sea.

The three of them walked in procession.

Abner was the lightest, of course. He was young, quick of foot, his eyes dependable, and he seemed to have developed a sixth sense for locating food. He carried only the twig, which he never tired of brandishing—his sword of vengeance.

Jack walked behind him, keeper of the weapons.

Monroe carried the provisions and the blankets.

Their progress was slowed now. The bank of the creek was treacherous; in some places the gravelly paths would suddenly give way to sucking mud.

In the afternoon they stopped to eat. Monroe squatted and got the water boiling for the lentils and fat they'd found the previous day. A wizened old black woman lay face down in the weeds, dead, and they'd plundered the straw basket she'd left behind. Jack had spoken some words over her body, and he'd prayed so nicely that Monroe thought he might be coming back to his old self. There was true charity and pity in his impromptu sermon, none of the rant and rancor of his campfire speeches, the gloom-laden silences, and the talking in riddles.

"This is Cox Creek," Jack announced to the other two as the poor stew simmered. "Be careful. It's deeper than it looks, children."

The sun was hot again today, and growing more brutal. Summer was almost upon them. The dragonflies seemed to arrive in squadrons, along with the beetles, the ants, the grubs, the gnats— the moist ground a rippling live thing under their feet.

Alert as ever, Abner heard the singing first. He scrambled to his feet.

Jack and Monroe could hear it too, quite clearly now. From the far shore of the creek the high, childish soprano notes wafted back to the three blacks, who listened in astonishment. More enchanted than apprehensive, Abner pointed over there. Two little white girls in bonnets, one singing a hymn.

They weren't alone. A white man, also hatted, stood near them. He was busy baiting the hook of a long fishing pole.

Jack pushed the other two behind him, hushing them. He watched as the white man cast his line into the water. By now the girls were lying on their backs, dozing in their dirty white dresses, their caps off and perched playfully on their feet.

The three blacks walked in silence until they found cover behind a stand of tall grasses.

"Who they?" Abner asked.

"Keep your voice down," Jack instructed.

"You reckon they been run off by soldiers?" Monroe said.

"Maybe," Jack said. "Everywhere you go, somebody runnin' from somebody."

"What kind of fish they getting? Can I fish too?" Abner asked. "I could swim over there right quick."

"Don't be crazy, boy," Monroe said. "What you gone do? Sit down to supper with them? 'Sides, you go in that water, suppose you lose your footing, hit your head on something. Big turtle eat you alive. You wanna get bit by one of them cottonmouths?"

After they'd watched the trio a while longer, the boy whispered, "They gone take us back?"

Jack said, "No, they not."

"That man look most like Master Peary," Monroe said. "Mas' Clarkson knowed him."

Jack did not appear to be listening. He turned to Abner: "Some branches," he said. "I need some branches. Get me three long limbs. Go."

With Abner dispatched, Monroe caught Preacher Jack by his good arm. "If it ain't soldiers, who is it chasing them?"

"The sun."

"What you say?"

"The sun. And the sword. Both burn like fire."

"What you send Abner outta here for?"

Jack didn't answer.

---

Jack turned the three branches over and over in his hands, weighing them. While Abner and Monroe looked on, he unwrapped the trapper's knives. Then he shredded the cloth in which he had been carrying them and began to tie the rags to the skinning knives.

The preacher was swift and precise in his movements, fastening the handles of the knives taut against the green wood. The rotting cloth seemed to turn to wire under his deft manipulation. The three pikes were perfectly straight by the time he set them down on the grass.

Next to them he laid the short ax.

"We ready now," Jack said when he was all done.

Abner could barely contain himself. "We ready to hunt?"

"No, son. We ready to eat."

The three bowed their heads to say grace over their portions. Monroe mumbled along with the other two, but his mind was somewhere else.

The three of them on this endless, bewildering path, freed, but not yet free. When Monroe lit out from the ruined plantation, he was looking to get his due—his land, his rights, his rest. He wanted to live. But this preacher, no, his path dead-ended right here.

The three white folks on the other side of the creek, also homeless. Maybe suffering with some ravaging pox. That sickness had taken the lives of hundreds in the past year. Monroe had a sudden image of the white man's naked body covered in boils.

How come there was no woman with those children? Maybe the Mrs. had been taken by a fever, the way Master Clarkson's older son's wife died. The younger Clarkson had been a mean son of a gun. Maybe these white people had kin that were all scattered or dead now, just like his and Jack's and Abner's were. Had the soldiers in blue strung them up, massacred them? Did Yankees do that to white folks?

Monroe couldn't stop thinking about the woman that Jack had run off that night. The shine of her face, like gingerbread batter. Her slender hands knotted together. He had wanted to take them in his and place them on his chest, assure himself he was still alive, feeling. Twenty minutes he was with her, and he was still mourning the life they might have made together, free. Why hadn't he run too when she and her uncle lit out? He wished to God that he'd had the courage that night to bolt, throw in with the two strangers headed for the Union Army camp. Ten seconds after they'd gone, he had sensed the fatality of his hesitation.

While his mind raced, Monroe kept staring at the three pikes lying at Preacher Jack's feet. And now they had taken over his thoughts so completely that he could no longer swallow his food.

He felt it, all at once, knew. He was dizzy with the knowing. His head jerked crazily, along with his heart, and then he was looking into Jack's eyes.

"Sit closer to us," Jack said.

But Monroe did not obey. He could see that Jack was sweating mightily. A stink seemed to rise from the preacher like swamp gas.

"Strength in numbers, brother," Jack said, reaching out for him. "Move close."

Monroe shook his head. It was all he could do.

Abner laughed at him. "I'm strong," the child crowed. "Monroe ain't strong."

"Yes he is," said Jack. "He gotta be."

The boy was restless, unchained. "I wanta hunt now," he demanded. In a burst of petulance, he kicked over the tin cup he'd been using to eat from.

"Soon," Jack said.

CHAPTER 37

## *Macon, Georgia, 2000*

Well, no turning back now. She was in Southland. Where it all happened—*it*. There were slaves just about everywhere in the U.S. at some point, Kofi had reminded her. Yeah, Big South cornered the market on black misery, but there was more than enough blame to go around the world twice.

She wished Kofi were beside her now. He'd given her tips about what to look for, where to go, what to ask. And he'd gifted her with a beautiful leather notebook. Just for luck, he said. His sureness that she would make a good scholar had bolstered her. But now her confidence was faltering.

Yvonne took a few deep breaths to steady her nerves. She opened her bag, found her notebook and pen, and then started up the long flight of washed stone steps to the County Hall of Records.

Thick accent aside, the older white woman at the information desk was most helpful.

Yvonne was alone in the reading room. As she leafed through the weighty cloth-covered annals for the county, from time to time she found herself losing focus. Page after page of statistics: births, deaths, election records, real estate sales, road expansions, bond issues, evidence of the area's inevitable modernization. Before her was the story of the city and surrounding townships in all their arid posterity. No wonder she was fighting sleep. Missing were the motorcar accidents, the political scandals, the picnics, the hurricanes, the wedding parties, the tragic nightclub fires—the meat and the beat of life, happy and unhappy. The *people* were missing.

But then a name jumped out at her, dry statistics suddenly brought to life. A death certificate issued for Willetts, Grady, age thirty-six. Yvonne saw the "N." next to the name. No big mystery to what that stood for: Negro. Cause of Death: Unknown—Suspicious.

*Suspicious*, to say the least. So it was true, what Bean had said; Lila Toomey had struck somewhere in this area. Then Yvonne looked at the date on the certificate: 1947. Not Lila. Couldn't be.

Yvonne picked up the pace of her page turning, surfing backward through time.

And there, in 1905, another Willetts. Paul, age twenty-one. Negro. Probable Cause of Death: By Human Hand.

*1905.*

A Willetts murder at the turn of the twentieth century. God-amighty, how many in between? she thought. How far back did it go? What the hell was this murderous thing about? Why did these Willettses— But, wait a minute. Hold it. You're forgetting something, Yvonne reminded herself. You've found the Willetts stuff. But what about Sarah's people? You're supposed to be tracking Lila Toomey and *her* people, remember?

Yvonne retraced her steps carefully but could find no mention of the name in any of the volumes—no property purchased by a Toomey, no babies born with the name, no deaths recorded. Willetts, yes, but not Toomey.

The Wilmington minister told Bean and Detective Sansom that Lila Toomey and her mother had come from these parts. Why no history on the family? Maybe Lila had changed her name, or simply taken a false one.

A note in boldface type at the end of one volume instructed that similar information for the years 1950 to the present was now available only on computer. Yvonne groaned. Kofi had warned her she'd likely run into that. "Don't panic if you have to go online," he said. "Somebody will show you how."

Yvonne hurried back to the information desk. She needed more help, she told the woman—*hep*, as it was pronounced by everyone she had encountered.

A young black secretary set Yvonne up on the spare PC and helped her access the records she needed.

Sure enough, more Willetts death records. One in the 1960s. Death occurred in the town of Galilee. Unknown causes.

At last, stiff from sitting all morning, Yvonne packed up her things. The work wasn't over, though. She'd received instructions on how to get to the public library, where she intended to search the newspaper archives. But she was tired and hungry. Amy Rice was expecting her at her home sometime in the afternoon. Maybe she'd be better off going to Amy's first, where she could rest and have a bite, and then hit the library later.

Amy Rice walked with a slight limp, but she moved swiftly. As she approached Yvonne in the driveway, a gentle wind blew against her flowered dress to outline her thighs. She beamed at Yvonne, hugged her strongly, and took the valise out of her left hand.

Amy's home was the airy essence of welcome—a pastiche of patterns and color, overstuffed armchairs, wallpapered nooks, framed photographs, comfy cushions, and billowy white curtains. There was a warm syrup quality to her voice, making it all the more startling when she cussed.

"You never been south before, right?" she said. "You're probably looking around and thinking, 'Where the fuck am I?'"

"Maybe a little. But the people I met this morning were all nice."

"We specialize in nice. Good or bad is another story, but we do know how to be pleasant. Long as you stay on the surface, motherfuckers are all nice."

"You have such a pretty house. Is this where you and Kofi's sister lived?"

"No. I moved out of that place after Laura died. You can pretty much imagine why."

"Yeah, I suppose I can."

"You must be worn out. Why don't you stretch out there? And let me offer you some iced tea. Then you can tell me all about your glamorous New York life. You like sweet tea?"

"Anything's okay."

"Good. We love our sugar down *heah*."

"Amy, your voice is funny. I mean, there's times when you sound like you're from *down here*, and times when you don't."

"Oh, that. I go in and out of my shit so much, even I don't know what I sound like. I am from the South, but I lived up north for a while too. In fact I met Laura up there. We went to Wellesley together."

"What kind of work do you do?"

"I'm with a university press. I work in Athens."

"Athens?"

"Yes. It's a lovely place. Very old. Very intact. Spared from the ravages of the Civil War, like Macon itself. But before I continue with my lecture, what about something stronger than tea? Maybe a glass of wine? I rigged up the kitchen sink so it comes out of the tap."

"I shouldn't," Yvonne said. "I've got a lot more reading to do."

Amy came back from the kitchen with a half-full bottle, and one not yet opened. After she'd resettled herself on the sofa, she said, "Kofi says you used to work in a prison. You must be a pretty tough bitch."

"Not really. Not enough to stay in that line of work."

"Maybe you know a lonely lady gangster about to be paroled? Life's *nice* down here, tell her. Warm ten months of the year. Food's good. Tell her my daddy's already paid for this house, so there'd be no question of rent. And I'm not *that* bad looking, right?"

"You not bad looking, period. And it sounds like maybe you the one who's lonely."

"Maybe."

"You never found anybody else."

"Not in the same way, no."

"That Laura must've been something. Kofi sure was crazy about her."

"Hmmm. Kofi's a nice guy. But that mother of theirs. Miss Mimi?" She shook her head.

"I hear she was nasty to you."

"Yeah, she was. But I'm not her kid, like Laura and Kofi. I have a bit more distance on the thing. I don't think I'd want to be Laura's mom. Temper from hell. She could be selfish, hard-headed, kind of a bully. So, yeah, Mimi wasn't as enlightened as she might have been. But I give her a lot of credit for taking little Benny in. At least he didn't have to be orphaned twice."

"Bean turned out as good as any boy there ever was."

"I'm glad. As for Kofi, I know he idolized Laura. But I bet he didn't really know her any more than I did. Sometimes I think the only reason she liked me was that I wasn't always trying to analyze her, or change her. I knew how to just let her be."

"It's funny. You and Kofi both talk like you not good enough. He's always measuring himself against his sister. He's not as brave or smart or this or that as she was. I don't think he's got the slightest idea what a good man he is. Now, why you giving me that big smile?"

"Look, we're girlfriends already, aren't we? I mean, we've got that instant-bonding thing going, right?"

"It looks like we do."

"Okay. So, you're in love with Mr. Kofi, aren't you?"

The question brought Yvonne up short. Am I? she thought. "I gotta be honest. I barely know what that means. In love. Sounds kind of foolish for somebody my age."

"Foolish, my ass," Amy said. "Something happens to your face when you talk about him. I think it's great."

Yvonne felt a warm and utterly foreign sensation wash over her. It seemed to come up all the way from her ankles. All the crazy shit that's going on, she thought, and suddenly all I want is to be sitting next to him somewhere.

"It's time I got going," she said a little while later, after Amy had cajoled her into drinking half a glass of wine. "I don't suppose there's a bus around here to get me to the library?"

"Fuck a bus. I'll drive you."

"I don't want to trouble you."

"Don't be crazy, Yvonne. I'm taking you to the library. And you know what else? You're not going on any goddamn bus tomorrow either. I'm taking you to Mount Meggs."

"I can't let you do that. Don't you have to work?"

"Who, me? We're going to make a day of it. Stop for lunch. Let you get a closer look at the glorious South. Maybe I could meet Carrie Joshua too, if you don't mind my nosy ass trying to horn in on whatever it is you want with her. Just give me a minute to put on some shoes."

***

"It's strange, isn't it?" Yvonne said. "Us black people all pretty much come from the South, but we're everywhere you can name. North. South. East and West."

"Ah, yes. The diaspora," Amy said, making a right turn and heading into the center of town. "But it hardly stops here in the States. Our peeps are in France, Italy, Germany. Shit, I went to Japan once: Negroes! We're everywhere, baby. Why do you bring that up?"

"I'm just thinking. Wouldn't be anything out of the ordinary for a family from down here to move out of these parts—leave Georgia, or leave the South altogether. Some go to Delaware. Some to New York. Maybe to California or someplace. Start new generations in a lot of other places. In the class where I met Kofi, he used to talk about the migration from down here after the First World War."

"That's right."

"There's these two families. Toomey and Willetts. I don't want to go into the whole thing right now, but the more I think about how wide they might be scattered, the more scared I get."

"You lost me. What's this about families? Is that what you're doing at City Hall—and the library? You know about Bean's family? You're tracking them?"

"Bean? No. What would he have to do with anything?"

Amy pulled up at the stoplight. She looked searchingly at Yvonne. "Why are you doing that?"

"Doing what?"

"Reading up on the Willettses."

It took a moment or two for Yvonne to react. But as she began to speak, the driver of the car behind them tooted once, signaling impatience.

"What's going on here, Yvonne? Do you or don't you know Laura adopted Bean from the Foundling Home in Cumberville?"

"And?"

"And he was just a baby when somebody killed his parents and his two brothers. Slaughtered them all. The Willetts family. It was about the most shocking crime ever around here. Laura thought it was better if her mother and Kofi didn't know about that part. Why are you bringing—"

Yvonne let out an awful moan that soon turned into a cry of terror. "Stop the car! I gotta call home."

Amy drove on, eyes wide.

"Stop this goddamn car, woman. I have to find a phone!"

Amy screamed back: "Phone! In my purse!"

## CHAPTER 38

## *The Bowery, 2000*

Twenty-six steps up to the third floor. Kofi's sweat blinded him as he climbed.

His hand shook as he fumbled with the locks.

When at last the loft door swung open he hesitated before walking inside. Usually, Bean's loft was filled with traffic noises and the clank of the workmen along Bowery as they soldered metal to metal, scraped gunk from old kitchen equipment, moved furniture, barked at one another in Chinese. But now there was only this preternatural stillness.

He stepped into the kitchen, looked around, then moved toward the front of the loft, past the alcove where Bean had set up his bookcases, TV and stereo equipment, and on through to his sleeping space near the cathedral-style window. Nothing out of the ordinary anywhere: In the far corner, the mountain bike

Kofi had given him as a birthday gift one year. Hooded sweatshirt draped over the back of a secondhand armchair. Loose change in a cup on top of the bureau. Clock radio silently running down the minutes. Bean had not rolled up his futon, but he'd pulled a blanket neatly over the mussy sheets.

Kofi retraced his steps back to the kitchen. He pulled a Heineken out of the fridge and sat down at the kitchen table, starting to breathe normally again. He made a quick call to Yvonne to tell her he'd arrived at Bean's place. The moment Bean came home, Kofi was going to tell him he shouldn't—couldn't—stay alone in the loft anymore. Bean was going to fuss and ridicule him, but there would be no two ways about it: he was leaving with Kofi. Bean's very name, or his blood, had apparently sentenced him to a short life. Some force wanted Bean to pay for somebody else's sin, or somebody else's madness. *God knows it's not rational,* Kofi thought, *but the facts are indisputable: If your last name is Willetts, you die. And you die horribly. You just do.*

Not this time, though. Kofi was going to grab the boy up and keep him safe.

Bean's train ought to be pulling into Penn Station pretty soon. Kofi looked down at his wrist to check the time, but then realized that he'd left home in such a hurry that he'd forgotten to take his watch. He noticed the array of clocks on a shelf in the kitchen, all with different times. Now what was that about? Oh, that's right, Bean was currently caught up in another one of his obsessions; he was buying and photographing all kinds of timepieces. Kofi pulled his cell phone from the pocket of his jacket, noted the time on that, and then tried again to get through to Bean.

Still no answer.

*Where the fuck are you, man?*

After he finished half the beer, he rose from the chair and

rechecked the whole apartment, including the banged-up armoire Bean used as a closet. All clear. *Just hang on,* he told himself. *It's all going to be all right. You're the one in charge now—the cooler head. You're the one who's got to protect Bean from this insane curse, and you have to save Yvonne from herself. They're counting on you. And so is Laura. Wherever she is, she's counting on you too. They all need mothering. They all need fathering.*

He went over to the bathroom then, suddenly in desperate need of a pee. He opened the door, relieved himself. But, on the way out, it occurred to him how odd it was that the bathroom door should have been shut. Why would Bean close the door to the head when nobody was at home? Almost as odd, the shower curtain was pulled all the way across the rod. He nearly laughed out loud; he'd had a memory of an old girlfriend's loony cat. Whenever he had to go to her place to feed it, he would look high and low for the animal, then find the mangy thing in the bathroom, trembling in terror behind the shower curtain.

Kofi looked down then, and noticed a dull yellow substance smeared along the rim of the tub.

He raised his arm as if to jerk the dark-gray curtain open, but then he paused. He had the sensation that some living shadow on the other side of the curtain was awaiting a cue from him, as if some mirror image of himself was aping his movements from inside the tub. Harpo Marx goofing on Lucy Ricardo in a make-believe mirror.

At the first tug on the curtain, he realized his mistake. He should never have remained in the loft after determining that Bean hadn't come home yet. And now, no matter what happened, it was too late.

The curtain gliding open on its metal rings made a sound like distant sleigh bells.

Sarah Toomey's hair fell in angelic ringlets to her shoulders.

Pure light from the tiny window high on the bathroom wall seemed to anoint her. In a sleeveless, skintight dress the color of a polished ruby, the nails of her bare feet painted to match, she was the picture of seductive loveliness. And her eyes were like leaping flames.

"I know you," he accused.

"Do you?"

"Yes, Sarah. I know you and I know what you are."

Sarah laughed, but made no movement.

"You are some beautiful. I give you that."

"So you find me beautiful. Did you hear that, Jeffrey?"

"What? My name isn't Jeffrey."

She laughed again. "Jeffrey says it's all right. He says I'm entitled to be loved." She leaned toward Kofi. "Do you love me?"

Kofi willed himself not to flinch. "Love you? Lady, I wouldn't touch you with sterilized gloves."

Sarah's body crumpled in on itself. "No," she said, voice breaking into bits, "of course you wouldn't. You know what I am."

"You're here looking for a man. Only he's not a man, not yet. You want to kill him."

She nodded.

"Why?" Kofi screamed into her face.

Sarah began to mumble. "Help me, Jeff. Hold me."

"You crazy bitch. What the fuck did my boy ever do to you?"

Her face twisted in agony, her eyes now flat and black. "I don't know."

"You won't get him. I won't let you get him."

"I have to," she said. "But you—you're not—"

He had only a second, he knew. Kofi propelled himself backward and into the kitchen, ripped open a drawer next to the sink and groped crazily in it for a weapon, his hand fastening around a cold piece of metal. Not a knife, goddammit. Where was the big knife? When he tore the hand free, he was grasping the long handle of a heavy steel instrument, one face of it smooth like the ball of a hammer, the other made up of pointy teeth arrayed in rows like so many guardsmen. A meat tenderizer. They sold these for a buck fifty at the wholesale place on the ground floor.

Sarah walked calmly out of the bathroom.

Kofi stared at her face as, unbelievably, it shifted and changed and melted. And her wondrous fairy hair—that was now all gray straw. He could only blink stupidly at the transformation.

He lifted the hunk of steel over his head. "Get back!"

She paid him no mind, walking steadily toward him as he inched backward. No more than a foot away from him now, she opened her black mouth.

Kofi brought the tenderizer down with all his force directly onto the top of her head. He could only stand and watch as Sarah's neck puffed to three times its size and then contracted again. He slammed the tenderizer down once more, this time catching her at the temple. Blood splashed back at him and shot out onto the wall, staining a row of white espresso cups on their little hooks.

With Sarah reeling, he calculated that another assault might finish her off. At the least, he might buy himself enough time to make it out of the front door.

But even as he moved in for the last blow, she was upon him. He cried out as his neck and shoulder were pierced by the screaming hot needles that were her teeth. A second later he was flung against the exposed bricks, his bones breaking, his eyes rolling up into his skull, heart pumping on red alert. He tried to speak through his cracked, aching teeth as he heard an unearthly swish above his head.

An odd thing happened as Kofi died. He did not die alone.

Past the pain now, in his death dream he was back in the rambling old apartment on Riverside, and all the people he loved were there with him. And all was well. He would not have to regret the loss of the years he might have spent loving Yvonne; nor regret that he had never managed to bring about a reconciliation between Mimi and Laura; nor be bitterly disappointed that he would not see Bean into manhood—because all was well. They were all teasing one another good-naturedly, laughing at Kofi's terrible puns. He had saved them, brought them all together, and they were under his strong and loving protection. He had saved—mothered—and fathered—them all.

## CHAPTER 39

# The Bowery, 2000

Minn could afford to be generous. He extended the bottle toward the black man, Homer, and watched as he took a long pull of the sweetly caustic brandy. When a younger black derelict, Knight, reached for the bottle, Minn did not try to stop him. Instead, he grinned magnanimously.

"That's good stuff, ain't it?" he said, retrieving his bottle. "And more where that came from."

Knight snorted. "Yeah, sure they is. You think I believe that bullshit you laid on Homer—about a bitch givin' you money?"

"Who give a fuck where he got it?" old Homer said, reaching for the bottle again. "Long as he got it."

"It ain't bullshit," Minn insisted. "I got forty bucks off her. She was so crazy she come back to me twice. She's got her mind set on finding this son of a bitch that cut her up. She'll pay any amount to find him."

"What sumbitch?" Knight asked. "Who cut her?"

"I got no idea," said Minn. "Somebody or other said she was cut. I got no idea. I told ya, she's nuts."

Minn gave the two a taunting look then. "Shame you brothers missed out on it. I tell ya, this gal was acting like it was Christmas Day. I reckon she musta had a thousand cash on her. Don't feel too bad about it, though. I heard her tell somebody she'd be back. Maybe tonight. Maybe tomorrow. Two of you might could get lucky yet."

CHAPTER 40

# NoHo, 2000

The Asian lady in the Prince Street boutique was surprised to see Sarah back in the shop so soon. She stepped forward to greet her, but hesitated when she noticed Sarah's odd expression.

Sarah was brimming over with the good news. "We're going to be married! We've decided to buy one of your beautiful rugs," she announced. "For our new home. We're buying a loft, even though SoHo is passé. Isn't that right, darling?"

Sarah was talking at thin air.

She repeated to the speechless woman: "We're going to be married. We decided a lovely little rug or maybe one of your lamps would bring us good luck in our new life. And we need some luck now, don't we, Jeff? That's right. We're entitled."

The concierge with the neat little haircut and cashmere twinset watched Sarah sweep past the desk at the Europa. She called after her, but Sarah did not hear; she was headed for the hotel bar.

She placed the bundled rug carefully on the seat next to her and ordered an apple martini. As she drank, the telephone console at the far end of the bar rang. The bartender answered, listened for a moment, and then walked back to her.

"That was housekeeping," he said. "The Do Not Disturb is still on your door. Don't you want the linen changed?"

"Soon," she said. "But not now. I don't want my husband troubled. He's very tired."

Upstairs again, she came into the suite and locked the door behind her. Jeffrey's awestruck eyes were open, his arms flung out in a gesture of perpetual welcome.

Sarah bent and greeted him with a long kiss on the lips. Then she stripped out of her clothing and stood under the shower for a long time. When she was done, she dressed herself in one of Jeffrey's clean shirts. Next, she unwrapped the new rug and laid it tenderly over his stiffened body. With a sigh, Sarah lay down next to him and was asleep in a matter of minutes.

## CHAPTER 41

# *Georgia Swampland, 1865*

Monroe wept for a long time, silently and apart. And then it was all done. He felt better now that he'd given himself over to events. There was an accepting peace in the knowing. He lay listening to the other two, allowing their voices to lull him to sleep. He was letting himself believe that he might sink into a deep place and simply never wake again. If there was any mercy in the world, God would make it so.

But then he was shaken by the sound of the thunder. He sat up.

Jack narrowed his eyes. "There," he said. "Hear that? There go the drums."

"That the sky," Monroe said. "That ain't no drums."

"It's the drums, fool! Means it's our time."

"What time is it?" Abner asked.

The preacher looked down at him. "Remember your big mama Ruth?"

But he did not give the boy a chance to answer. He went on: "Remember Joshua and Lucy? Hester and Martha and Little George and Trish. Gustus. Simon. Millie. Norbert. Willy and Alberta and Casper."

Abner nodded yes, though in fact he had no idea who they were.

But Monroe remembered some of them.

Jack was intoning the names of slaves from the Clarkson place. Generations of them. Men. Women. Old Aunties. Children. All of them dead now, by sickness or overwork, by hanging or drowning. A few had actually died from old age. And one or two had simply vanished in the night.

"Why you talking about them?" Monroe asked mildly.

" 'Cause we gone see them again," Jack said.

The thunder was growing louder.

Jack's deep laughter ricocheted off the water as he handed the short ax to the child. He proffered one of the handmade pikes to Monroe, who took it without a word.

Moving fast, Jack took off toward the creek bed. He was making a raspy, unearthly sound from way back in his throat, and Abner, close behind him, was doing a childish imitation of the war whoop.

Monroe did not echo their screeches, but he kept pace. Faster they ran. Faster. *I am strong*, he thought. *And I'm not. I am free. And I'm not.*

Jack went crashing into the water, his soldiers bringing up the rear. They were across the stream in what seemed like seconds.

The white man looked up in astonishment. He had been turning a whole fish on an improvised spit over the fire. Jack's pike went through his throat cleanly.

The man fell convulsing to the ground. Jack put his foot on the man's neck and sawed the head off just below the entry wound.

The little girls were hysterical, screaming, crawling, scratching at the dust. But Abner had them penned, constantly kicking them back.

Jack took the severed head and held it up to heaven for a moment. Then he lay it atop a wave in the creek. In a minute it began a slow drift downstream.

Then the preacher grabbed the pike that had impaled the white man and drove its point into the shallow creek bed. He lifted the headless body and stuffed it upside down onto the pike.

Watching in awe, Monroe again smelled the preacher's foulness.

"Put them in!" Jack ordered Monroe. "Stick 'em straight up in the creek."

Monroe could see that the preacher meant the remaining two stakes. He did as he had been told.

"Now, Abner!" Jack called to the boy. "Strike your holy blow."

Abner flung himself upon the girls, ax raised high above his head.

"As I said, boy. As I said!"

Abner did not kill them right away. He chopped off each child's arms. He and Monroe dragged them to the water's edge where they tied the girls' small bloody frames to the stakes. The youngest child was dead, but her sister was still screaming, green eyes making crazy orbits in her head.

"*Feast!*" Jack cried into the wind. "Feast on their flesh."

As if in answer to some water god, the creatures would come up. Scenting the blood, the ancient snapping turtles would fill their mouths with baby flesh. The snakes would hiss and lick and puncture white skin, infusing the little bodies with vile black poison. The girls would molder and bloat and rot in the Georgia sun.

Monroe's clothing was wet and streaked with gore. Jack said it didn't matter; the ship was right there on the horizon and they'd be given robes of gold as soon as they stepped aboard. He took the others' hands in his. And the free men staggered forward in a kind of dance.

## CHAPTER 42

# Mount Meggs, Georgia, 2000

They'd hardly said a word to each other since Amy's alarm clock went off that morning. But now, halfway to Mount Meggs, the two of them were full of talk again.

"Okay," Amy said firmly. "Kofi thinks you're sane. You sure look like you're sane. We got through last night and you didn't try to strangle me in my sleep or anything. I've had my coffee. The sun is out and here we are driving to see Carrie Joshua. But you know what? I don't believe a word of that shit you told me."

"You think I made it up? Maybe me and Kofi are pulling your leg?"

"No. I mean, I'd be freaked out too if I had two friends named Willetts get killed, and then I read all the stuff you read yesterday. And yeah, that quilt looks scary and everything. But . . . but you and Kofi have got to be in the grip of some kind of mass hysteria, Yvonne. What you're saying—what you're thinking—things like that just don't happen."

Yvonne sat silent.

"They just don't, Yvonne."

"All right."

"I bet after you show her that photo she's gonna say those bones and stars and all the rest of that stuff on the quilt don't mean jack shit. And as for that ugly motherfucker in the middle of it—he's just a very unfortunate-looking brother."

---

Carrie Joshua wore her white hair in two plaits, which she braided each morning with some effort, owing to her arthritis. She was not especially tall, but, given her overlong arms and torso, there was something treelike about her, and her enormous gnarled feet in rubber flip-flops were rather like old chestnut-colored roots.

She seemed neither pleased nor displeased at Yvonne and Amy's arrival. When they came upon her on the front porch, Carrie Joshua's face was still, eyes impassive behind the lightly tinted lenses in her spectacles. They remained so while Yvonne poured out thanks to her—she knew what an imposition this was, and was so sorry that Carrie had been unwell. Hopefully she would not take up too much of Carrie's time, since she had to get back to New York as soon as possible.

Carrie Joshua's curiously neutral gaze continued. Yvonne did not quite know what to make of it. But once she ushered the visitors into her home and lowered herself slowly into a parlor chair, she was gracious and welcoming.

Though she could barely make out the details of the photograph that Yvonne showed her—the failing of her eyesight was galloping these days—she listened intently to her visiting scholar's questions about story quilts. She would interrupt Yvonne periodically and dispatch Amy here and there in the house. Into the kitchen to fetch a cold drink; into the back room where on a shelf she would find an illustrated text or a notebook that Carrie wanted Yvonne to see; into the bedroom to retrieve a vintage quilt from one of the cedar chests.

Amy returned from the latest mission. "I think I'm about as close to heaven as I'm ever gonna come," she said dreamily. She was holding against her face a yellow quilt with what seemed like thousands of tiny jonquils hand-stitched in a sublime lavender.

"Yes, it's a pretty one." But that particular one wasn't old at all, Carrie said. A neighbor had done it just a few months ago, and Carrie was going to present it to her grandniece as a birthday present.

"Your man," Carrie said after a minute. She was looking in Yvonne's direction.

"Mine?" Yvonne asked.

"Yes. The face on your quilt. Black snakes in his hair and all? I'm not able to see him too well, but I'm pretty sure I know who he is . . . was."

Stunned, Yvonne couldn't speak. Instead it was Amy who said, "Who he *is*? Really?"

"Yes. It isn't so hard to figure out."

"You must be kidding. That shit—I mean, that stuff has some meaning? It's for real?"

Carrie Joshua smiled, more or less. "That's the question. Isn't it, young lady? Was Preacher Jack Willetts real or was he not?"

At the mention of the name, Yvonne's spine tightened. "What did you say about a preacher?"

"It was once said," Carrie began, "that a slave preacher known as Jack Willetts massacred a family—part of a family, at any rate. They were white folks. It happened a while after Emancipation."

"White folks," Yvonne repeated. "Were they called Toomey?"

Carrie shook her head. "Possibly. But I don't know that name."

Amy's next comment died on her lips when Yvonne shushed her. "Never mind about the name," she said. "Please, just go on."

Carrie resumed: "Willetts, according to the legend, beheaded a white man on the banks of a swamp, and mutilated his daughters. It was unspeakable. He left the man's body on a pike for the crows. It was a terrible act of retribution for all the terrible acts visited on our people. The little girls were tortured, left cut up and bleeding in the water. The snakes did the rest, along with who knows what other creatures. Days later, their mother came upon them."

"God have mercy," Yvonne said. "It probably drove her stone crazy."

"Indeed it might have. And it seems that Willetts himself had slowly gone mad over the years. As the story became known, the image of Preacher Jack began to show up here and there. As often as not, on quilts."

Yvonne shook her head. "I'm trying to put this story together in my head. You saying that everybody knew what this preacher did? That it was common knowledge?"

"I don't know if I'd say that."

"What happened to him? Was he caught? Did they hang him?"

"He was never seen again."

"How convenient," Amy said.

"Understand," Carrie said, "there's no way to know how much, if any, of the story is true."

"True or not," Yvonne said, "why would Negroes want to put

something like that out there for other people to see? Man on that quilt looks like the devil himself. Why would they want to be reminded?"

"Maybe," Amy said, "because they weren't ashamed of what the guy did. They were proud, glad he took his revenge. Like Nat Turner."

Carrie snorted. "No, ma'am. It had nothing to do with black pride. Far from it."

"Then why would they be so eager to display him?" Amy said.

"They didn't," Carrie said. "The mad nigger preacher was not a Negro icon. It was something perpetrated by whites. Jack turns up in sensational fiction from the era, in whispered tales used to frighten naughty white children into behaving, and on quilts stitched by the lily-white hands of southern women. I imagine those were being turned out with some regularity during Reconstruction. Take the story far enough, and you have the distinct possibility that a few black preachers wound up at the business end of a rope because they bore some resemblance to Jack Willetts."

"If he ever existed," Amy said.

"Yes," Carrie said. "If he existed. You may be familiar with the kind of work I've done for most of my life. My attempts many years ago to recover the records from some of the plantations where Jack Willetts likely would have come from—nothing but dead ends."

"Do you believe in him?" Yvonne asked. "You think the stories are true?"

"I don't think they're true, and I don't think they're not true. As I said, I could find no real evidence."

Carrie Joshua was the expert. She was saying the jury was still out on the question. Yvonne knew what she believed, though. In her mind, Willetts had been as real as the brushed-velvet settee under her ass.

Still, the story, as Yvonne said earlier, had not yet come together in her head. What did all those horrible things have to do with Sarah Toomey and her mother before her? And Lila's mother before her. What tied them together?

There was no way to delve into that without narrating all the events that had taken place in New York—Bitty, her brother, the peril that Bean faced. Yvonne was calculating how to approach the thing, where to begin. Would Miss Joshua believe her? Where in hell to begin? She'd just have to begin at the beginning.

But a question from Amy saved her the trouble.

"I don't suppose," Amy said to Carrie, "there are stories about the white man's wife? After she found her children."

"Ah," Carrie said. "So you do know more than you've let on."

Neither responded.

"Or perhaps not," Carrie said. "It's just that you mentioned the wife."

"No," Yvonne said, "we don't know what you mean."

The old scholar had Amy brew a pot of tea before going on with the story. "Keep in mind now," she cautioned as she stirred sugar into her cup, "while that horrific image is supposed to have been propagated by white racists, the tales I've gathered about it have all come down to me from our own people. Great-grandmother to grandmother, and so on. You surely realize how much room there was for false memories, mistakes and embellishments and outright inventions. Here is what was said:

"The woman found her daughters in that horrific state. Yes, she was their mother. And yes, the dead man was their father. But she was not the white man's wife. Nor was she white."

"Fuck me," Amy said. "She was a slave. Wow."

"That's right. A slave."

"And the little girls—children of rape?"

Carrie said, "Rape, certainly, no matter how you look at it. But they were her babies. Why were the girls with that man but not their mama? We don't know."

"I'm betting it wasn't for a good reason," Amy said.

"We don't know," Carrie repeated. "But you can imagine the woman's anguish. Who couldn't?"

Yvonne's hand moved involuntarily to her mouth. Somehow, she knew what was coming next.

Carrie said, "The final part of the story is that the beautiful woman was able to wade through the tangle of deadly snakes and snapping turtles unharmed, so that she could bring her daughters ashore and bury them.

"She swore that the man called Jack Willetts would pay for what he had done, and go on paying into eternity. In other words, his descendants would meet the same abomination of a death that her children had. Of course, this last bit takes the story out of the realm of historical speculation, and into the realm of—"

"Fantasy," Amy said.

"Well, folklore at any rate. And you can't verify a folktale. The same way you can't prove or disprove a song—or something illustrated on a quilt.

"But that doesn't mean the slave Willetts didn't exist. Nor that his actions in the swamp were fictional. And as for the man having sired children by a comely slave woman . . . that story is almost too common to mention."

"And how do people explain why all the poisonous snakes and stuff didn't kill the mother as well?" Amy said.

"She may have been dead before she stepped into the water. That seems to be the consensus."

"She what? Oh, wait a minute. She was a ghost. Or a—shit,

I don't know. Some kind of spooky creature. Now I *know* it's all bullshit."

"Do you?" Carrie said.

No answer from Amy.

Could things be true without being real? Yvonne thought. True without being true. "In this folk story. Legend. Whatever you call it," she said. "Do they give the slave woman's name?"

"Name?" Carrie Joshua said. "No. She doesn't have a name."

*But she does*, Yvonne wanted to say. *She does have a name. Sarah.*

———

It was time for them to leave. But Yvonne wanted to catch up with Kofi and Bean before she and Amy set out.

She had been calling New York every couple of hours, unable to reach either of them. Yesterday, when she'd phoned Kofi with the stupefying information about Bean's history, he'd rushed out of his apartment, telling her that he'd stay in touch. But there had been no word from him since his all-clear at the loft.

Did Bean know now what kind of danger he was in? That he was part of the insanity? Had Kofi whisked him away from New York—away from Sarah Toomey? Did the child believe him? Was he frightened? Was he safe? Kofi had friends out on Shelter Island. Maybe he and Bean had headed out there. Maybe they were on a plane headed for Sweden. Even better.

Again she took Amy's cell phone in hand, walked into the adjoining room, and tapped in Kofi's number. Still no answer. Not at his apartment and not on his mobile. She switched to dialing Bean's loft again, allowing the phone to ring at least ten times. Then, just as she was about to disconnect, the phone was picked up.

A low noise in the background. But no one spoke.

"Bean?"

Silence at the other end.

"Bean! It's Yvonne. Who is this?"

The boy's voice was unrecognizable. All she could hear now was a faint lowing, like the helpless bleat of a newborn farm animal.

"Jesus God— Is that you, Bean?"

He broke into full-out weeping then.

"Oh, God. Tell me what's wrong."

"No."

"Is your uncle with you?"

"No."

"Who is that talking then? I hear somebody talking. Who's there with you?"

"People. From the police."

Yvonne beat down the urge to scream. "Where is he, Bean? Where is Kofi? I need to speak to him."

"Kofi," he choked out. "Kofi's dead."

Yvonne grunted once, and then went quiet. She held the small silver unit to her ear, listening to Bean sob between words, not hearing much until the very end: "I found him when I got home. I don't . . . understand . . . I can't . . . It was . . . He was all . . . broken up. They took him away in a bag."

They took him away. The words banged against her brain, settled in her chest. No Kofi. No more.

"Where is Sansom?"

"Downstairs. He said I have to pack some things and clear

out of here. Because it's . . . the lab people . . ." He took to wail-
ing again.

Yvonne could no longer feel the floor beneath her feet. She
didn't know how long she'd been holding the phone to her ear
listening to the sound of Bean's gasping sobs.

Now he was speaking again. "He's gone."

It broke her heart.

"You're okay, baby. It's gonna be okay."

"What should I do?"

"Get your things and go down to Sansom. Stay with him,
you hear me? Tell him I said you have to. Don't you leave his side
till I get there. I'm coming home now. Soon as I can get a plane
out. All right?"

"Yes."

Yvonne rang off a minute later. Both the other women were
in the room with her now, staring worriedly at her face. She
placed the phone gently down on the back of a chair, and then
fell weeping into Amy Rice's arms.

CHAPTER 43

## *The Bowery, 2000*

Sarah was dressed all in white wool, her hair in a chignon, when she checked out of the hotel. She gave a dazzling smile to the concierge as she paid the bill.

"My husband's already left," Sarah said. "He asked me to be sure and tell you we had a wonderful stay."

"Thank you. Did you need help with your bags? Where are they—still in the room?"

"They've been taken care of."

The concierge did not understand, but said nothing further.

"Goodbye now," Sarah said.

The young woman did not return the goodbye. She watched Sarah move briskly toward the exit. *Beautiful woman, handsome man, acting as though they're on a honeymoon perhaps. Do Not Disturb sign permanently on the door. But something is off, something is wrong. He disappears. She's in and out of the place constantly. Shopping bags from every high-ticket boutique in the neighborhood. Then, this morning, another guest complains about a queer odor somewhere on their floor. Look at the way she's moving. Seems to be in an awful hurry all of a sudden.*

As Sarah swung through the revolving doors and out onto the sidewalk, the concierge picked up the phone and punched in the extension for Security.

Sarah headed east across Prince Street. Her steps in the strappy high heels she wore were strong and purposeful.

"Ooooh, Miss Prada. Work it, girlfriend!"

She turned to see who had spoken. A shapely black man in a tight-fitting brown leather skirt and high heels, snapping his fingers in her direction.

Not comprehending, she hurried on, glancing back at him.

On Bowery, once again she turned north.

Her footsteps never faltered; she seemed to be on an absolute trajectory. In her mind's eye, she saw the entrance to the building—and, yes, there was a kitchen-supply store directly to the left of that door. She did not know why she had to find that loft building again. She did not know why she had to enter that rusted door again, climb the long flight of stairs. She only knew that it was near, and that her entire being was focused on getting there. She was so focused in fact that she did not notice the white derelict hobbling alongside her.

Minn, the drunk to whom she had given money the other day, was asking eagerly, "You find that fella?"

Sarah shrank away from his touch. He stank. She took several steps backward and suddenly found herself in the grip of a muscled arm, a hand across her mouth. She was dragged brutally into the cool and darkened interior of a construction site across from the men's shelter. One shoe pulled off in the struggle.

The strong young man, Knight, held her fast while an older black man searched her. He ripped her purse open, pawed through it, dropped it, and kicked it aside. Minn bellowed something unintelligible, and then Homer began to pry into the top of her dress.

Unable to breathe, she began to twitch violently. But the more she attempted to wrench away from Knight, the more harshly he restrained her.

Sarah bit all the way through Knight's finger, bit until her upper teeth almost met the bottom ones. He let out a strangled yip, and then punched her forcefully in the face.

They all seemed to be on her then, their collective body odor strong enough to make her swoon. Homer tried to stuff a filthy rag into her mouth.

But Sarah would not be held down. The men were startled to find the tide turning. She was fighting off the trio, unvanquished by Knight's blows. She felt her neck engorge nearly to the point of exploding. Her eyes met Homer's and she heard him scream before he turned and gimped frantically away through a thick plastic curtain.

Two of them left now. She recognized the young one—

*But no, that was impossible. This young man was dead. She'd seen him die with her own eyes. She'd seen the old master's brother use his brown leather boot to kick the boy's head in, one witheringly hot afternoon. She'd seen the flies drinking his blood, she'd seen two of the old ones dragging him off the field by his feet.*

Knight hammered at her in panic.

Kill him first, Sarah thought.

*The smell of cannabis in the air. A short, dark woman holding a microphone. Peals of laughter turning to tomb-like silence. "Those motherfuckers in the Caribbean was downright creative about the thing. You know? Like this one massah who needed to make an example of somebody who wasn't movin' fast enough. He slit this dude open from neck to penis and filled his belly with hot coals. Yeah, like that motherfucker was a baked potato."*

A collective gasp from a crowd of horrified listeners. Someone burst into tears.

You need to kill this one first, she said to herself. Bite and tear until he is nothing but bones and black pus. The poison rose into Sarah's throat.

But, just before her tongue split and her skin turned brittle and crusted, she ceased fighting, her body going limp.

They kept pounding at her, but she felt nothing. Sarah was watching images on a constantly changing screen behind her eyes: Blood and slime on a windowsill. She heard a grown man's unholy cry as he flew through glass. A woman writhing on the tile floor of a public bathroom. And she herself was one of the players in the insane movie. She saw herself with blood in her mouth. She recalled the oozy warm feel of it on her clothing. She was staring down at a handsome young man, nude, inside a dressing room. He looked torn in half.

And there she was again, with a blade in her hand—slashing—

*I am laying with a white man. Opening my legs to him. I grasp at his long hair as he enters me. I've come to crave that moment, live for it. I am wallowing in his desire for me, his need for me, he is helpless, I am helpless. I am filthy with lust, glorious, shiny, afire, and at the same time feel I'm dying. I ought to be dead. And soon will be dead. I say to him what he always says to me, I watch his lips move—"I love you." But no sound comes from my mouth. I can't speak. In my sleep, in my dreams, I am killing him.*

*God help me, who am I? I won't have a name until I can hear him say it. And he is saying it now, I think. But I cannot hear it!*

*We have these babies. He holds them close to his body when he plays with them, for hours sometimes, while I sleep. Or I wake up and see him on the spindly piano bench, watching over us, and suddenly, with no prelude, we are tumbling, grunting, rutting in that wicked hot place again. It's a way of feeding ourselves, because we have no food. Heedless. I feel I'm inside his body, seeing me through his eyes. Lovely. Loved. Happy. Hopeless. Captive. Insane. We are right to keep the door to our world locked. Outside it, hell waits.*

"There's something in my hand," Sarah said out loud.

Knight punched her again.

*Have I killed him? Have I killed a white man? If I did, surely I will soon be dead. They will whip me. They will hang me. Some of the hangings they make a spectacle of, hack off body parts, set fire to the swinging body, burn you alive. Others are completely perfunctory. Snapped neck. You're here, you're gone, you're alive, you're dead.*

*The deep-black woman tells the others that the white man is my brother. That his papa took my mother just as he took me. Sin upon sin upon sin. But Old Fanny knew that it isn't true; I'm born not out of his papa but out of his papa's brother. Fanny ought to know, because she was there when I was born. She washed me my first day in this world and she washed my mam on her last.*

"But I deserve to be loved," Sarah said. "Didn't he say that?" she asked Knight. "He said, We're going to Spain. Maybe we'll never come back. We're going to a movie. We're normal, Sarah. We're going to eat together and fight and go hear music and all that shit. And his laugh. Jeffrey's laugh is marvelous. He makes me laugh too."

*That Arlette. She don't walk on the ground no more. She walk on the air. And Monsieur René, a man who found his reason for living. Dress her in her gray dress. Two empty cradles. We gone bury her babies.*

*"Okay, sugar. Go ahead and kill me."*

Sarah was at the distressed wood desk, writing with great concentration on a sheet of hotel stationery.

"What's that you're doing?" he asked.

"Writing you a letter."

"A letter. What does it say?"

"Everything I feel."

"What a goofball you are. Why don't you just say it? . . . I'd like to hear you say it . . . This little idyll is just about over."

"I know."

The room was warm. *I need to taste you . . . all day . . . right now . . . What do I taste like? . . . Tell me how much.*

A brilliant blue scarf . . . "This much."

Teeth. Blood in my mouth.

Spent and weeping, and laughing crazily. *"Okay, sugar," he said. "Go ahead and kill me."*

The first sliver of reality poked through the fog in Sarah's mind. She was fighting off two men in a dusty construction site.

*"Keep it with you forever."*

*"My beautiful fucked-up Sarah."*

A letter opener near her left hand. She plucked it from the desktop and in a single movement plunged it into Jeffrey's chest, ripping upward. He fell to the floor heavily, hitting her shoulder on the descent.

*Jeffrey is dead. Arms open forever. Perpetual welcome. Perpetual rest. There's a beautiful rug there to keep him warm.*

Jeffrey is dead.

She heard a horrible ricocheting scream. It was her own. It brought her to her knees on the dirty ground.

*Oh my God. Where can I find a stick? I will poke my eyes out. I hope they stone me. I hope they burn me alive. Please, please burn me.*

There was a phrase people used. Always said wistfully. *The love of my life.*

Without Jeffrey, there is no love, and certainly there is no life.

All those women. Looking for a man. Looking for love and kindness in a man. She found one. It was as though God was tired of toying with her. He'd decided to let her be happy at last. Once. Stop the endless cycle, the search, the pledge to revenge a wrong no one even understands.

*There was that enchanted hour. Nothing happened, really. They were swimming lazily from one end of the pool to the other. Or just lying in the blue-green water, holding hands. If ever she had felt right, felt she was exactly where she belonged, it was there, in that quiet hour. Lucky. She couldn't stop smiling.*

*And now the idyll is over.*

She called his name then—finally she could say it—*Jeffrey, I love you*—and surrendered to the present moment. She would not say another word. She would die bleeding and defiled, but silent.

After they raped her, Sarah crawled only far enough to find a heavy stone. She handed it to Knight. In a martyr-like gesture, she knelt before him, head bowed. "Please."

———

Kyle Sansom took Bean's canvas duffel and threw it onto the back seat of his car. He held Bean firmly as the young man's slender legs threatened to give way.

Bean let himself be placed onto the passenger seat. In silence he watched Sansom light a cigarette while he spoke with two other plainclothes cops. Bean, in an automatic movement, no thought behind it, picked up the camera in his lap, aimed out the side window, and snapped the three men. His eyes still teary, he pointed the Leica at the rusted iron door of his building and shot that.

Besides the police activity centering around the loft building, there was commotion going on farther downtown as well, at the site of the new facility that NYU was building. He could hear sirens roar up and suddenly stop a block south of where he sat.

In a while, Kyle Sansom, struggling to conceal the confusion and fear on his face, tapped at the window. Bean lowered it.

"How're you doing there?" Sansom asked softly.

"All those cops back there," Bean said, "all those for Uncle Kofi?"

"No. Not for him."

"What happened then?"

"There's a woman they found."

"Is she dead too?"

"Yeah."

Bean nodded and rolled the window up again. His elbow struck the shutter on the Leica, now resting on the dashboard. He would find out months later that he'd just taken a picture of the pale and cloudless sky over Manhattan.

It was an eighteen-year-old skateboarder who spotted the dead woman's body. Officers Albers and Perreau were in the patrol car that the kid flagged down.

By the time they reached Sarah's body, the massive sand-colored reptile was halfway out of her chest.

At first Albers thought he was hallucinating.

But Perreau saw it too. "Good Christ, look at that thing! What the fuck is it?"

"Kill it!" Albers screamed. "Shoot it."

"Shoot it? Look how that motherfucker's moving around. What am I—Annie Oakley? Gimme something! Gimme that two-by-four."

Perreau raised the plank high. But on its downward arc, he froze. He'd heard the sounds the creature was making. *Sweet Jesus. It's talking.*

Albers heard it too. A mournful cry that turned into high-pitched wails. The hysterical shrieks of a woman. The terrified wails of a little girl.

The two policemen looked at each other in disbelieving stupor.

Albers suddenly exploded. *"Kill it!"* Then both fell upon the thing with boards, bricks, hammers, anything within reach. They pounded it over and over. Finally, Perreau drew his weapon and emptied it into the head.

Albers realized that he had to get hold of himself, stop shaking. And he tried. But it was no good. He couldn't stop shaking and he couldn't stop screaming: *"Kill it! Kill it! Kill it!"*

Perreau was holding him now, tight, anchoring him, as though Albers might just fly up to the top of the makeshift tent. "All right, all right," Perreau said. "You're okay now. We both are. It's dead now. Look."

But when they turned toward the thing again, it wasn't there.

## CHAPTER 44

# *New York City, 2003*

Kyle Sansom waited at the bar until Yvonne finished her shift.

He had been checking in with her every couple of weeks since Kofi's murder. And he felt especially protective of Bean.

Then, in the autumn of the year that followed, there was that event that seemed to scramble everybody's priorities. So many ties strengthened, so many destroyed. After 9/11, Kyle cherished the bond he'd established with Yvonne and Bean even more, looking on them as family. The loving protectiveness was mutual. They could no longer imagine life without Kyle's friendship.

Yvonne walked up behind him, put her hands on his shoulders. "Still drinking club soda, I see. Good for you."

He turned on the barstool and embraced her. "How's it going?"

"It's going. You know."

"Everything still okay with the kid and his dream girl?"

"Lord, yes. They're the original two peas in a pod. I'm so glad he's got somebody. Alena is such a sweet thing. And she loves him to pieces."

"Almost sickening, huh?"

She laughed. "You shut up. He deserves it. He's had it so damn hard."

"I know."

"I know you do, and I have to thank you again for the way you always looking out for him."

"Sit down and have a drink with me," he said.

The bartender poured a red wine for her, and the two sat without talking for several moments. Yvonne broke the silence: "You talk to Richard and Sheila lately?"

"Nah. I don't talk to much of anybody besides you and Bean. I mean outside of the job. There's always the job. Nothing left over after that."

"Well, that's wrong, Kyle. You should be with other people. You ought to find somebody. Get yourself a woman, huh? Don't you think it's about time?"

"I'm holding out for somebody like Alena. Beautiful as all get out and looks at me like the sun shines out of my ass." He gestured to the bartender for another drink. "And you? You out there beating the bushes, looking for a worthy man?"

"Not me. I had me a worthy man, didn't I? Don't expect to find another one up to that level. Nowhere in this life anyway."

Yvonne stopped talking. She thought she had seen tears shimmering on the lower rims of his eyes. After a few minutes she stood, placed a palm on his cheek. "What we go through . . . God. What we all been through . . ."

He nodded.

"It's such a nice night," she said, and took his hand in hers. "Why don't we walk a bit."

---

They were almost the same height. Alena was all legs, just like Bean. She liked to borrow one of his wifebeaters and wear it with her jeans—so they looked like twins, she said.

Tonight they ordered in. Pizza from the good place on Eleventh Street. They drank wine, they smoked a bit of weed, and now they were lying, legs entwined, on the new futon that Kyle Sansom had given them. "You're both skinny, and I know how close you are, but you need room to stretch out when you sleep," he said.

Sleep. It was months after Kofi died before Bean could sleep. Now, he fell off every night in Alena's arms. And when he was snatched awake by one of the nightmares, she was there to murmur assurances to him, swear her love for him, kiss his eyes. When he woke up crying, she cried with him, and rocked him, and kissed him on the mouth, and soon they would be making love. Bean moving inside her rhythmically, looking into those infinite emerald eyes, finding in them love, yes, and so many other things he could never catch hold of. *Please, please don't ever let her leave me. I won't survive.*

Her lips right next to his ear: "Take more," she would say sometimes.

*Please. Just the thought of it hurts, literally hurts me.*

Alena placed a wedge of sweet orange between his teeth.

"Where did you just go, my love? What were you thinking about?"

"Karma."

"What about it?"

"About how it was the best day of my unbelievably weird life, that day I came into the café, and saw you. It's how I know there really is such a thing as fate."

"Um hum."

"What? You don't think it was fate?"

"Fate that I was doing a double shift and it was me who waited on you?"

"Yeah. No question, it was meant to happen."

"You're too superstitious. But you know what? To celebrate our *destiny*, I'm going to get up and make you a delicious cappuccino."

"You don't have to, babe."

"I know. I like to do things for you. Like that beautiful song on your Uncle Kofi's record—all for you, body and soul."

"My little woman from Planet Wonderful, who are you? What did I do to deserve you?"

She smiled over her shoulder.

"Tell you something else," he said. "It's no accident we're both orphans. My mom and dad were killed in that car crash when I was a baby. You and your sister were adopted but you were raised by different couples. And then, well, then she died."

"Then she died. Right. And I don't even remember her. We were too little when we got separated. Except, I do have that dream about her. Regularly."

"In the dream, how do you know she's your sister? Does she look that much like you?"

"Yes. Or she kind of *is* me. You know how dreams are. Anyway, we've got on these prissy white dresses. And we're about to get, like, baptized by a white-haired old preacher. By the banks of a river. Just like in some corny old movie about black people looking up to heaven, hollering and shit."

Bean poured himself into his jeans and pulled out a chair at the table. "One day we're gonna be corny old black people. I mean, I hope. No baptizing in the river though. Gotta draw the line somewhere."

She gently placed his coffee down before him, let her delicate fingers walk across his back. "Something else, m'lord? Back rub? Hand job?" She laughed. Tinkling. Bawdy. Goofy. All at the same time.

"Yeah, let me think about it. I'll get back to you in a minute." He lifted the hem of her tee shirt and kissed her stomach. "Hello in there . . . Anybody home?"

"Oh no, mister," she said. "Don't *even* . . . How about some biscotti?"

---

They turned the TV on but soon grew bored and began to talk to each other, ignoring the screen.

"I forgot to tell you," Alena said. "Your girl is getting a raise. I'm gonna be sort of the manager when Evan's not there."

"Great." He paused there for a minute. "And that's because you deserve it, right? Not 'cause he might still be trying to get in there."

"It is not. He said it's because he trusts me. And he's never met anybody as *controlled* as me. He says I'd be able to keep a cool head and handle things that would freak other people out.

Anyway, he hired me even when I couldn't remember the name of the place where I worked before. That's trust, right?"

"*Please hire little me. I've been working like crazy, but I can't remember where.* You don't really believe he bought that, do you? Come on, he took one look at you and thought—I think we know what he thought."

"Well, maybe. But I can tolerate a little harmless flirting. I'm not a child."

Bean recalled sitting in the café once, talking to Evan, the boss. "What a sweet, even-tempered girl," Evan had said, looking admiringly at Alena stacking saucers near the milk frother. "And drop-dead gorgeous. How'd you get so lucky?"

But then, after she'd worked in the shop for a while: "I'm having some second thoughts about you," Evan told Alena one evening as she was counting the cash. They were done for the day. "I have a feeling you might not be quite as cool as everybody thinks you are."

She opened her eyes wide and coyly batted her lids. "Oh? Who's 'everybody'?"

"Yeah. You know how to keep things bottled up, don't you? All nice and tidy and 'nothing disturbs a hair on my head.'"

Alena looked on him with an indulgent smile, but there was mockery in her voice. "Now, how many glasses of that wine have you had, Evan?"

He ignored that question too. "I wonder if one day you're going to just let it rip. I mean, like a major volcano, like a nuclear apocalypse. I got a feeling maybe when you finally do blow, man, it's gonna be epic."

Bean cracked up when she repeated the conversation to him.

"You laugh, my love," Alena said, "but perhaps he's right. Who knows? Maybe you wanna watch your step. 'Cause when it happens—if it happens—it's gonna be fuckin' epic, man."

## RHODE ISLAND RED

Nanette Hayes's day is not off to a good start. Her on-again, off-again relationship with Walter is off . . . again, and when she offers a fellow busker a place to stay for the night he ends up murdered on her kitchen floor. To make matters worse, the busker turns out to have been an undercover cop. And his former partner has taken an immediate and extreme dislike to Nan. When she finds that the dead man stashed a wad of cash in her apartment, cash that could go to help his blind girlfriend, Nan's desire to do the right thing lands her in trouble. Soon she's on the hunt for a legendary saxophone worth its weight in gold. But there are plenty of people who would kill for the priceless instrument, and Nan's new beau just might be one of them.

Crime Fiction

## COQ AU VIN

Nanette's life is finally getting back to normal when her mother calls her with some upsetting news: Nan's beloved bohemian aunt Vivian has gone missing. Normally this is par for the course with Viv, but this time the circumstances surrounding Vivian's disappearance are rather troubling. Would Nan be up to brushing up on her French language skills and flying to Paris to track her down? Would she ever. Now swanning about her favorite city, Nan has a hard time keeping her attention on the task at hand . . . especially after she meets handsome violinist Andre, a fellow street musician from Detroit. But trouble has a way of finding Nan, and her search for Vivian lands her in the underbelly of historic Paris and in the crosshairs of some of its most dangerous denizens.

Crime Fiction

In the third book in the Nanette Hayes Mystery series, Nanette is on the rocks. Heartbroken and alone, she finds what comfort she can at the bottom of a bottle. But her life seems to turn around when she's given a voodoo doll, so much so that Nan seeks out the doll's creator, Ida, to thank her. Unfortunately, the meeting doesn't go so well, and Ida ends up with a bullet in her head. Guilt-ridden, Nan resolves to get justice for her new friend, only to find that Ida was hiding some dark skeletons in her closet. Now plunged into a dangerous world she doesn't understand, Nan will have to team up with some unlikely allies, like her estranged father, a high school principal, and Leland Sweet, an NYPD officer with whom Nan has some major history. But will Nan solve Ida's murder or fall victim to the same forces that brought her down?

Crime Fiction

VINTAGE CRIME/BLACK LIZARD
Available wherever books are sold.
vintagebooks.com